## 'My lord, I have a proposal for you.'

De Rohan shuddered visibly. 'Much as I am flattered by your attentions, I had set my sights on a bride with, shall we say, more feminine attractions.'

'I meant a proposition. Marriage was truthfully not what I had in mind.'

'I had not realised you were suggesting a more clandestine arrangement. I regret, however, that I must still decline your offer.'

Maude fixed de Rohan with a disparaging glare. 'I had no such thing in mind. I wished only to offer you my services as a mercenary.'

**Elizabeth Henshall** is married with two young sons and lives in Cheshire. Following a degree in French and German, she had a variety of jobs before deciding to give up office life. A year in Germany teaching English convinced her that this was certainly more exhausting! She now teaches French and German at a local secondary school and finds her life is indeed very busy. Fascinated in particular by local history, Elizabeth enjoys writing and researching with wine at hand.

**Recent titles by the same author:**

MADSELIN'S CHOICE
BETRAYED HEARTS

# THE KING'S
# NEW MAN

### Elizabeth Henshall

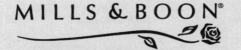

**MILLS & BOON**®

*All the characters in this book have no existence outside the imagination of the author, and have no relation whatsoever to anyone bearing the same name or names. They are not even distantly inspired by any individual known or unknown to the author, and all the incidents are pure invention.*

*First published in Great Britain 1998*
*Harlequin Mills & Boon Limited,*
*Eton House, 18-24 Paradise Road, Richmond, Surrey TW9 1SR*

© Elizabeth Henshall 1998

ISBN 0 263 80802 5

*Set in Times Roman 10½ on 12 pt.*
*04-9806-82782 C1*

*Printed and bound in Great Britain*
*by Caledonian International Book Manufacturing Ltd, Glasgow*

# Chapter One

*North of England, 1107*

The bunch of wild spring flowers landed in the centre of the river and was immediately borne away by the fast-moving current. Maude watched the scattered buds until they disappeared below the surface of the treacherous water. She brushed back some of her wayward hair with a dirty hand and quickly wiped away any suspicion of tears. Sniffing loudly, she turned back towards the forest and scanned its perimeter with a practised eye.

There was no one yet in sight, but this was a wild and dangerous place. The Forest of Bowland was fully deserving of its dire reputation. Despite more than forty years elapsing since William the Conqueror had decimated the population in the area, pockets of outlaws still lingered. It was a haven too, for traitors and rebels who sought protection from King Henry's spies. The few Norman nobles who remained lived in constant danger of attack. Consequently, as highly skilled mercenaries, Maude and her brother earned a reasonable living by offering their services to vulnerable keeps.

Maude clambered nimbly up the incline of the river bank, grateful for the freedom permitted her by breeches and tunic. She sat on a nearby log, hoping she would not have to wait long. With her knife and bow in easy reach, Maude cast her eyes once more in the direction of the forest. Satisfied that she was alone, she leaned back to allow the mid-April sun to warm her cold skin. There was no escaping the hateful sound of the river any more than she could avoid this meeting.

'Maude?'

Maude slowly opened her eyes, taking a few moments to focus on the dark shape of the man before her. Stocky and of middling height, Geoffrey Gant appeared not to have changed much in three years. His thin blond hair clung damply to his head. The leather hauberk he sported was stained and filthy and very much in keeping with his un-savoury character. Maude could feel his cold eyes staring at her unconventional attire.

'Did you think I would not come, then?' She eyed him with distaste as she rose to face him.

The broad shoulders shrugged. 'We did not part on good terms and you were always headstrong, my lady. There was every chance you would do something foolish.'

'I've grown up,' she replied with asperity. 'I had to.'

Her accusation was ignored. 'You still look like a boy, Maude. No wonder you aren't wed.'

Her skin prickled as Gant leered at her and she pulled her cloak about her. 'My appearance has nothing to do with my lack of suitors, as well you know. However, I do not wish to rake over old coals. You summoned me here to discuss my brother.' Maude returned his stare. 'What have you done with Philippe?'

He was unlikely to be fooled by her curt tone since her devotion to Philippe was well-known. Despite his rather bovine appearance, Geoffrey Gant was not a stupid man. Ostensibly they were alone, but Maude was certain he had his men positioned in close range. It was unlikely he would take any chances with her and he had proved three years ago how much of a lying, evil coward he was. Shifting position to look over his shoulder, his face moved into the bright sunlight and Maude could see how the years had indeed taken their toll on him. For a man of twenty-five, Gant was not wearing at all well. Guilt, she supposed, could do that to a man.

'He's safe. For the moment.' His reply was guarded.

Bristling at the man who had changed her life and who was now making a fresh assault on her hard-won peace of mind, Maude took a step closer. 'Say what you have to and then leave me be.' For Philippe's sake she could not allow her temper to get the better of her.

'I have him to ensure your co-operation, Lady de Vaillant.' He allowed time for his words to sink in. 'Since I know how close the pair of you are, I feel certain that you will be keen to ensure Philippe's survival.'

'And how do I know for certain that you have him?' Maude glared at him.

Gant smiled, displaying his yellowed and broken teeth. 'Such a lack of trust in one so young, Maude.' Without taking his eyes from her, he lifted his arm and beckoned to someone in the forest behind him.

Within seconds, Philippe was dragged from the shadows. Maude could not prevent a gasp of horror when she saw what they had done to her brother. 'By the Face of Lucca,' she breathed, 'what have you done to him?' From the way he held himself, she surmised that one of his arms and possibly several of his ribs were broken. His thick, black hair was matted with blood and his handsome face swollen and bruised.

'He needed a little persuasion,' Gant explained coldly.

'You might have killed him,' Maude ground out, her eyes riveted on her brother. 'There was no need to be so violent with him.'

An unpleasant smile lit up Gant's puffy face. 'Oh,' he said quietly, 'I think there was every need, my lady. At least now you know how serious I am about your co-operation.' He raised his hand and repeated the gesture. Philippe was dragged away.

When she could no longer see him, Maude turned back to Gant. 'Why exactly do you require my co-operation?' she demanded. As she watched his face carefully, Maude noticed how the gaze of his soulless blue eyes shifted about restlessly. Being the son of a man exiled for treason, Maude reasoned he would have to be on the look-out for trouble all the time.

King Henry had banished Gant's father, Hugh, more than a year ago for plotting to free the King's brother, Duke Robert of Normandy. After the battle of Tinchebrai in Normandy, Henry captured the Duke and had him permanently imprisoned. Several of his barons, however, held land on both sides of the channel and were willing to support whichever of the brothers offered them most. The feckless, but wildly generous Duke seemed an attractive alternative to the cruel and greedy Henry, whose harsh regime did not find favour with many of the old Norman aristocracy.

When suspicions about Hugh Gant emerged, the old man fled to Normandy and his English lands were consequently forfeit to the Crown. As nothing had been heard of his only surviving son since, it was assumed that Geoffrey had returned to Normandy with his father. Maude had felt some satisfaction at that because Geoffrey was obsessed with the estate. He had already sacrificed much to become the heir and she had grave doubts about his sanity.

'Henry has bestowed my lands on one of his new men, a Breton by the name of de Rohan.' Gant's eyes glimmered with emotion for the first time. 'But it's my land and I intend to keep it. No court favourite is going to take what's mine.'

A mixture of scorn, anger and hatred welled up within her, but Maude fought against the impulse to kill him there and then. He still had Philippe and his life was more precious to her than anything else. 'And what exactly do you need me for?'

Gant took a deep breath as if trying to control his inner emotions. 'I want you to become part of his household.'

Maude heard the words, but they did not sink in. 'Part of his household? By the Face of Lucca, Gant, are you mad? I have no intention of setting foot in that place ever again.'

For once the shifty blue eyes bore into her and the light of the fanatic gleamed from them. 'If you want your brother to live, then you'll do it.'

Schooling her expression, Maude lifted her chin. 'And how exactly am I supposed to achieve this feat? Thanks to your last performance there, the people think I'm possessed by the devil. They'll not have forgotten me.'

A short laugh escaped his lips. 'My people will do as they're told. I still have men loyal to me.' He smiled, assessing the extent of his power over her. 'I hear de Rohan is eager to ally himself with a rich heiress.' He glanced briefly at her bedraggled appearance and reached out to pick up one of her thick, black braids. It fell from his grasp as Maude jerked her head away from him. 'Failing that, I have it on good authority that the man has a reputation as a highly skilled lover. It may be that I'm doing you more of a favour than you think, Maude.'

Her cheeks burned at the lewd implication. 'You know

as well as I do that no man will come within a bow's length of me for fear of damning his soul.' She could hear the deep thudding of her heart and willed it to slow down. 'Have you any other suggestions?'

Ignoring her sarcasm, Gant glanced at Maude's bow and knife. 'De Rohan has been most distressed about several recent attacks on his person. He has spread the word that he is most keen to take on a man with special skills who will guard his life with his own. It would seem that the Breton is somewhat lacking in the art of defence.' The yellow teeth were bared as Gant pondered this particular piece of information with some pleasure. 'He's no more than a defenceless peacock.'

Several thoughts whirled around Maude's mind at that moment, but one stuck out above the rest. 'I'll not kill him. Not even for Philippe.' Her family might not be of the highest rank, but their honour was paramount.

'My dear girl, you mistake me.' His voice was lower, more confidential. 'I require only your presence in the keep and regular reports about his plans. You are to gain his trust. That's all I ask.'

Maude snorted in disbelief. He truly was mad. 'De Rohan is not likely to take on a woman like me. There are plenty of skilled men he could choose from. Most hereabouts are good archers and in dire need of work.'

'Ordinarily I might agree with you,' Gant said. 'But he really is desperate for someone with very accurate skills, Maude, and I'm sure that as soon as he finds out how very special you are, he'll offer you more than enough to make it worth your while.'

'Nobody,' she said slowly, 'is going to take on a woman accused of harbouring the devil within.'

'He might, if he thought such a reputation would keep enemies at bay.'

'What enemies?' Maude demanded, her dark eyes narrowing.

Taking his time deliberately, Gant walked casually to the top of the incline and looked down at the river. It was dangerously swollen thanks to the heavy spring rains. Maude kept her eyes averted, preferring to see if she could catch sight of her brother.

'He's a courtier with the king's favour and plenty of enemies. No doubt several irate husbands would be happy to hear of his death.' That particular sentiment seemed to bring a secret smile to his lips. 'De Rohan is, above all, an ambitious man, though, who values his life.'

None of this made any sense to Maude. 'Look, I am tired of playing these games with you. If you don't want to kill him, what do you want with him? I really don't understand.' Her patience was now beginning to wane.

'Death,' he announced quietly, 'would be far too simple and would not address the problem at all.' His eyes stared down at her almost unseeing. 'I wish to get my land back and restore the name of Gant. My father was no traitor, but it is said that the king suspects de Rohan of treason. I must prove it.'

Maude shook her head in confusion. 'And if I fail to arouse his interest?' She remained still, awaiting his reply.

'Oh, you will not fail, lady,' came the soft, certain reply. 'If you do, then Philippe will also end up in the river.'

Maude closed her eyes. He was mad, but there was nothing she could do about it. She bowed her head. 'Very well, then. What now?'

Gant turned to her, his victory close. 'You'll hear from me for I have loyal spies everywhere.' His hand reached out to pull her chin up so that he could look into her eyes.

'Not afraid to touch me?' she taunted and tried vainly to pull away from him.

He shook his head and smiled. 'Not whilst I still have your brother.' His hand dropped to his side, apparently satisfied that Maude was convinced. 'De Rohan is to hold a special fair on May Day with a competition to find the best archer. I will expect you to be there, my lady. And I have absolutely no doubt that you will win, one way or another.'

The de Vaillant keep hugged the wild north-western coastline that had suffered successive attacks from the Seawolves, Vikings and Scots. Small, grey and as weatherbeaten as the terrain about it, the keep barely struggled to survive against the backdrop of the cold sea and the damp marshes. Even on a bright spring day such as this, Maude reflected, the greys and greens of her birthland were as dour as the people who inhabited it.

Her horse grazed peacefully as she stopped to look across the last valley. The wind ruffled the sea and brought with it the sound of the gulls and the smell of the seaweed. Two small fishing boats bobbed along the outskirts of the wide, sweeping bay, and past the grassy dunes beyond the keep, Maude could see several figures on the rocks collecting mussels. She breathed deeply of the tangy air and allowed the brief feeling of peace to envelop her. This had been her home for nineteen years, but the sheer joy that had once existed for her here had been snuffed out three years ago by Geoffrey Gant.

It was a strange and isolated place where few Normans settled permanently. Of the original band of men brought by Roger of Poictou, only five families now remained. Since de Poictou had been banished for taking part in a rebellion against King Henry early in his reign, most of his Norman tenants had chosen to return to their homeland where the weather and the people were more hospitable. Despite the Earl's hasty departure, there remained in the

King's mind, at least, the question of absolute loyalty from the remaining Normans. He had had the last shire reeve hung on grounds of treason.

It was well known that Henry was obsessive about plots and assassination attempts, and his network of spies went some way to forewarn him of any possible trouble. For this reason the King was keen to distribute forfeited land amongst court favourites whose futures depended completely on his goodwill.

This Breton, de Rohan, was probably one such man despite Gant's accusation. He was, no doubt, an ambitious peasant whose fawning and clever tongue had advanced him greatly in the King's eyes. Maude sighed wearily. She felt nothing but scorn for such people. Honour and trustworthiness were beyond their ken. This Breton would discover firsthand, though, that such advancement brought with it a life of danger. De Rohan would not last long.

Maude turned her attention to the de Vaillant keep and the small village huddled within its palisade. The native English were an odd mixture of Angles, Norsemen and a few Danes who viewed the mantle of Norman oppression with the same stoic indifference they viewed everything else. Norman and peasant alike depended on each other to survive. What, she wondered, would the villagers of Gant's keep make of their new lord? If her memory served her aright, they were a cowed and miserable group, whose fear of Gant kept them in their place. That would be just how he wanted it.

Her heart sank as Maude pondered the problem of finding work in the Breton's household. Once he heard of her reputation, she doubted de Rohan would allow her to stay. The king's men were outwardly as pious as their king; any suggestion of allying himself with an evil woman would be a definite hindrance to his ambitions.

By the time she reached the keep, Maude had still found no solution to the problem. As she dismounted, the guard offered her a cheery wave. 'Best hurry, my lady. Bronwen's been searching for you.'

'Serious?' she asked rather anxiously. Bronwen was not a woman liable to flap around for nothing. Her temper was legendary and few were willing to cross her.

'Visitors.' The man nodded in the direction of the keep. 'From Silverdale.'

Elfie! Maude's frown disappeared. She hadn't seen her friend for months because of the dreadful winter weather. Quickly making her way to the stable, Maude rubbed down her horse, promising Lark an extra apple on the morrow in recompense.

Maude found Elfie in the comfortable solar, warming her hands before the fire. The long, silver-blonde hair and changeable blue-grey eyes were inherited from her English father. Like him, Elfie was tall and slender with a kind heart and a gentle nature. From her Norman mother came her dogged determination that could be most impressive. Having known her since birth, Maude had learned much about dealing with difficult men from Madselin of Silverdale.

Elfie turned and grinned at her. 'Have you been out hunting? We've been here ages and nobody seemed to know where you or Philippe were.'

'Something like that,' answered Maude evasively, coming to stand by the fire. She chose to ignore Elfie's questioning look and pulled off her cloak. Her heavy braids fell over her shoulders and she shook her head. 'We heard about your father's accident. How's his leg mending?' Elfie could always be distracted by talking about her beloved father. Edwin of Silverdale could do no wrong in his elder daughter's eyes.

For once, Elfie's customary smile wavered. 'Not good,'

she said shortly. 'The wound is not healing and my mother is fretting. If it doesn't improve, my visit to Cheshire will have to be postponed.'

Maude tilted her head to one side to look up at Elfie, who was a good deal taller than her. 'I did not know you had planned to go.' She doubted very much that it was the heat from the fire that caused Elfie's cheeks to glow. Her recent betrothal to John de Courcy was more likely to be the reason.

The question hung between them for a moment or two. 'Well, I think I should,' confided Elfie, bending down to place another stick of wood on the flames. 'It might be better to sort out any problems. John was supposed to visit last month, but we received only a brief message to say he could not come. There's been no word since and I would like to know if…well…' she glanced up shyly '…if there was anything wrong. Although, if my father is ill…' Her voice trailed off.

Maude nodded. John de Courcy was proving a remarkably unenthusiastic bridegroom, despite the fact that Elfie was beautiful, well-dowered and consequently much sought after. Five proposals from heartbroken suitors had already been rejected. Edwin and John's mother, Ghislaine de Courcy, had grown up together on her estate in Cheshire and they had been keen to unite their families in marriage. Although the betrothal had been planned since Elfie's birth, the contracts had only been agreed last Yuletide. It would seem, though, that Elfie was keener on this marriage than John de Courcy.

'We had planned to go next week,' Elfie continued, sitting down on a stool. Pulling her skirts up to her ankles, she stretched out her feet and allowed her wet shoes to dry before the flames. Her voice sounded so miserable that

Maude placed her hand on her friend's shoulder and gave it a gentle squeeze.

'Perhaps if Bronwen were to tend Edwin?' Maude suggested. 'She still has ways of healing that are unknown to many hereabouts.'

Elfie shook her head. 'My mother would never consider him being tended by anyone but herself. You know how she is.'

Aye, thought Maude not a little jealously. Madselin fussed over Edwin and all four of her children like a mother hen. Edmund and Adam had escaped to be squires to Sir Richard d'Aveyron, leaving Elfie and little Hawissa to bear the brunt of their mother's over-zealous solicitude. Maude's own mother had died giving birth to her. Bronwen, the Welsh-born midwife, had looked after her and Philippe ever since.

'Maude?'

The question pulled Maude from her private thoughts. Elfie was watching her carefully.

'Aye?'

'Something is wrong, isn't it? I can tell, you know.'

Maude hesitated, torn between keeping her secret and her longing to confide in her friend. There was no one else she could talk to. She looked around the room as if checking to see that they were truly alone. The flickering torches on the walls gave the solar a gloomy light that cast strange shadows on the tapestried walls. But for a small table and a few more stools, they were undisturbed. Sheepishly she lifted her hands in a gesture of despair. 'It's Philippe.'

'I knew it. You've been acting most strangely, even for you.'

Maude ignored the implications of her words and frowned at the flames. 'Geoffrey Gant has kidnapped him.'

'What on earth for? With all due respect, Maude, everyone knows how little money your family has.'

'Aye, but it's not the money he's after, it's me.'

After a few moments silence, Elfie cleared her throat. 'After what he put you through…er…I mean…'

Maude put an end to Elfie's embarrassment by holding up a dirty hand. 'He wants me to do something for him. If I don't agree, he'll kill Philippe.'

The details were quickly told and Elfie just stared at Maude. 'He's mad,' she managed to say after a short while.

'What choice do I have?' Maude muttered angrily, scratching away some mud from her tunic with a jagged nail. 'If it's the last thing I do, I'll kill him.'

Sensibly, recognizing the dangerous limits of Maude's patience, Elfie retreated into deep thought. 'I think I heard my mother discussing this Breton with Beatrice d'Aveyron the other day. They thought they were alone…' She cleared her throat in embarrassment at admitting she had been listening to a private conversation.

'Go on,' Maude urged curiously. Any piece of information could prove useful. It was certainly better than nothing.

Elfie's cheeks flamed a little and she drew closer to Maude. 'Well, it seems that William de Rohan is very popular amongst the ladies of the court. Apparently, his skills as a lover are…' she lowered her voice to a whisper '…very much in demand.' Elfie glanced around the room again and moved even closer, as if she truly feared that spies would leap out from behind the wall-hangings. 'Beatrice had heard that the King was jealous of him and had him sent as far away as possible.'

Dark eyes locked with grey-blue and all that could be heard was the crackling of the fire and the screams of the gulls outside.

'Oh,' seemed a most inappropriate response to such news, but it was the only one that emerged from Maude's open mouth. Despite her contempt for such a defenceless man, her curiosity had nevertheless been stirred. Finally, her mind struggled to put her thoughts into some sort of order.

'Well, aptitude in the bedchamber is no substitute for skills of combat up here. No wonder Geoffrey Gant was smug.' She sighed heavily. 'It'll be like a lamb to the slaughter. I know to my cost how ruthless the man can be when it comes to his land.'

Elfie nodded in resignation. 'What if you were to explain to de Rohan?'

An unladylike snort told her what Maude thought of that suggestion. 'He's more likely to throw me in the river for witchcraft than listen to anything I have to say.' Brushing her heavy hair aside impatiently, Maude sat forward and placed her chin in her hands. 'How am I ever going to get anywhere near the keep?'

'Well, if anyone can win an archery competition, you can,' said Elfie helpfully.

Gratifying though Elfie's faith in her skills was, Maude shook her head doubtfully. 'I'd never get through the gate.'

'Not as Maude de Vaillant, true. But you can pass well enough as a boy if no one looks at you too closely.' Elfie stared at Maude's slender form critically. 'With a bit more dirt and tight binding, I'm sure it would be easy enough.'

It was a ludicrous suggestion, but Maude did not dismiss it out of hand. 'And what about Bronwen—how am I going to explain about my absence? Even if I did manage the whole thing, I have no idea how long I'm going to be there for. She's going to be making a fuss about Philippe soon, too.'

Bending forward, Elfie pulled off one soggy leather shoe

and tested her frozen toes against the heat of the fire. 'If you were to come with us to Cheshire,' she spoke slowly as if piecing together the words in her mind, 'no one would worry about you then, would they?'

'But your mother...?'

'Is unlikely to come and would be grateful for your protection. She rates your skills most highly, you know.' Elfie sat back. 'If I could persuade her to allow you and Edmund to come, then it could work. When we get close to de Rohan's keep, we could arrange for a messenger to summon you to Philippe's latest secret mission. That way, you will be free to spend as long as you need there without arousing suspicion. No one will worry about Philippe either.'

Maude stared at Elfie in complete astonishment. Any reply she was about to make was disturbed by a fit of girlish giggling outside the solar. Maude and Elfie looked up in surprise as the door burst open to reveal Madselin and Bronwen clearly indulging in some uncharacteristic and most unmatronly discussion. As soon as they realised they were not alone, the two women schooled their expressions into ones more appropriate to their age. Both women were tall with dark, silver-flecked hair and dark eyes. The Welsh woman's sun-browned skin betrayed her low-born status. Bronwen recovered her voice first. Fixing her gaze on Maude, she advanced into the room.

'Well?' she demanded. 'Where have you been? The patrol has been searching for you since midday.'

Long accustomed to Bronwen's sharp tongue, Maude toyed with the idea of lying but rejected it when she saw the light of battle in her eyes. Bronwen always seemed to know anyway. The woman's uncanny intuition had often caused her much grief when she was a child and Maude had often wondered if there was any foundation in the rumours that Bronwen was a witch. Her preference for following in the old ways of pagan worship and her knowledge of healing had disturbed more than one priest's peace of mind. Such rumours had done little to help Maude's own reputation either, and outsiders tended to view the pair of them as an evil influence to be avoided at all costs.

'Looking for Philippe,' she said eventually. 'I wondered if he had gone further upriver and might be lying injured somewhere. His horse has been restless this past week and Philippe has been complaining of him rearing up suddenly.' All of which was true enough, thought Maude.

The hard expression on Bronwen's face softened and some of the fight left her. 'Well, you should have told me. It's too dangerous to go out on your own these days. The patrol found a group of travellers attacked only yesterday on the north road. Two dead and one badly injured. If you go out, you'd be wise to take some men with you. This shire reeve is too busy filling his own coffers to deal with outlaws.' She shook her head and sighed wearily.

'You know as well as I do that I'm safer on my own than relying on that pack of lack-wits,' came the testy reply. Maude gave Bronwen a challenging look, but Bronwen wisely refrained from leaping to the defence of the keep patrol.

'Did you find anything?'

'No.'

'I had no idea that Philippe was missing,' said Madselin, breaking the growing tension between the two. 'What happened?'

Bronwen shrugged her thin shoulders, the lines on her once-handsome face drawn deep. 'He went out hunting two days ago and we've heard nothing of him since.'

Madselin turned from the fire, black browns drawn together. 'He's been gone for longer than this before. You know Philippe when it comes to earning money. De Meschin's mercenaries have been in the area. Most likely he's gone with them to fill his purse.'

Maude bit her tongue to stop herself from contradicting Madselin, but she could not prevent her cheeks from heating. It was, after all, a good enough excuse for his disappearance for the time being. 'Well, if he has gone with them, he should have let us know.' Her lips pressed into a tight line of disapproval.

'Well,' said Madselin confidentially, 'even the most sensible, reliable men can act somewhat unpredictably when it comes to love. Edwin was much the same,' she added wistfully.

'Philippe is not unpredictable,' retorted Maude hotly, although even as she said the words, she knew there was more than a grain of truth in what Madselin had said. Much as she hated to admit it, Philippe had developed some inexplicable infatuation for Louise de Moresby. Admittedly the girl was young, pretty and had nice ways with her, but she was completely helpless and unable to defend herself. If her keep was besieged, thought Maude disgustedly, Louise would most likely swoon. Fortunately, Louise was an heiress of some standing and highly likely to contract a marriage with a man who had the King's favour, so Philippe's passion would never get the chance to flower.

They had met Louise the previous summer when her father had called upon Philippe's services as a mercenary to defend them against the unwanted attentions of an over-ambitious suitor. Ever since then, Maude had often caught her normally earnest brother staring into space with a faraway look in his eyes. He had said nothing specific to her for there was little need. She knew Philippe as well as she knew herself.

All the same, he seemed to be very preoccupied with

earning large amounts of money, to the detriment at times of his safety. Of late, they had even begun to argue about his obsession and Philippe was increasingly more withdrawn. Maude had wondered if there was more to it than he had told her and his secrecy was most hurtful. They had always told each other everything.

'If he wants a wife, I'm sure Philippe will do all sorts of things you wouldn't expect,' responded Madselin. 'They can be most surprising, you know.'

'Philippe doesn't need a wife,' burst out Maude, her dark eyes flaring with anger. 'He has us.'

Bronwen and Madselin exchanged knowing glances. 'He's twenty-one,' Madselin said gently to Maude's mutinous face. 'You have to accept that he might marry one day. He's strong and handsome and will make an excellent husband.'

Suddenly her head began to ache unbearably. Making her way to the narrow window, Maude pulled open the shutters and breathed in the fresh, smoke-free air. Outside, the gulls screeched in unison over the small hillock beyond the palisade where her parents and two of her brothers were buried. Maude could see quite clearly the markers of their graves etched against the backdrop of the darkening sea. Her father, Ivo, had been laid to rest alongside his wife four years ago after he had succumbed to a bout of the lung fever that killed so many in this part of the world.

Ivo had never taken to Maude, no matter how hard she had tried to please him. She had done everything she could to make him proud of her, but the most she got was an indifferent grunt. Her skills at archery and hunting were the best for miles around.

Gyrth, the head villager, acknowledged openly that she was better than every one of her nine brothers, but the man whose approval she craved preferred to ignore her. The only one who had ever shown her any love was Philippe. He valued her skills and her intelligence, ignoring the protestations of the other men, and would increasingly take her with him as another mercenary. After all, what else did she have?

Bronwen came to stand by her, her eyes concerned. 'If you've another of your headpains, I'll make you up a chamomile tisane.'

Ashamed of her childish outburst, Maude smiled wanly up at the face of the woman who had staunchly remained with her. In her own way, Bronwen had loved her, too. Over the years, she had made it clear that she did not want to be there and that the only reason she stayed was to fulfil the promise wrested from her by the dying Isabella de Vaillant. Bronwen had been forced to kill Isabella to save her unborn child, and in return, she had vowed to Isabella that she would protect Maude for as long as she was needed. It was a bond that could not be broken.

'I'm sorry, Bronwen,' she muttered. 'I'm just worried about Philippe. The tisane would be most welcome.'

For no more than a fleeting moment, a strange look came over Bronwen's face. It was as if she had been drawn suddenly to a place far beyond them. 'You have no need to worry,' she said quietly. 'Philippe's destiny is a happy one.' Bronwen turned then and left, leaving Maude staring after her in confusion. Bronwen often said such strange things, but this had more poignancy than usual.

'Mother?'

Madselin eased herself on to Maude's vacated stool and looked across at her daughter expectantly. Elfie used the exact same tone as her husband when he had come to an important decision.

'Do you think Maude could come with me to the de Courcy manor? If Edmund were to come too, then you could stay with Father.' Elfie smiled over at Maude. 'It might do Maude good to have a change and she would be able to discuss mercenary tactics with John's father and brother.' She leaned forward to place her hand on her mother's knee. 'I'd feel happier if she was there, too.'

Maude held her breath as Madselin thought about the suggestion. 'Well, I'd have to talk to your father and Bronwen about it first.' She eyed Maude's pale face and dirty tunic. 'But I think it might be a good idea.'

Maude's smile wavered. She was not at all sure that she agreed.

# Chapter Two

Maude's heart was almost in her mouth as the forbidding outline of de Rohan's keep came into sight. It had been three years since she had last seen it and the place had lost none of its oppression. Built on a high mound, the keep towered above the hovels of the village, much in the way of a master standing over his slaves. That was how the Gants had liked it.

The May Day celebrations were underway, and as the villagers and visitors swarmed over the hill below the keep, Maude could hear the music and the laughter. The maypole had been set up at the bottom of the hill and its brightly coloured ribbons floated in the wind. Every now and again, a small child would chase one of the ends and yank it in devilment.

Soldiers mixed freely with the crowds, their metal helms glinting in the sun. De Rohan wished to stamp his authority on the occasion, that much was clear. Casting her eye over the crowd, Maude was disappointed to find no sign of him, although he could have been any one of the men down there. From all that she had heard about him, though, Maude was fairly confident that he would be easy to spot.

Popular courtiers, she was sure, would be keen to attract attention to themselves.

Beyond the maypole, several peasants were being directed to erect the butts for the archery competition. Maude narrowed her eyes to judge the distance and smiled to herself. It would certainly be far enough to separate the skilled from the unskilled. All she had to do was remain calm.

As her gaze shifted, however, Maude's spirits fell. There was just the small matter of the river, which wound itself around the bottom of the hill like an evil serpent. If she was to enter the palisade, then she would have to cross the river.

Gritting her jaw, Maude urged Lark back into the shadows of some trees. A furtive glance around assured her that she was alone. Maude dismounted and quickly pulled off her thick riding habit. Underneath she wore a filthy pair of breeches and a grubby tunic of most uncertain origin. Bronwen would never have allowed even the meanest beggar to wear such garments, but all things considered, Maude had decided the dirtier and tattier the better.

Elfie had been as good as her word. Madselin and Bronwen had capitulated in the end and the party had set off early that morning for their trip to the de Courcy keep. Edmund, Elfie's older brother, had displayed characteristic impatience at their journey being interrupted so early on, but he had paid scant attention to the messenger who had requested Maude ride on to meet Philippe on a secret mission. By the look of relief on his face, Maude was convinced he was quite grateful, since he had ever been nervous in her company. The two girls had silently wished each other luck before pressing on to their fates.

The sound of the rushing water echoed in her ears and Maude felt vaguely sick. Only the thought of Philippe stiffened her resolve. Lifting her chin, she marched down the slope with Lark in tow and hoped that she didn't look as dreadful as she felt. If she ever made it to the gates, it was highly unlikely that she would be able to shoot an arrow anywhere near the target.

'You'll not be crossing the river that way today, unless you've got a handful of silver.'

The words stopped Maude in her tracks. Looking around wildly for the owner of the voice, her gaze alighted on a very thin, and extremely dirty youth, whose ragged garments were in a far worse condition than her own. She had been so engrossed in her own thoughts that Maude had failed to notice him sitting cross-legged and motionless beside a bush. So much for her tracking and hunting skills.

When she said nothing, the boy hauled himself to his feet and looked her up and down suspiciously. 'You're not from these parts, are you?'

Rough though his accent was, Maude was probably far more fluent in the local English dialects than she was in Norman French. 'No,' she replied firmly, quelling her growing concern. He was, after all, just a child. Mentally, she reminded herself about the knife she had hidden under her sleeve. 'You?'

His breeches flapped around his twig-like limbs and Maude wondered how he managed to walk at all. Gleaming blue eyes peeped out from beneath a hedge of light brown hair that appeared to be teeming with lice. A filthy hand obligingly reached to scratch his scalp, confirming Maude's suspicions.

'I live over there, beyond the bend in the river. You can't see it, though if we got a bit closer you'll probably be able to smell it.' The words were delivered with a certain amount of confidence that drew Maude's attention. The child certainly had some pride.

'Why can't I cross here?' she asked curiously. 'There's a bridge, isn't there?'

'Not any more. The new lord had it pulled down for some reason. Old Osric is the ferryman and he's right mean. It'll cost you more than you've got.'

Money was as ever in short supply and she couldn't afford to waste it. The two silver bits hidden under her tunic would only stretch to bread and cheese, and possibly a little wine. 'You know another way, then?' Maude knew what was coming, but she had to ask anyway.

''Course, but it'll cost you.' The boy assessed her tattered garments and then stared quizzically at Lark. Clearly her tatty appearance and the possession of a horse were at odds. 'What've you got?'

Maude pursed her lips tightly. 'Some bread and cheese. I'll share it with you if you can get me across the river.

At the mention of food, the boy's eyes lit up. 'Follow me.'

Half-expecting a trap, Maude's eyes scoured every inch of the path as they made their way towards the broad bend in the river. Somewhat nervously she pulled the knife down from the folds of her sleeve and allowed it to drop snugly into her grip. Just the feel of the weapon gave her more courage. It was a bit of a surprise when the boy came to a stop and gestured towards several huge yew trees that grew close to the river bank.

She looked blankly at the trees and then again at the boy. 'I'm sorry,' she muttered with a frown. 'What do you expect me to do exactly?'

The boy sighed and shook his head. He clearly thought he was dealing with a complete witling. 'There's a rope just below the surface of the water. All you have to do is hold on to it as you cross. Easy. The current's right dangerous, but it's a bit slower here.'

Maude could feel the colour draining from her face. It was not wise to display any sort of fear before strangers, but try as she might, Maude could not dispel its grip on her. 'Easy?' she croaked faintly.

Concerned that his next meal was slipping out of his reach, the boy looked at her more closely. 'You're afraid, aren't you?' he stated with confidence after a moment or two. 'Can't you swim, then?'

'Yes, I can. It's not that. I just can't do it. The water makes me feel ill.' Maude allowed her gaze to travel to the water. It rushed past at an alarming speed and she could feel her stomach beginning to churn. 'Is there another way?'

'No. Only Osric.'

Disgusted with herself for allowing such weakness to take control, Maude dropped Lark's reins and sat down on a log. She put her knife back up her sleeve since she was not in any obvious danger from the boy. 'I can't afford him,' she said miserably.

Her companion sat down at her side. He stank abominably.

'You need a bath,' she said, remembering the lice.

He just grinned. 'My name's Hoel. What's yours?'

'Maude.'

'You're a girl!' He paused for thought, but any other comments were interrupted by a deep growl coming from his stomach.

'Have you had anything to eat today?' Maude studied him a bit more closely. He looked about ten but was probably older.

'Not for a couple of days.'

Well, his need was greater than hers. She got up and pulled the food she had from her saddle pouch. 'Here, then. Take this.'

Hoel's blue eyes just stared at the fresh bread and cheese as if they were pure poison. 'Why don't you want them?' he asked suspiciously.

'I'm not hungry,' Maude replied. 'It's being near the river.' She pushed the food at him once more and this time, Hoel grabbed it as if his life depended on it.

Within seconds, Hoel had stuffed the lot into his open mouth, reminding Maude very much of a hungry fledgling. Once finished, he brushed the crumbs from his lap and looked up at her. 'Why are you here, then? There's probably lots of places holding a fair.'

'I need work nearby. If I win the archery competition, I'm hoping de Rohan might keep me on.' Maude moved tentatively towards the river so that she could view the keep more clearly. It would be difficult to attack, thanks to the steep mound it was built on, and de Rohan obviously feared attack or he wouldn't have had the bridge pulled down. Gant's only hope would have to be from within, and she would provide the link. She very much hoped that she hated de Rohan on sight. It would make things so much easier.

Hoel joined her. 'You're a girl,' he pointed out carefully. 'It's not likely that the new lord will take you on. Besides, Thorston will beat you.'

Maude gave him a withering look. 'That's why I'm dressed like a boy. And who's Thorston?'

Picking up a small stone, Hoel chucked it in the river. 'He's one of us. An outcast. Best archer I've ever seen,' he added gravely with all the certainty of a seasoned soldier. His gaze flickered over her tight lips. 'Are you any good?'

'I'll have to be if I'm to beat Thorston, apparently.' Maude scanned downriver. 'What's beyond the bend?'

'That's where us outcasts live, though I doubt we'll be

there for long. The new lord won't probably like it, Alfred says.'

Deciding it would be better not to know who Alfred was, Maude sat down on the log whilst Hoel continued to throw stones. 'How long have you been an outcast?' For someone so thin and so patently hungry, Hoel appeared quite cheerful.

He sniffed and wiped his nose on his filthy sleeve. Maude was certain his tunic had never been washed. 'Ever since I can remember. My mother died and I was looked after by her friend until she died too. Thorston found me and we've been together for a long time. We joined up with Alfred and his family not so long ago. There's quite a merry band of us now, though the villagers don't like us.' He scratched his body vigorously.

'Miserable lot they are, an' all. Frightened of their own shadows, I reckon.' He sighed. 'If Thorston gets taken on, he'll find me some work, too. Be nice to eat regular meals,' he added wistfully.

Pangs of guilt shot through her, but Maude firmly willed them to the back of her mind. She could not afford to be sympathetic. Philippe's life was at stake. Anyway, there would be many others in similar plights also taking a chance in the competition. 'Well,' she said. 'I wish you and Thorston luck, then.'

Satisfied that all itches were well under control, Hoel turned his attention back to Maude. 'Why does a girl need such work? You didn't actually say before.' His tone was accusatory.

Maude hesitated. 'My brother's being held for ransom so I need the money for him. I've heard de Rohan is prepared to pay well.'

He eyed her tattered clothes and then the horse with suspicion. 'Did you steal the horse?'

'No. She's mine.'

Hoel nodded his head thoughtfully, clearly putting his mind to the situation. 'You're in disguise, then. Nobody is to know who you are, otherwise the people who took your brother will do him harm.'

As a piece of logical deduction, it was most impressive. Maude stiffened. The boy was quick, too quick. If she stayed with him too long, it could be dangerous. Before she could say anything, though, Hoel suddenly sprang to his feet.

'Come on, then. You'll get nowhere staying here. The competition starts at noon.' He squinted upwards towards the sun. 'There's not long left.'

There was just the river to cross. She stared at it, feeling its evil fingers waiting for her just below the surface. Maude's skin turned clammy and cold as the fear spread right through her body. She inched her way down to the river's edge, her hands shaking. Hoel pointed to the end of a thick rope attached to a tree. It had slithered below the surface of the water and into its murky depths. 'S'easy. Just hold on tight to the rope.'

Maude shook her head, hardly even able to look at the water. 'It's no use.'

Hoel frowned. 'Wait a moment,' he said before disappearing into the undergrowth that bordered the river. A minute later he reappeared, dragging a makeshift raft of several thin saplings. 'We used this for Hulda when she was pregnant. What d'you think?'

Her gulp was perhaps not quite the response he was expecting. 'I'll pull it,' Hoel said quickly. 'You could just sit behind and close your eyes.'

It was clearly the only way she was going to get across the river today. Weakly and with dreadful foreboding, Maude nodded. She had to think of Philippe.

Rigid with fear, Maude sat huddled behind Hoel, holding on to his stinking, skinny body for fear of her life, uncaring of fleas or any other vermin he might host. Hoel held Lark's reins so she could swim alongside. Having the horse there somehow gave Maude the feeling of solidity on one side of her at least.

It was a crossing she never wanted to repeat. Time seemed to pass in slow motion and it really looked as though they would never get to the other side—ever. Maude was soaked thoroughly and shivering with fear and cold.

All of a sudden, Maude could feel Lark pulling upwards as she found solid ground to walk on. Sighing with relief, she was just about to send up a prayer of thanks, when Lark stumbled, pulling the raft and its two occupants off balance. She hit the freezing water with a thud. A second later, Maude found herself engulfed in thick mud. A thin hand grabbed at the back of her tunic and with surprising strength, hauled her to the safety of the bank.

Spluttering with terror, Maude lay on her back, staring at the sky. Soft white clouds floated above. She blinked and realised she was still alive. Elbowing herself into a sitting position, she made a vain attempt to drag off the mud clinging to her sodden tunic. Lark and Hoel had suffered similar fates.

'We were lucky. It was shallow where she fell,' explained Hoel as he spat out some of the river water.

A sound like rolling thunder approached and Maude turned her head sharply. They found themselves surrounded by a small group of horsemen.

'Nothing more than a couple of filthy peasants, my lord.' A guard with beady black eyes stared down at them in disgust. Maude returned his look with feeling as she struggled to her feet.

'Much as it may be a foolish question, Riddell, I feel curious as to why a peasant would have such a fine-looking horse?' The question was delivered in a deep, languid voice that sent cold shivers down her spine. It was him, it had to be. If it was de Rohan, though, he was certainly no rough Breton peasant.

Maude turned in the direction of the voice and anything she was about to say died in her throat. The man was blindingly handsome, but there was more to it than that. Tall and well built, William de Rohan's presence struck Maude de Vaillant with the power of a Viking's war axe. The auburn hue of his dark hair glinted in the sun as he pushed it back from his brow. Contrary to the dictates of the King, his hair was shoulder length and unbound, framing an almost beautiful, sun-weathered face. She had a fleeting vision of soft, brown eyes, black brows and a carefully barbered jaw before remembering the role she was playing. Like Hoel, Maude fell to her knees with her head bowed in respect.

'Well?' The voice prompted her in a passable attempt at English. 'Are you able to explain yourself, lad?'

Swallowing hard, Maude mustered her voice and ventured a glance at de Rohan. What struck her was the awareness in those eyes of his, as if they saw right through her. This was going to be far harder than she thought. 'I'm come for the archery, my lord.'

The dark eyes continued to assess her. She could feel them on her. Eventually de Rohan sighed, reducing the tension between them. 'And the horse?' He smiled wanly at his companions before addressing them in Norman French. 'God's truth, these northern peasants have no conversation. We can only hope our sojourn here is short-lived.' His own chestnut stallion appeared to be fixing Maude with a glare similar to the one directed at her by the unfortunate Riddell.

Dressed in a sumptuous green cloak and soft leather boots, de Rohan looked the epitome of a king's courtier. Maude could quite see why the vain King Henry might wish himself rid of such masculine perfection. It was certainly no surprise that he was popular with women. Irritated by her own clumsiness and underestimation of the situation, Maude attempted an uncertain smile. 'I borrowed the horse from the head villager. If I win, I'm to send him some money…my lord,' she quickly added.

Two pairs of brown eyes collided at her slip of etiquette. Maude held her breath and hurriedly busied herself brushing the mud from her hands. Forgetting to tack a title on the end of a sentence was a punishable offence, certainly in the eyes of most nobles. She had to learn quickly or she would not last long.

'And where are you from?' The question was politely put, but Maude was certain she could hear a trace of humour behind the words. Looking up once more, she found the handsome face smiling down at her benignly. Had she imagined his perception? Looking at him now, Maude found it hard to believe. Perhaps the river water had addled her wits.

Maude waved her hand vaguely in the direction of her home. 'Over there, my lord.'

'Ah, I see,' came the languid reply. 'And the ferry was not to your liking?'

Darting a questioning glance at Hoel, Maude frowned up at him. 'He was a bit too expensive, my lord.'

'Riddell, I thought I had made it quite clear that there was to be no charge for the ferry today.' Despite the rather resigned note in his voice, Maude detected a command that had not gone unnoticed by the unfortunate Riddell.

'Aye, my lord. The ferryman was made aware of your wishes. I'll remind him again.' The swarthy face of the guard grimaced as he wheeled his horse around and headed off towards Osric.

'Well, lad.' De Rohan moved his huge horse closer to Maude before leaning down towards her. 'I shall look forward to your performance at the butts shortly.' Maude raised her eyes to his and for a few heartbeats it was as if they were completely alone in the world. His mouth broadened into a smile, displaying a set of uncracked, white teeth and a dimple in his chin. 'I'm sure you will prove most entertaining.' His gloved hand reached out to pluck a large, dripping leaf from her shoulder before going on to close her open mouth. For a dreadful moment, Maude had thought some of her hair had come loose from its bindings and she held her breath.

Straightening once more, de Rohan shook his head in contemplation of her bedraggled appearance. He reached into a pouch at his belt and threw her a silver coin. 'Compensation for your ruined clothes.' He held up his hand as Maude opened her mouth to protest. The dark eyes glinted down at her, clearly enjoying her discomfort.

'Please, do not concern yourself, lad. I shall not be out of pocket since I fully intend to retrieve the money for your clothes from the ferryman. My apologies for your distress.' Another heartwarming smile apparently constituted their dismissal.

Once de Rohan and his party were out of earshot, Maude let out the breath she had been holding. 'Damned popinjay,' she muttered, following his green cloak with her eyes. 'I thought he was going to have me hung for horse-stealing.' She tugged at her boots and emptied them of river water.

'You didn't sound like a peasant and he didn't believe it either. Brighter than he looks, I think.' Hoel grinned at her as he ruffled his hair in the breeze. 'Things look as if they might be interesting. I'll come with you.'

His assessment of the situation was very accurate, thought Maude irritably. She had thought outcasts were supposed to be stupid. It would seem that she had met the exception. 'Suit yourself,' she muttered as she pushed her hair further under her cap. 'But don't you dare say another word.'

Hoel's only reply was to hold out his hand. With a heavy sigh, Maude slapped the coin into his palm. 'By the Face of Lucca, Hoel, you'd better earn it,' she threatened, and stalked off towards de Rohan's keep.

Hoel stopped at every one of the market stalls filled with mouth-watering delicacies, clearly determined to spend his money. There were several stalls lining the route to the gate, and progress up the hill was made even slower because of the crowds milling around. Mouth-watering smells wafted in the air and she stared longingly at the pies. It was only when one young serving girl gave her a shy, blushing smile that Maude remembered why she was there and hurriedly pushed herself in the direction of the palisade.

All entrants to the competition had to enrol in front of the main hall itself. The guards on duty paid them scant attention, and Maude found herself finally within de Rohan's keep. Though how long she would stay there was anyone's guess.

Tall, square and sturdily built, de Rohan's keep was impressive. The recent downpours, however, had turned the bailey into a mudbath and several planks of wood had been placed over the worst parts. Maude and Lark eyed the foul puddles that remained with disgust as they picked their way to the public pen. Stabling Lark was essential and Maude was glad to see that de Rohan had at least made adequate provision for the horses.

Her heart was beginning to beat faster as Maude looked

around. Despite the warmth of the day, she felt cold and clammy. Doubtless it was because of her wet clothes, but she shivered all the same. Hoel went in search of Thorston and left her to enrol. It wasn't until he actually left her side that Maude realised how much she had enjoyed being with someone else. The only person she really spoke to these days was Philippe and he had been so hard-working and preoccupied of late that she had begun to feel very much alone.

As Maude approached the crowd of men and youths waiting to put their names in for the competition, every eye seemed to fasten on her. They were a rough-looking lot and few appeared to consider her much to worry about. Several of the men who stank of rancid ale were already becoming loud and quarrelsome.

The soldier in charge was the same Riddell she had come across earlier and he was clearly at odds with this particular duty. Sweat trickled from under his metal helm and into his bush of a black beard. Short and muscular, the soldier faced the rabble before him with an aggressive stare designed to gain attention. Cold, black eyes passed dismissively over Maude and focussed on the huge lout standing next to her.

He reeked of sweat, filth and ale and his matted fair hair was no doubt home to much else besides. Unable to stand still, he reeled into Maude on several occasions. Maude assessed his chances of even making it to the butts fairly poor, but the lout was welling with bravado. Trying to distance herself from him, Maude found herself trapped by the press of bodies around her.

'When's it all starting?' he snarled. 'Some of us 'ave got kids dying for want of food.'

When he opened his mouth, the stench about him was worse. The soldier placed his hands on his hips and visibly willed the man to be quiet. He ignored the warning signs, but those standing close to him sensed the trouble and tried to edge away.

The soldier's voice carried loud and clear. 'I want no troublemakers. You're out.'

A hushed silence spread over the crowd. The lout himself appeared stunned by the pronouncement. 'I've as much right as anyone else here,' he railed suddenly.

'You've as many rights as I allow you,' Riddell retaliated. 'The lord doesn't want drunkards, he wants good archers.'

The crowd murmured their agreement. The man just spat onto the ground. 'I'm better than any of this lot,' he hissed.

'That's as may be, man, but you're drunk. Be off.' Riddell did no more than nod in the man's direction and two burly soldiers began to push their way towards him. Clearly now appreciating the gravity of the situation, the man began to panic. Maude dodged his flailing arms as best she could but there was too little space. In a desperate attempt at escape, the drunkard simply hit out at the nearest obstacle. With one mighty swing, his fist collided with Maude's face and she crumpled in a heap into the mud.

'She's coming round, my lord. I'll take the leeches off now.'

Maude's blurred eyesight took in only the outline of a face above her, but her mind latched on to the significance of the word 'she'. Struggling to her elbows, Maude discovered that she was no longer wallowing in the mud, but had been placed on a wooden bench inside. Feeling very dizzy and sick, she waited until the buzzing noise in her head subsided a little before attempting to open her eyes. Her right eye remained closed and throbbing. Gingerly she prodded it to find out the extent of the damage.

'Hold still, girl.' The voice sounded mildly irritated. 'I
don't want to lose the leeches. They're about to drop.'

Maude felt two slight tugs around her swollen eye and
wondered if she was going to be sick. 'Hmm. They've
helped a bit, but you're not a pretty sight.'

Shakily, Maude pushed herself up to a sitting position.
A loud rushing noise roared through her. When it finally
abated, Maude cast her good eye about her surroundings.
The old woman who had tended her was dropping two
swollen leeches into a casket and muttering what sounded
like endearments to the creatures.

She was obviously in the main hall of de Rohan's keep.
The room was square and lofty, with thin window slits
allowing little light to penetrate the gloominess, even
though the shutters were wide open. A good fire burned at
the far end, despite the warm weather. Smoke and the smell
of sweet apple wood drifted in the air. Benches and trestle
tables lined the sides of the hall, and the wooden walls were
covered in a variety of threadbare hangings.

Soft laughter drew her eyes and Maude found herself
staring at William de Rohan once more. He had discarded
his green cloak and was attired in a brilliant tunic of scarlet,
embroidered exquisitely with black thread. Tight black
breeches completed his attire. Maude knew she was staring,
but it was hard to look away. Goblet in hand, de Rohan
was smiling tenderly into the eyes of a most attractive
woman with butter-blonde hair. The couple were surrounded by an adoring gaggle of youths and girls who were
almost tripping over themselves to attract his attention. His
eyes, however, were focussed on the beautiful woman before him.

They were watched in turn by a brown-garbed priest, a
giant of a man with short red hair, and an older man of
middling height with iron-grey hair. The latter's eyes were

fixed on the couple with an expression that Maude found oddly alarming. There was a strange half-smile on his lips, but his eyes were cold and haunting. He was not a man she would wish to tangle with.

Her movements must have caught de Rohan's eye and he turned to her, raising his goblet in salutation. 'Not dead yet, then?' The languid drawl echoed across the hall, causing Maude to tighten her lips. She was determined this arrogant peacock was not going to draw her into saying something foolish.

Maude raised her hand to her damaged eye. 'Still alive, my lord,' she managed to say. Hauling herself to her feet, Maude steadied herself on the nearest table.

'Tell me,' de Rohan asked of her, watching Maude take a few tentative steps towards the door, 'is it the habit hereabouts for girls to dress as boys? A quaint northern May Day custom, perhaps?'

The crowd about him simpered and snickered at his question. De Rohan beamed, clearly pleased with himself. Everyone awaited Maude's reply.

Tired, sick and hungry, Maude's patience was fast running out. Gritting her teeth, she gave herself one last chance at polite conversation. 'I thought it best, my lord. I doubted if I would be allowed to enter the archery competition as a girl, despite being better than most of the men round here.'

'Ah, I see. And you are prepared to swim the river and brave the local drunks to do it. Such courage is utterly breathtaking.' His eyes roved over her entire length and gleamed as if amused in some way. He looked at her as a man looked at a woman and she was clearly found wanting.

Acutely aware of her dreadful condition, Maude blushed furiously, although whether from shame or anger she really couldn't tell. Skeins of her dark hair hung in muddy tangles

about her face, her eye was throbbing and her tunic ripped
in several places. Lifting her chin, she decided that the only
thing to do was attack. If there was anything she had
learned from her time with Philippe, that was it.

'My lord, I have a proposal for you.'

A gasp of disbelief escaped from de Rohan's audience.
'A proposal!' he repeated with that maddening smile still
pinned to his lips. 'Well, my dear, I have to say that I have
been offered many proposals in my time, but none from
someone so clearly…er…determined to gain my attention.'
He grinned, enjoying her discomfort and making a joke of
it.

Before Maude could say another word, he had lifted up
a slender finger to halt her words. 'But I really feel that I
must stop you there. Much as I am flattered by your attentions, I had set my sights on a bride with, shall we say,
more feminine attractions.' His eyes lingered on her dishevelled hair. 'I really don't think we would make an attractive couple, my dear. Our garments are just not compatible.' The man shuddered visibly.

All about them, the crowd hooted with laughter at his
set-down. Maude longed to throttle the arrogant peacock
with her bare hands, but fought down the impulse for Philippe's sake. Taking a deep breath, she looked at him with
steady eyes.

'Perhaps you misconstrued my intentions, my lord. I
meant a proposition. Marriage was truthfully not what I had
in mind,' she ground out, her cheeks burning with the humiliation. If she ever came out of this in one piece, Maude
mentally promised herself satisfaction at de Rohan's ex-
pense.

De Rohan picked up the flask of wine and filled two
goblets before sauntering towards her. His unexpected de-
fection silenced the audience, and Maude noticed that even

the guards were watching the proceedings with interest. He stopped before her and held out a goblet. Maude debated whether or not she could afford to refuse but decided in all probability she couldn't. Snatching it from him, she mumbled her thanks.

'Forgive my hasty assumptions, my dear,' he continued gravely and on a far more intimate level. The man was standing close to her and Maude was very much aware of his height and his attractiveness. It made her feel uncomfortable. 'I had not realised you had a more clandestine arrangement in mind. I regret, however, that I must still decline your offer.'

This time it was Maude who gasped out loud. Blushing a fiery red, she stared up at him open-mouthed. 'I had no such thing in mind,' she spluttered, her wine slopping to the rushes at her feet. His height meant that she had to take a step back to look the man directly in the eye. Summoning every ounce of the haughty de Vaillant courage at her disposal, Maude fixed de Rohan with a disparaging glare. 'I wished only to offer you my services as an archer and bodyguard. No more than that, rest assured.'

Close to, she could see how the dark barbered stubble was already growing back. Somehow, so familiar a male irritation comforted Maude in this nightmare. At least de Rohan didn't have everything easy. Presumably he did not grow a beard out of vanity. He would hardly want to hide all that beauty, after all.

Suddenly, without warning, tears welled in her eyes. Uncertain whether it was his reminder about Philippe or simply a combination of all the factors, Maude found her lips trembling. Swallowing hard, Maude was determined the brute would not see her cry, but she felt so tired, hurt and sick.

If he noticed anything amiss, de Rohan made no mention

of it. He sipped delicately at the wine before placing the goblet carefully next to hers on the table. 'Do you have a name?' he asked eventually.

'Maude,' she sniffed, wiping her nose with her sleeve. 'I'm able to track, hunt and use a knife, should the need arise,' she added, rallying a little. 'I work as a mercenary. Few in these parts would turn me down.'

His eyes turned on her sharply. The alertness was back. 'Tell me, Maude, why such an expert is in need of work, then?'

She could feel those eyes of his on her and wondered then if she could ever suffer his arrogance for more than a minute at a time. 'I've heard you pay well and I need the money.' The words were snapped out with impatience and frustration.

De Rohan merely twitched his lips. 'You put things so forcefully, Maude, that I am indeed tempted to let you convince me. Riddell!' He had not changed the tone of his voice, but the faithful guard appeared at her elbow within a heartbeat. 'Take her to the butts. I'm sure Maude will prove most entertaining.'

Maude closed her eyes, wondering whether she would ever survive the humiliation she had suffered at the hands of this enigmatic peacock. All the same, it would be most satisfying to wipe the smile from his well-formed lips.

# Chapter Three

'Well, FitzCount? What did you make of her?' William de Rohan narrowed his eyes to scan the line of archers milling around the butts. His gaze came to rest on the bedraggled figure of the girl. She had once again reverted to her disguise, deciding that the men might give her more of a chance as a youth. This brave deception had caused him an inner smile. 'Most entertaining wench I've laid eyes on for years,' he added as an afterthought.

The two Bretons had managed to detach themselves from the crowd that dogged their heels at every turn and were grateful for the brief respite. Brian FitzCount stroked at his red beard thoughtfully and followed his friend's line of vision. 'She's got spirit, no doubt about that. Interesting to see how she does. Is she part of it all, do you think?'

'Undoubtedly.' De Rohan raised a brow at FitzCount's craggy face. 'Do you think I was wrong to turn her down, perhaps? I thought I'd make her sweat a little.'

FitzCount gave a shout of laughter. 'I'll warrant she itched to kill you on the spot for those set-downs. She's no peasant, that's for certain.' He paused for a moment to watch Maude examine her arrows. 'Wonder what she looks like without all that mud? You might regret those hasty refusals yet, de Rohan!'

De Rohan laughed. 'Whatever plan young Maude is party to, rest assured she is not going to prevent me from finding the traitors and marrying a lovely, witless and charming heiress as my reward. It's taken years to get this far and the King is unlikely to refuse me anything if I bring in the plotters.'

FitzCount slung a thick arm around de Rohan's shoulders. After twenty years as part of Henry's entourage, they had both learned from a very early age that the art of dissembling at court was their greatest weapon. De Rohan had used his good looks and charm to fight his way to the top, but FitzCount could tell that the façade was getting harder for his friend to maintain.

'Aye,' he agreed affably. 'Let's hope you're right. If Bertolini has anything to do with it, though, he'll be up here to snatch all the glory. You'd best watch him, William. He could make a lot of trouble for you.' Theobald Bertolini was in charge of the King's spy network across the land and was always pushing his big nose into anything that would increase his own power. Ruthless and silent, the men of the court had to watch themselves in his presence. 'Although I can't say I envy you the young heiress. A comfortable widow is more in my line.'

De Rohan shook his head. 'A simple, adoring girl with nothing more in her head than pleasing me and choosing pretty gowns is all I ask. She'll give me her land and her money and I'll give her endless numbers of children and the King's favour. A perfect match.' He drew in a tired breath. 'I've had enough of money-grabbing, scheming women to last a lifetime, Brian. I've no more stomach for dancing to the King's every whim either. I want to be my own man for once and I'll do my damnedest to succeed this time.'

They both watched Maude flex her shoulders before practising an experienced and very steady draw on her bow. Despite her appearance and the now badly swollen eye, Maude had an air of determination that marked her out from the rest of the competitors.

'Well, at least you know she's not after you for your pretty face, de Rohan. Just your money.'

De Rohan grinned. 'Honesty is a valuable quality in a woman. It might be interesting to see if money is the only thing she's after. She could prove most diverting.'

A broad smile spread slowly over FitzCount's plain face. 'Thought she might.'

When Riddell called out the roll of names, Maude filed along with the rest of the competitors. A huge crowd surrounded the whole area and there was nowhere for her to escape even if she had wanted to. For a brief moment, Maude wondered about Geoffrey Gant and the spies he had boasted of. She scanned the faces of the villagers, but saw nothing more than misery and fear there. Well, it was too late to back out now.

The large bag of silver offered by de Rohan had attracted many men keen to display their talents. The size of the purse was perhaps also the measure of de Rohan's view of his own worth. He was afraid, it would seem.

Thinking back, Maude was not at all convinced of de Rohan's helplessness. He was well made for a courtier; although he affected a languid, lazy appearance, she had seen those dark observant eyes and the shrewd calculation behind them. There was far more to William de Rohan than met the eye and, much as she hated to admit it even to herself, she was curious to find out more.

The audience stood noisily watching as the competitors took out their arrows. Behind her, Maude could hear children squeal, mothers shout and men laugh. Music drifted around them, mingling with the smell of baking pies and roasting meat. Brightly coloured banners flapped and whirred loudly in the wind. Above it all, the sun shone, bathing the whole scene in a peace that she had not felt for a long time. Maude's anxiety thawed just a fraction.

Each man had to fire three arrows in the first round and the best twenty remained. Her hands damp with nerves, Maude took a deep breath before drawing the string back. In that split second before she fired, a deep calm invaded her. This was for Philippe. The first arrow thudded into the target with gratifying accuracy. Her next two landed in the same area. She was through.

For the second round, the men were moved further back to weed out more of their number. Each one was offered a skin of ale or water but, remembering the sergeant's dislike of drunkards, Maude opted for the water. It was warm and tasted as if it had come from the river several hours earlier. Her mouth was as dry as dust, but she had no desire to make herself even more ill. Maude threw the ladle back into the pail in disgust.

Within minutes, a servant had tapped her on the shoulder and produced a goblet of wine. Maude looked at the boy quizzically and he pointed to the older man with the iron-grey hair and beard she had seen before in de Rohan's hall. He was standing at the front of the crowd, his hands placed possessively on the shoulders of the woman with the blonde hair. The woman shifted a little nervously under his grip, but the man paid her no heed. His eyes remained levelly on Maude's face as she sipped at the wine. He gave no encouraging smile; indeed, it was as if he were assessing her true mettle. Gratefully, Maude tipped her head in acknowledgement of his favour before turning back to the targets.

The next three shots hit their mark with unerring accuracy. Only five competitors now remained. Two were older, experienced men who looked as though they might have been mercenaries at some stage. Broad-built and dishevelled, their long, greasy hair was tied back with leather thongs. They could fight their way out of a difficult situation with their eyes shut.

The other two were younger and, although smaller in build, their accuracy was impaired only by the distraction of the crowd. The youngest was, in fact, Thorston. To Maude he looked little older than Hoel, but he must have been about fifteen. Less grubby than Hoel, Thorston had that same air of neglect about him. Hunger and worry were etched deep in his face.

The next targets, however, drew a gasp of surprise from the crowd. Five apples had been threaded on to a piece of string and hung from a branch. Each man had five shots at their own string. Caught up by the breeze, however, the apples danced about, making the task significantly more difficult. Whoever had devised this, certainly knew what he wanted.

Maude glanced over her shoulder in the direction of the couple. William de Rohan was now standing next to them, his arms folded across his chest and his eyes riveted on Maude. The fact that he had come to watch at all was proof to Maude that his interest had been piqued, if only a little. Deep down, a thoroughly feminine smile of satisfaction spread through her. She turned back to the target.

The two older men did well. Each made three apples apiece before the wind and the vibrations of the previous shots snatched away victory. The third youth scored two and spat on the ground in disgust. Thorston took his time

and split four apples. His face beamed pink with the flush
of success. Maude swallowed hard before pulling up her
bow to aim. The crowd held its collective breath and all
noise seemed to cease.

The first three arrows found their mark, but the fourth
shot past when the wind pulled the string suddenly to one
side. Not wanting to waste her last shot, Maude knew she
could only tie with Thorston if she hit the apple. This had
to be a certain victory or it would all be pointless. The fifth
arrow sliced through the string and all five apples plunged
to the ground.

The crowd shouted and hooted their approval, and
Maude could feel her pride swell inside just a little. Thorston stared at the apples in disappointment, but he recovered enough to offer Maude his hand. He had recognized
the skill and stood down. She decided he was older than
he looked.

When Maude looked back at William de Rohan, there
was a slight frown on his face. Good, she thought. So much
for his condescension. The man at his side was smiling,
too, but it made her feel odd even though it wasn't directed
specifically at her. There was no good reason for her to
think it, but all the same Maude held her breath. A pre-
monition, perhaps? Alerted by the look on her face, de Rohan glanced at the man and said something that wiped the
smile from his face and caused the woman's hands to flutter
nervously.

Shaking her head, Maude turned away, only to come face
to face with the priest. A flash of recognition crossed his
face and Maude could feel the colour draining from her. It
was the same priest who had bayed for her blood three
years ago. Could anything else go wrong?

The cheering ceased as de Rohan approached Maude and

Thorston. Carefully he took a weighty purse from his belt and smiled at both of them.

'I declare this youth to be the winner,' announced de Rohan. Maude and the boy looked at each other in confusion as de Rohan handed the money to Thorston with a flourish. The crowd, too, remained silent, clearly bewildered by the decision. Maude could do no more than gape at de Rohan who was ignoring her and beaming at Thorston. Finally it was the lad himself who tried to settle things.

'But it was not me, my lord. I did not win the competition. He did.'

'But you scored four apples, did you not?' De Rohan smiled at him, all concerned.

'Aye, but he did better. He sliced the string itself. Used his head.' Thorston's simple words echoed around the silent audience.

'Ah, yes, of course. But you see, I did not ask anyone to slice the string. I wanted them to hit the apples.' De Rohan offered a sympathetic smile to Maude before placing an arm delicately around Thorston's puny shoulders.

Aye, Maude did see. He wanted someone who would follow orders to the hilt. Nor did he want a woman. There would be no place for her here. Closing her eyes briefly in disappointment, Maude then smiled at Thorston. 'Congratulations, then. I wish you luck.' Pushing her hand at Thorston, the two nodded solemnly at each other before Maude turned to leave.

'A moment, lad.'

Forced by etiquette to return, Maude faced William de Rohan with a tight smile. 'Aye, my lord.'

'A token of appreciation.' He tossed a smaller bag of coins at her and Maude caught it deftly. 'I'm sure your head villager from…over there…will appreciate his share.'

So he had seen through the plan and was very much enjoying rubbing her nose in her failure. Her eyes flashed with a mixture of pain, anger and frustration. What on earth was she to do now? The bag almost seemed to be burning a hole in her hand. 'Most kind, my lord.'

Slowly she turned to go. As she pushed herself through the crowd, a small hand closed over her wrist. 'I thought you won.'

Hoel's blue eyes gazed earnestly up at hers.

'Aye, well, things aren't always as straightforward as they seem. I'm pleased that your friend won, though,' she said gruffly, trying to keep the bitterness of losing from her voice. Philippe's fate had depended on her success. What now?

'Well, he said your shot was the best he'd ever seen. You should have seen the expression on his face! Poleaxed, he was. I was standing right by him.'

'Maude de Vaillant!' The name boomed out across the crowd, turning her blood into ice. 'Show your face, if you dare.' The priest had declared himself.

Slowly, she pushed Hoel from her. 'Go to Thorston. Now!' she commanded urgently.

Hoel looked up at her and nodded. Maude took a deep breath as the crowd fell away before the thin figure of the priest emerged. He stopped five paces in front of her, his grey eyes burning into her.

'Daughter of the Devil,' he accused. 'What evil do you make here now?'

A shaft of sunlight streamed on to her face at that moment, causing a gasp of disbelief amongst the onlookers. 'I came to use my bow and did so honestly,' she replied as calmly as she could. Terror was clutching at her heart, though. 'I have done no harm.'

'You draw evil wherever you are,' hissed the old man. 'People die around you. You are marked.'

Maude saw the faces of the people frown as they trawled their memories. Some recognised the name. Fierce whispers circulated, followed by angry heckling.

'I've done nothing,' she protested quietly, hoping a calm voice would placate the suspicious nature of the people.

'Riddell. Escort this woman to the gate. I'll have no trouble here.' William de Rohan's voice cut through the jeering. He had strolled casually to the priest's side and had gracefully placed a hand on his sleeve. Almost without noticing, several of his men had appeared and were barring the crowd from pushing forwards towards Maude. 'Take her away.' Despite the languid tone, Maude could hear the insistent command in his words. Riddell heard it, too.

Maude and de Rohan exchanged glances for no more than a moment, but she knew then that she owed her safety to him. The crowd were ready to pull her apart had he not calmly intervened. She couldn't help thinking that this was another perfect excuse for not taking her on.

Riddell gripped Maude firmly by the arm and pulled her wordlessly down the slope to the palisade gate. Some of the villagers ran alongside them, pelting her with mud and bits of discarded food, but they lost interest when Riddell took a swipe at them with his sword. The gates were heaved open and Maude found herself hustled to the other side. 'My horse,' she babbled, suddenly remembering Lark. 'My horse is still there.'

'Lord de Rohan says to come back when it's dark. He wants a word with you. The horse will be safe until then, I reckon.' For a soldier, Riddell had a wide repertoire of facial expressions and Maude was not at all impressed by the sneer he was offering her.

Jerking her arm free of his grip, she glared at his swarthy

face. 'If my horse comes to harm, I warn you now, Riddell, I shall hold you responsible.'

The sneer broadened into a broad smile. 'It's not the horse I'd be worrying about if I were you, wench.' He pushed her roughly back. 'Now be off.' The gate slammed shut.

It seemed like hours had passed before her heart returned to normal and Maude was able to breath a little more easily. Still desperately worried for her brother and bone-weary from the strains of the day, Maude decided her best plan would be to get some sleep. After all, who knew what de Rohan had planned for her. Despite his reputation as a womaniser, her appalling appearance had already earned his scorn so she felt quite safe on that count. It was the way he seemed to know exactly how her mind worked that disturbed her. Even Philippe had never really managed that.

Drawn to the river, like a moth to the flame, she followed the path as it meandered westwards. Her eye and her head throbbed unmercifully and she longed for fresh water or one of Bronwen's tisanes. After a while, she came to the spot where she and Hoel had crossed the river. It was overgrown with long grass and low, spreading branches. Crawling into the darkest spot, Maude wrapped her cloak about her and fell into a strange and dream-filled sleep.

'Maude?' The wind whispered her name again and she tried to shake it off. 'Maude?' This time it was louder and accompanied by a hand on her shoulder. 'Maude. Wake up.'

Slowly, she opened her one good eye, but it was her nose that warned her. 'Hoel?'

'Aye? How did you know?'

Maude sat up as best she could and pushed her hair back. As far as she could tell, the sun was much lower and the wind stronger. She must have been asleep for several hours. She smiled up at the cheeky face. 'Instinct.'

Hoel frowned. 'I was worried about you. I knew you'd not go far without the horse so I came to look for you.' His eyes rested on her bruises and her pale skin. 'I've brought something for you, but it's not much.'

'Hoel!' she said in genuine surprise. 'How did you know?' She took the wineskin and drank her fill. It was a very good quality.

Hoel shrugged his shoulders. 'De Rohan put it down and forgot about it. Thought you'd need it more than some villager.'

The wine was strong and soft and slipped down her throat easily. When she had finished, Maude lay back and breathed more easily. The wine had calmed her quite considerably.

'You'd best come with me.'

Obediently, Maude climbed out from her refuge and walked with him around the bend of the river. A small encampment nestled amongst the trees. Piles of rubbish and the raw smell of human excrement fouled the fresh breeze to such an extent that Maude's empty stomach heaved. There were three lean-to hovels made of narrow tree trunks, branches, moss, leaves, reeds and any other natural materials that lay nearby. Several children ran up to them, clamouring their welcome. Hoel held up a handful of stale pies and loaves as well as some freshly-killed rabbits and took them over to a tall, dark man who was tending a cheerful fire with great care.

'This is Alfred,' he announced to Maude. 'He and Hulda look after us here.'

Alfred turned his head and knelt back to survey Maude. He took in her bruises, her muddy appearance and her wan face with no more than a faint sigh before wiping his hands on his breeches and hauling himself to his feet. 'Welcome, then, stranger.' He placed his hand on her shoulder. 'You're welcome to food and shelter.' His eyes were kind and Maude found herself warming to this man.

'My name is Maude,' she said. 'I'd be glad to accept your offer, if I could wash first.'

A thin, sharp-faced woman with a grubby baby on her hip emerged from one of the huts. Strands of thin, brown hair fell from an untidy braid. Despite the lines of worry on her face, Hulda retained an air of youthfulness. A pair of earnest brown eyes studied her carefully. 'You'd best come with me, then.'

Within a short while, Maude found herself sitting before the fire, chewing on roasted rabbit and stale bread. She had been joined by seven children who were just as thin and dirty as Hoel and Thorston.

They all sat in companionable silence, chewing on the hot meat, when Thorston arrived.

'Thought you'd be in the hall with the new lord.'

Thorston grinned, his teeth shining in the half-light. 'Me, too,' he said. 'But I decided it wasn't right. I told de Rohan that Maude had won fair and square and I couldn't rightfully accept the winnings. I gave them back to him,' he added cautiously. Alfred said nothing.

Stunned, Maude just stared at him. If there was anything these people needed, it was money. 'What did he say?' she asked.

'Not much. Said if I changed my mind to come back tomorrow.'

'I see.' She wasn't at all sure that she did. These people were desperate for food and certainly couldn't afford such expensive principles. 'And will you?'

'I reckon I might,' he grinned. 'Just wanted to make my point.'

A broad grin spread across Maude's face. 'Well, I'm most grateful, anyway.' She wondered what poor de Rohan had made of all of this. He must be finding life in the north rather unnerving when starving peasants rejected his generosity for reasons of conscience.

For all their poverty, they were a happy group, taking care that each received their share of food and attention. When they had finished eating, Maude took her leave of Alfred and his family.

'If you need shelter for the night, girl, you're welcome.' Alfred nodded down at her anxiously. He was genuinely concerned.

Maude smiled at him, warmed by his sincerity. 'I have to get my horse, but if I need somewhere to stay, I'll be back.' With the dusk drawing in, safe company was a welcoming thought.

Hoel and Thorston accompanied her back to the keep, their simple chatter taking her mind off her meeting with de Rohan. Halfway up the hill, Maude stopped. There was a strong smell of smoke. Looking up, she could see an orange light above one of the stalls.

'The keep's on fire,' she whispered. 'I must get Lark out.' She was certain that the inhabitants would be safe but there was no one to look out for Lark. 'No one will notice me. I'm going to get her.'

Thorston and Hoel ran after her, but they had not gone far when the sound of hoofbeats reached their ears. Maude stopped to listen. They were fast and there were two of them, she decided. Narrowing her eyes, Maude could just about make out two dark shadows racing from the palisade gates. Instinct warned her that this was trouble. Their only escape would be across the ferry.

'Run to the ferry and stop them getting on,' she shouted at Thorston. 'Shoot them if you must, but try not to kill them.' Without hesitation, Thorston nodded and hared off towards the ferry.

'Get some stones. As many as you can.' Hoel accepted his orders as Thorston had.

At least it wasn't yet fully dark; if these were no more than messengers, she'd be able to tell as soon as they drew close. In view of de Rohan's difficulties, however, it would be wise to be cautious. Who knows how grateful he might be? It would be worth a try at least.

Maude ran as fast as she could to the flat land that stretched between the village and the ferry. Higher up the mound, torches were streaming towards the palisade gates like living light. The horses were being followed.

She positioned herself in the shadow of a large tree and waited. The first person she recognized on the lead horse was the blonde woman who had made de Rohan laugh. The man doubled up behind her was no more than a dark shadow. She was struggling and crying out for help. Unwilling to risk hurting her, Maude turned her attention to the second horse whose rider was alone.

Her arrow hit him deep in the shoulder and he landed with a heavy thud. Hearing the noise, the first rider half-turned to look over his shoulder. He drew his horse to a standstill, realising that his escape over the ferry was no longer possible. Thorston had planted himself firmly in front of the raft.

'Put the woman down.' Maude stepped out of the shadows, her arrow pointing at the man's neck. As he turned, she recognised him as one of the men who had taken part in the archery competition earlier. One of the mercenaries.

Her answer was a cold sneer. 'I'm afraid of no girl, whether marked by the devil or not.'

Maude stared at him, watching his eyes assessing his different options. Not far behind him came the sound of chasing hoofbeats. Suddenly, he spurred his horse forward, urging him towards the river. He had decided to take the risk and swim across on the horse. With the current being so strong, he would have his hands full just guiding the horse. If she shot him in the river, the woman was likely to drown.

The rope. She remembered the rope. 'Hoel! Throw the stones close to the horse and keep him going downriver,' she shouted. Beckoning to Thorston, Maude ran to the place where the rope was tied.

Hoel carried out her orders perfectly. The horse shied away from the splashes made by the stones and soon enough, the strong current carried them further and further downriver. The rider was already losing control and the horse was beginning to panic. Gripping on to its mane, the woman screamed pitifully in terror.

Maude knelt down at the edge of the river, testing the slimy rope in her hands. This was no time to think of her own fear, but it was nevertheless creeping through her body like an evil mist. 'When I give the word,' she whispered to Thorston, 'shoot him in the shoulder.'

If he was surprised, he gave no sign of it. A brief nod acknowledged her order. Maude was suddenly reminded of de Rohan's insistence on wanting someone who would obey orders without question. She decided he was right.

As the horse flailed closer to the rope, Maude heaved on it so that it lifted clear of the water. She yelled to the woman. 'Grab the rope. Reach out and hold on to the rope.' Maude's voice carried to the terrified hostage and the woman shrieked even louder. 'You must do it now or you will die. Take hold of the rope with both hands.'

With seconds to spare, the woman snatched her hands from the horse's mane and reached for the thick, slimy rope. At the same time, Maude shouted the command to

Thorston. The kidnapper did no more than utter a short
scream as the arrow lodged deep in his shoulder. Within a
heartbeat he had slithered into the black water and disappeared.

Maude was holding on to the rope, but it was beginning
to slacken as the woman clung on for her life. Suddenly,
two soldiers leapt from nowhere into the river and two
more grabbed the rope from her hands. The men from the
keep had arrived. Maude breathed a huge sigh of relief as
the woman was plucked from the water and dragged to
safety. She was frightened and wet, but safe.

'Well, Maude. A most impressive performance.'

Maude turned to find William de Rohan standing no
more than two paces behind her.

Anything she was about to say was interrupted by the
woman hurling herself hysterically into his arms. 'William!' she cried. 'You saved me. I was so afraid.'

She clung to him as if her life did, indeed, depend on
him. 'You're safe now, Gundreda,' he murmured, looking
down tenderly at the woman in his arms.

'I think it would be best if I take my wife, de Rohan.'
The older man with the grey hair appeared suddenly from
the shadows. For a minute or two, the men stared at each
other, locked in some struggle. Finally, de Rohan nodded
and offered a smile.

'Of course.'

The other man did no more than grab his wife quite
roughly by the wrist and pull her back to his horse. De
Rohan watched them silently before turning back to Maude.

'You'll be staying in what's left of my keep, tonight.'

## Chapter Four

An overwhelming urge to run away assailed her, but Maude stood her ground as she was subjected once again to the disagreeable scrutiny of William de Rohan and his entourage back in the safety of his hall. A strand of hair dangled irritatingly over her cheek and she batted it away.

'So, Maude. My thanks for your quick-witted actions. I am utterly grateful that you were able to save Lady de Vere.' He was watching her carefully.

'I did tell you earlier, my lord. My skills are, indeed, most impressive.' Maude levelled her gaze at him and was surprised to see that he found her outspoken attitude worthy of a smile. In her experience, most men did not normally appreciate her frankness.

'So you did, Maude. So you did.' For no more than a brief moment his eyes held hers, as if he were weighing her up. She, in turn, was mesmerised by the flash of interest that had kindled in his eyes. It was not at all hard to see why he was popular with women. Reminding herself hastily that this was a man used to getting his own way by means of charm, Maude stiffened her resolve. William de Rohan was not going to make an easy conquest out of her.

'Remind me of your skills, Maude,' he continued in that

lazy drawl. 'I am beginning to think I made a grave error of judgement in turning down your propositions and proposals.' He picked up a goblet of wine and was obviously more intent on entertaining his adoring audience than in finding out more about his heroine. His hall was crowded with people who seemed to have nothing better to do than hang on his every word. Well, one woman had seen through his insincere charm and Maude was determined he was not going to get the better of her.

The only other person who did not seem to share this blanket adoration of de Rohan was the man with the grey hair and beard. If this was Lord de Vere, then she was in the company of the infamous shire reeve. He sat quietly to one side, drinking his wine and contemplating the scene before him. There was an air of satisfaction about him that seemed somewhat out of place after such a frightening event. His wife was clearly recuperating elsewhere.

Sighing heavily, Maude glared at de Rohan. 'My brother's skills as a swordsman are much in demand and I have often accompanied him on his missions. He was proud to have me at his side.' She sniffed briefly to allow this information to sink in, pleased at the rather aghast expressions on the faces of her audience. 'I am an excellent archer, tracker and hunter and am more than adept with a knife, if need be. My skills with a sword are considered by my brother to be competent.'

A stunned silence followed her words. De Rohan moved to stand before her. 'Perhaps I should be speaking to your brother, then?'

'Philippe is not available at the moment,' she snapped, two red blotches staining her cheeks.

'Pity,' he replied with maddening resignation. Gently, he reached out to pluck a twig from her hair, rearranging a few straggly hairs to his own satisfaction. 'So, we have only your word about your skills?' he asked, raising his brows in question. His familiars sniggered somewhat unkindly behind him.

'My word is good enough for most in this area,' she replied with asperity. 'The name of de Vaillant is an honourable one.'

De Rohan tilted his head to one side as if thinking deeply before looking over to the red-haired man she had seen before. 'What say you, FitzCount? Have you heard of the de Vaillant name before?'

FitzCount gave his friend a measured look. 'I recall hearing of one Ivo de Vaillant who was vassal to the traitor de Poictou.'

It was an insult designed to goad her. What with her tiredness and her throbbing eye, Maude's patience finally snapped. 'There was never any doubt about my father's loyalty to the King. Every member of my family behaves with honour and I shall endeavour to maintain such conduct. I am, however, tired of wondering why I am being subjected to such scrutiny since I was clearly not involved in the abduction. Whatever you wish to say, I sincerely wish that you would get on with it. My lord.'

The whole hall seemed to hold its breath as they waited for de Rohan's wrath to explode. Maude could feel them all expecting, nay...hoping for her downfall. All de Rohan did, though, was to place his fingers over his mouth and break out into a genuine smile of pleasure. Against her will, Maude could feel her prickliness abating just a little. His charm and good humour made her feel as surly as a maltreated peasant.

'My dear girl. You northern women are endearingly frank.' He reached out to touch her bruised eye. 'It would also appear that you have a most hardy and enduring disposition. However, it would assist me to know why you want to place all your varied talents at my disposal.' Despite his charm, the man's mind was as sharp as a razor.

'I told you before. I have need of your money.'

'Ah, yes, of course. I should have remembered. Women and money are, to the best of my knowledge, inseparable.' There was an odd glint in his eyes as he said this, but Maude dismissed it as being part of his interminable wit. At least his adoring audience liked it. 'Unfortunately, Maude, we courtiers are notorious for our lack of money. You would be greatly disappointed by my resources, I fear. Hence my desire to wed an heiress.'

'But you did offer a large purse for anyone offering particular skills to protect you from danger,' she said carefully, wondering where on earth the man was taking the conversation now. She would never involve herself with a courtier again.

'I did, indeed,' he replied quickly. 'But have you not considered marriage yourself, Maude?' He eyed her wild, tangled hair and torn tunic with a certain amount of humour.

'No,' Maude replied frostily. 'No man would contemplate marriage with me.'

His smile broadened. 'You surprise me. I would have thought that any number of northern lordlings would be keen to have so accomplished a wife. An expert archer for a helpmate ought to be *de rigueur* in these parts.'

Open laughter broke out around them, but they were facing one another as if no one else existed. Maude shook her head in disbelief. 'You heard the priest, my lord. I'm a marked woman.'

'Ah yes. The priest.' He sighed heavily before turning back to face his followers. 'Is he here?'

The silence that followed was answer enough.

'I assume you have an answer to such an accusation?' De Rohan turned back to face her, all humour gone.

'An accident of birth, my lord. My mother chose to die in order to save me. It was no more than that. Ever since, though, I have been blamed for any accident, tragedy or suffering which occurs in my vicinity. Such a reputation has had a dampening effect even on the most courageous of our...er...northern lordlings.'

'I quite see.' William de Rohan leaned against the table and stared at her in a most speculative way. After taking another sip of wine, he placed the goblet firmly on the table as if having come to a decision. 'Were it not for the fact that I am currently engaged in negotiations of marriage myself, I would naturally reconsider your proposal, Maude. I'm sure I would feel entirely safe in your hands.' It seemed this *double entendre* was popular with the men. Maude preferred to stare at him woodenly. She refused to encourage him in his antics. 'A solution, however, does present itself which may benefit the both of us.'

Maude could see FitzCount and de Vere watching him very carefully. The rest of the crowd shifted on their benches, no doubt expecting another witty set-down. 'I am eager to hear your suggestion, my lord.' Maude was suddenly very tired of all this and just longed for a comfortable pallet. It had been a very long day and she really was not in the mood for much more of his particular humour.

Flicking pieces of fluff from his beautiful tunic, de Rohan sighed. 'My reputation as one of the King's new men goes before me and the need for good protection in these wild lands has been made very apparent. My own sword arm is perhaps lacking in strength and I admit to a certain concern for my safety.'

He was lying, she knew he was. The man's body was shaped and honed as well as any well-practised mercenary, and she had seen enough of those these last few years. Accordingly, Maude merely raised a disbelieving brow. 'Much would depend on the nature of the danger, my lord, don't you think?'

De Rohan nodded. 'I see you have it exactly. You truly have an acute grasp of the situation, Maude. It is a most encouraging thought.'

'Well, you know, I'm not at all sure that I do,' she said slowly. 'Perhaps you could enlighten me as to the exact nature of these dangers, my lord.' If he could play with her, then she could give him as good as she got. Maude offered him a wide-eyed, innocent look.

A surprisingly brown hand dismissed her question with a very graceful gesture. 'Outlaws, traitors, disenchanted nobles...perhaps even an outraged husband or two...' De Rohan looked directly at the grey-haired man. 'Would you think that covered it, de Vere?'

De Vere managed only a tight smile. 'I'm sure you have thought of everything, de Rohan.' His voice conveyed the impression of boredom, but the faintest flicker of his eyelids betrayed his interest. No love lost between those two, then, thought Maude. This was hardly surprising if de Rohan was foolish enough to flirt openly with the man's wife. For all his cleverness, the man still had a foible or two.

De Rohan ignored any hint of irony and looked straight at Maude. 'I am constantly in danger, Maude. You cannot conceive the number of nights I have been kept awake by my condition.'

The man was playing to his audience again whilst keeping her dangling. They both knew what he was leading to and de Rohan was deliberately humiliating her. The crowd burst into outright laughter at his innuendo—even the dour FitzCount was hard-pressed to keep a straight face. Maude could feel her calm slipping.

'I fear your "condition" is likely to deteriorate significantly the longer you remain in these parts, my lord. It might be best if you sought professional help from the King's court, then.' She smiled at him tritely, pleased that he had obviously not expected so fast a reply. Clearly the man had no idea what living with an army of brothers was like.

'Ah, Maude, I think it's too late for that.' The dark eyes twinkled down at her in a very courtier-like manner. 'Would you be my protector?' De Rohan stood very close to her and it was almost as if he had forgotten the rest of the hall.

She fixed him with a disparaging look that Philippe would have warned de Rohan about. 'That very much depends on what you're prepared to pay me.' The man seemed to think that all women were hell-bent on getting their hands on his silver, so she would not disabuse him of that supposition just yet.

'That,' he pointed out very quickly, 'depends very much on your worth.'

'I see.' The wretched man was going to demand a performance from her. For a languid courtier, de Rohan had seriously hidden depths.

Maude eyed the teeming puddles in the bailey with distaste. She was not going to enjoy this spectacle at all. Her opponent, a confident, well-built squire of about sixteen named Thomas, had accepted de Rohan's challenge with bad grace, clearly put out about having to fight a woman. He cast glowering eyes in Maude's direction. Their audience knew no such apprehension. From the smiles and cheery expressions, they were keen to gloat over her downfall. Several of his soldiers held torches aloft to light the area of battle.

De Rohan had commanded a demonstration of her swordsmanship, since that, he had concluded, was her weakest skill. Maude smiled inwardly at that, since her 'weak skill' was more than likely far better than the boy's.

The two of them stood opposite one another, swords gripped tightly, lips compressed. De Rohan and FitzCount stood at the top of the steps to the hall, surveying the scene in companionable silence. If anything, de Rohan looked rather grim, but Maude dismissed it as a trick of the unsteady light.

At Riddell's sign, Maude immediately stepped back, the heavy sword braced before her. Thomas, looking for a quick and heroic end to the fight, knew no such caution. His blade sliced towards her three times before he thought to change his pattern. Heavy on his feet, Thomas was no match for Maude. She evaded his attack quickly and effectively, then darted towards him with a would-be mortal lunge.

Shocked to the core, Thomas could only stare at the ripped tunic and the small red stain that signalled the end of the demonstration. Gracelessly, he threw down his sword and gave Maude one last grimace before storming off to attend to his wound. Maude knew she had merely scratched him, but the damage to his pride was far greater. Sighing heavily, she turned to de Rohan to await his decision. The assembled crowd were gratifyingly silent.

'The girl was most impressive. I wonder how she would fare with a larger man?' De Vere's gravelly voice boomed across the courtyard. All eyes turned to him, but de Vere ignored them. His full attention was on de Rohan.

They were, decided Maude, most adept at squeezing blood from a very dry stone. Pushing her hair back from her swollen eye, Maude tilted her head in silent acceptance of this further challenge.

Riddell was not a simple boy, however, and Maude eyed him with some apprehension as he stood before her. She was not much in favour with him and Riddell did not look as if he had a soft heart.

De Rohan had decided that knives might offer an interesting challenge and had clearly chosen his captain with the aim of defeating her soundly. Small in stature, but broad and brawny, Riddell would require far more thought than Thomas. Her slight weight put Maude at a significant disadvantage and demanded a greater degree of cunning. Having seen him deal with the louts that afternoon, Maude knew Riddell would not squander his energy, nor would he give her any quarter. Well, she had fought men like him before and won. All she had to do was adapt and improvise.

Riddell had planted his feet wide apart and his knife was held, point upwards, at waist height. Maude could feel the eyes of the crowd burning into her almost as if they would set her alight, but her courage did not fail her. Narrowing her eyes, she stared hard at her enemy, for that was what Riddell now was. He was not about to underestimate her in the same way Thomas had.

Slowly, very slowly, the pair began to circle each other. Their movements were controlled and well-practised, as if they were dancing. Suddenly, Riddell's knife slashed at her with the speed of an arrow and Maude jumped back to avoid it. Minute after minute, the pair circled, slashed and jumped, waiting for that vital error or that lowering of the defences that would let a blade through. Riddell's heavy body was surprisingly light in movement, but sweat was dripping from his shaggy mane of black hair. His swarthy skin shone red in the torchlight and his dark eyes seared into her. A seasoned soldier who was used to fighting—but used to fighting men, Maude reminded herself.

The mood of the crowd was now uncertain. There was

no smiling or laughter. Maude lunged but Riddell was there before her and his knife ripped through the sleeve of her mangled tunic. A slight smile formed on his lips as the soldier sensed victory. Maude allowed him to think it, at least.

Nearer and nearer he edged, ready to strike. When the blade came, Maude threw herself to the ground and rolled away from danger. As she leapt to her feet once more, she was clutching a lump of dirt and threw it at the soldier's face. Startled for no more than a moment, Riddell lost concentration. In that second, Maude took advantage and kicked the knife from his grasp. He made no move to retrieve his weapon, merely straightening himself in the direction of de Rohan. He had conceded.

William de Rohan descended the steps from the hall and made his way through the crowd. 'A most unorthodox method, Maude, but effective.' His eyes were luminous in the flickering torchlight and she was certain there was a hint of admiration there.

'Well?' she pressed him. 'Do you hire me or not?'

'My dear girl,' he replied with maddening humour, 'from now on I remain open to any offers you might care to make. I am entirely in your hands.'

Ignoring such irritating wit, Maude speared him with a withering look. 'I offer you my protection for the summer in return for one hundred silver marks.' It was an audacious suggestion, of course, but Maude surmised that de Rohan, now convinced as to her suitability, would pay handsomely for his protection. How she was going to survive a summer with this arrogant, lying peacock was another matter. Philippe, she decided glumly, had much to answer for.

'Whatever.' He dismissed her demands with that careless gesture of the hand again.

Maude pursed her lips. Maybe she should have bartered

herself for two hundred marks. No doubt she would earn every piece.

'But,' he continued in that soft voice that did not bode well, 'I shall expect constant protection. You will remain at my side at all times. Wherever I am.'

Maude flushed at the implications, but raised her chin as she faced him. 'Very well.'

'Excellent.' He turned to FitzCount, who had just lumbered up behind him. 'Do you not agree, Brian?'

FitzCount blinked rapidly down at Maude's dirty, bruised face. The mutinous look in her eyes caused him to shake his head ruefully. 'Let's hope she's worth it.'

Still somewhat nonplussed at the success of Gant's unlikely plan, Maude found herself ushered to William de Rohan's personal chamber. The room was plainly furnished, but there were touches of luxury in the shape of an exquisitely carved oak chest, a thick green bed coverlet and a leather-bound box lying on the table by the fire. She also noticed that the rushes of the floor had not been changed for some time and that the walls were covered in soot from the wall-sconces.

Suddenly the door was pushed open and two servants staggered in, carrying a large barrel. Close behind followed de Rohan himself. After instructing the men to bring wine and food as well as hot water, he stood before the fire, inspecting Maude. His face had lost that maddening smile, and bore once again the alert, probing look that made her feel rather nervous. 'Well, Maude. I trust you did not find your demonstration too demanding?' He reached forward to look more closely at her swollen eye.

Stepping back hurriedly, Maude managed a weak smile. 'You wished to see further proof of my skills. I would not have expected less.'

His sharp eyes watched her jaw tighten in determination
and the wretched man smiled. He reminded her of a cat
playing with a mouse. 'You appear to have led a rather
unusual life, Maude. My experience has always encouraged
me to believe ladies spent their time on needlework, gowns
and trinkets.'

A vision of the lovely Lady de Vere sprang to mind and
Maude's spirit drooped a little. 'My father had led a rough
soldier's life, my lord, and with nine sons found a newborn,
motherless daughter somewhat of a vexation. Most of my
time was spent with Philippe and the village boys. Naturally they had little knowledge of needlework or gowns.'

'Naturally not,' came de Rohan's admirably grave reply.
'But your loss is clearly my gain, Maude.' He looked at
her then, his eyes searing in to her. 'We do have much to
discuss, though.'

This worrying change of attitude was interrupted by the
return of the servants with mounds of food, wine and water.
Not entirely sure which bodily function was to be dealt with
first, Maude raised a brow in de Rohan's direction.

'Drink and food first, I think,' he said tactfully. Gracefully indicating where she should sit, de Rohan set about
offering Maude a selection of delicacies that had her mouth
watering. It had been some time since she had sat down
with Alfred and his family, and one small piece of rabbit
was not likely to staunch an appetite like hers for long.

Her evident pleasure in the food clearly held some fascination for de Rohan. He watched her every bite until finally Maude placed her knife on the table and looked up
at him. 'By the Face of Lucca, man, if you're waiting for
me to commit some grave error at your table, I would prefer
you to say so now. It makes me very nervous having you
watch my every move.'

It also made her very nervous having so handsome a man

sit no more than a handspan from her body, but Maude refrained from mentioning that.

'My apologies, Maude,' he said with rather fetching concern. 'It's just that I have never seen a lady eat so much.' Realising his further breach of etiquette, de Rohan flushed a little whilst clearing his throat.

So the perfect courtier was capable of the odd mistake? Graciously, Maude shrugged. 'If you had to share your table with an assortment of brothers, their offspring and any other visitors, you would quickly learn to eat whatever you could as soon as possible or die from starvation.'

Her words were delivered with such earnest conviction, that for a moment, de Rohan stared at her in disbelief before the subsiding flush on his cheeks returned with renewed heat. Then he laughed.

'You do know how to make a man squirm, Maude de Vaillant. I see you learnt much from those brothers of yours.' His eyes were alight with humour and, in truth, it was hard not to respond to him. Hard, of course, but not impossible.

She set her goblet down on the table firmly and looked at him. 'What did you want to discuss, my lord?' The quiet tone of her voice had a sobering effect on de Rohan and his smile was withdrawn.

De Rohan stared at her for a moment before rising and going to stand before the fire. The long, lean lines of his body were visible in the firelight and Maude wondered why he wished to conceal the fact that he was a knight trained in warfare. If it was obvious to her, it must be obvious to everyone else. Finally he turned to look at her. 'This is a dangerous job, Maude. Several men have been killed trying to protect me so far. I wish to make it plain to you, that's all.'

Maude stared at him for a moment before pushing back her braid. 'I know,' she said simply. 'It doesn't matter.'

A soft knock at the door shattered the silence between them and the closeness that had somehow crept between them for a short while was swept away. De Rohan's courtier-like smile was pinned firmly in place.

It was the woman with the butter-blonde hair, Lady de Vere. Close to, she was not so young as Maude had thought, but her skin was as soft and lovely as a peach.

The woman sighed with relief when she saw de Rohan and her hands fluttered about her face. Clearly she was still unnerved by her ordeal and seemed completely unaware of Maude's existence. 'William,' she said breathlessly, 'I was so frightened. I thought he would kill me.'

There was indeed a plaintive note of fear in her voice which drew sympathy from de Rohan. He placed his hands on her shoulders. 'You were very brave, Gundreda.' He smiled down into her pretty face and brushed a tear from her cheeks. 'You must stay here until you are recovered.'

Gundreda bowed her head. 'I don't think that Piers...I...I shall have to see. You know how it is?'

There was an unmistakable tremble to her voice when she mentioned the name. De Rohan's smile disappeared.

'Whatever you decide, my dear, your wishes will be accommodated.' He squeezed her shoulders once again before gently putting her from him. 'Tell me. I am puzzled about how you came to be taken.'

With shaking fingers, Gundreda pushed back some loose strands of hair. 'I was walking with Piers when the man rode past. He...I...heard him coming but I had no idea what was happening.'

'And Piers?' de Rohan questioned lightly. 'What did he do?'

Gundreda wrapped her arms around herself and began to

sob. 'I'm sorry,' she mumbled. 'I can remember nothing more.'

'Of course not. Forgive me?' De Rohan gave her a gentle smile. 'Come, I'm sure you wish to meet your brave rescuer?'

For a moment, Gundreda looked surprised to see Maude in the room, but she rallied quickly. 'You are so brave. I'm sure I would be dead if it weren't for you.' Her blue eyes shone with genuine tears and Maude felt her conscience prick a little for thinking the woman was less than sincere.

'I'm sorry you got so wet,' she said.

Gundreda made a brave effort at a smile. Ice-blue eyes swept over Maude's mud-spattered and torn appearance. They stopped at her bruised eye. 'You look worse than I do.'

Inwardly, Maude held her breath at such bravado. She had been right about the woman to start with. Her outward smile, however, betrayed none of her disbelief. 'I'm sure that would be true were I not bruised and muddied anyway, my lady.'

A rather strangled sound came from de Rohan's throat as he interrupted their conversation, no doubt thinking it might deteriorate into something far worse. 'Actually, Gundreda, I wondered if you might be able to render Maude some service. I fear she is in need of a bath, but I possess none of the things considered vital by most women.'

The words tumbled out quickly and Maude found it hard not to smile. The composed and courtly William de Rohan was really rather anxious! 'That will not be necessary, my lord. I can bathe at another time,' said Maude calmly. She certainly had no desire to have Gundreda de Vere on hand witnessing her toilette.

De Rohan fixed her with an outraged eye. 'I insist. I know for certain that you have already bathed in the river, been mauled to the ground by some uncouth peasant, halted an abduction and defeated two much larger opponents in hand-to-hand combat. Hot water is just what you need.'

Too tired to argue with him further, Maude relented. 'Very well. If you insist.'

'Is that a capitulation, Maude?' he asked innocently when Gundreda went out in search of the necessary vials and salves.

'Not at all. A mere break in the skirmish, nothing more,' said Maude with her nose in the air.

'I think, Maude de Vaillant, I am going to enjoy my sojourn here far more than I had anticipated.' He smiled at her then with heart-stopping brilliance. 'I'm sure you will be worth every silver mark you earn.' Without warning, he picked up her dirty hand and delicately kissed her fingertips. Then, his eyes still on hers, he stood back, bowed slightly and left the room.

Maude followed him with her eyes. She thought perhaps she agreed with him.

The bath was a joy above all things. Scented hot water lapped around her shoulders and filled her with a sense of such well-being. Closing her eyes, she tried to forget about Gant and her real role in this keep.

'Is the water to your liking?' Gundreda had returned with her basket of salves and medicaments.

'Why, yes, my lady. I am truly grateful for your assistance, but there really is no need,' Maude added warily.

Gundreda dismissed her words with a flap of her delicate white hand. 'If William de Rohan wishes me to help you, then I shall. Besides, I'm grateful to you myself.'

Setting down her basket, she busied herself selecting several concoctions that Maude eyed with concern. Generally, other women were afeared of her and reacted by being hostile and even spiteful. This was understandable, of course, but wearing on the soul.

'Now. Let me look at your face.' In fact, Gundreda was sounding more like Bronwen and a pang of homesickness washed over Maude. Face to face, Maude assessed her as being in her late-twenties. The yellow colour of her hair was fading and there were fine lines about her mouth and eyes. Nevertheless, Gundreda de Vere was still a very lovely woman. She certainly had no cause to feel jealous of Maude!

Gently her finger touched Maude's bruised eye, causing the younger girl to flinch a little. 'I'm sorry for your hurt,' she said quietly, 'but it will not last long.' She smeared some vile-smelling salve on Maude's injuries. 'This should help to reduce the swelling. The worst will be gone in a few days' time.'

'My thanks.' Maude wondered if she had deliberately chosen the worst-smelling concoction on purpose. Gundreda's laugh caused her to look up.

'I know the smell is dreadful. That, too, will disappear.'

Maude must have looked unconvinced because the woman continued to smile at her. 'William has had personal experience of this salve on many occasions. He'll not worry about it.'

Her facial expression must have conveyed her disbelief, because Gundreda continued, unabashed. 'Oh, aye. Don't be deceived by those looks of his. Sir William has a mind of his own and will not be an easy man to protect.' A strange expression settled on her face, almost as if she thought she had said too much. 'Now,' she said briskly, 'let's wash your hair.'

Sitting quietly before the fire drying her hair, Maude cast a glance at Gundreda. The two had lapsed into an almost companionable silence.

'You've known him a long time, then?' Maude needed as much information as she could get.

'Aye. Since we were both young. I was part of Henry's court along with William and FitzCount. Since I married Lord de Vere, though, I have not seen as much of them as I would have liked.' She sighed a little. 'William was deeply in love with me before I married,' she added with becoming coyness. 'We had wanted to marry, but the King would not hear of it. I was too useful to him, or at least my beauty was. I have always hoped that if something were to happen to Piers…that perhaps we could still wed.'

'How long have you been married?' Maude asked, taken aback by such unsolicited information.

'Three years.' For some reason, Gundreda's face closed up and there was a definite tension about her. 'My husband is an old friend of the King's. We live a little way to the north of here.'

As her tone was one which did not invite any further questioning, Maude subsided into silence.

Gundreda resumed of her own accord. 'He's much older than me, of course. I was lucky to make such an advantageous match for I had no dowry to speak of.' Her voice trailed off to a whisper as her body leaned towards the warmth of the fire.

'You'll be leaving soon, then?' Maude asked. It was hard to know what to make of Gundreda de Vere.

She sighed slightly. 'Be very careful, Maude. William de Rohan is a good, kind man, but the one thing he cannot tolerate is betrayal of his trust. With good reason.'

Any words Maude might have said seemed to stick in her throat. Swallowing rapidly, she simply nodded. Had Gundreda noticed something, then? She glanced quickly across to the now-silent woman. In the flickering of the firelight, Maude was certain she had seen tears in Gundreda de Vere's eyes.

## Chapter Five

The fire in the solar had long since died down, leaving naught in the grate but a pile of smouldering ashes. Streaks of the dawning light filtered through the shutters bathing everything in an eerie grey fog. In that strange, half-light of the early hours, even the worst men gain an unexpected innocence and vulnerability. As he stood watching her, William de Rohan thought Maude looked impossibly young and virtuous.

She had spent the night in his solar, the room next to his chamber, accompanied—for safety's sake—by his squire, Thomas. Theoretically, the room was a retreat from the noise of the main hall for himself and his guests, but in practice it was rather filthy, offering little in the way of comforts. Contrary to expectations, Maude had made no protest when he told her to sleep on a makeshift pallet there, but she had been near to passing out by then. Thomas had viewed the whole idea with much less equanimity and had settled down on the far side of the room with sullen bad grace.

He smiled grimly as he watched her stir a little. Even in her sleep, she was somehow aware of another presence nearby. Well, he amended, perhaps just his. She turned, affording a good view of her black eye. Damned if the girl didn't have the heart of a warrior and the courage of a king. For all that she was a lying, avaricious woman, he had woken this morning with a feeling of anticipation, of being in control for a change. It felt good.

William walked silently to her side, reminding himself of all the girl had done yesterday. Skilled and clever she most certainly was. She had also defended herself just as adeptly with her wit, and he remembered how much he had enjoyed that. It had been a very long time since a woman had chosen to cross swords with him—perhaps too long. He sighed. She was young and very small, but there was far more to Maude de Vaillant than met the eye. It was going to be quite a challenge finding out the truth from her, but, he found, that didn't bother him one bit. He wasn't so sure he could say the same for young Maude, though.

Grinning to himself, he gently prodded the sleeping Maude with his foot.

'Get up, Maude. There's work to be done. If I'm paying you a fortune, I do intend to get my money's worth.'

Maude shot up, putting him very much in mind of a startled, squawking falcon. Dark eyes bored into him from beneath an unruly blanket of wild, black hair. 'What is it?' she croaked, looking round the room in confusion. 'What's happened?'

De Rohan smiled down at her, completely ignoring the look of dawning anger on her face. 'A lovely day, Maude. Nothing more than that. A good time to view the keep.' He looked over at Thomas, who had also shot from his pallet at the first sound of his voice. The boy was now glaring at him as if he had completely taken leave of his senses. 'Thomas. What are you thinking of, boy? Fetch some water for Maude.'

The boy dragged himself to his feet and stalked from the

solar, muttering certain vile imprecations that did not bode well for either Maude or himself.

Left alone, Maude sank back into her pallet. 'I had no idea you were such an early riser, my lord. You should have warned me.'

'I like to think of our relationship as a journey of discovery, Maude. Surprises can be so exhilarating, don't you think?'

He had dressed carefully in good courtier fashion with his beautiful green cloak draped over his shoulders. Beneath it was a long tunic of darker green with brown breeches. The barbering of his heavy growth of stubble had resulted in several nicks about the chin, but William had persevered so that his skin was smooth. He wanted to make a good impression on all of them, especially Piers de Vere.

Maude pulled the blanket tighter to her body. 'No,' she muttered. 'I don't.'

William sighed. 'Come, Maude. I do hope you aren't going to be one of those difficult women who have no humour?'

'You pay me to protect you, my lord, not make you laugh,' she pointed out with a warning edge to her voice. 'If you wanted humour, you should have taken on a jester.'

There was a momentary silence. Dim as the light was, de Rohan could see her look of complete disgruntlement. 'Get dressed, Maude, and we'll see if we can't improve on your humour.' Dropping a pile of clothes on top of her, he turned to leave. 'I hope these fit. Thomas was very loathe to part with them. But I'm sure he'll forgive you in time. Don't be deceived by his sullen nature.'

Then he left her as she placed her head in her hands, muttering several oaths he had never heard before. Aye, he was going to enjoy this immensely.

* * *

Together they toured the cellars in the keep which were used to store casks of wine and barrels of salted meats. One area had been set aside as a dungeon and evidence of fairly recent usage had been left for them to contemplate.

The dark, dank rooms made Maude shiver. There were several rough pallets covered in slimy hay and leg irons chained to the walls. All Maude could think of was Philippe and how he might well be living in such a place. She knew she would do anything to save him from this fate.

'By the Face of Lucca,' Maude whispered as de Rohan waved the torch in a wide arc. The putrid smell was now overpowering and Maude put her hand over her mouth. It was all she could do to stop herself from being sick. They moved wordlessly back towards the steps.

'Quite barbaric, don't you think?' was de Rohan's only comment as they went up.

Maude was left with the feeling that she had been shown the dungeons as a warning.

The ground-floor area was inhabited by the soldiers who had accompanied de Rohan from the south. Judging by their swarthy appearance and guttural language, many also came from Brittany. Their accommodation was basic, with just a few tables and benches for them to use in their free moments. A small group of men were arm-wrestling when they walked in. The moment the soldiers noticed de Rohan, they stood to attention in silence and awaited their lord's pleasure. De Rohan merely smiled and waved them about their duties.

'Your men are very keen to do their duty, my lord,' Maude observed.

'Riddell is a hard taskmaster,' came the reply. 'I fear they are more concerned with his temper than with mine.'

Privately, Maude doubted that since she had seen the expression on the men's faces. These were seasoned soldiers, not simply guards forced into doing their duty. Respect from such men was earned, not dragged from them with harsh treatment.

'Worm fodder,' announced Maude. 'That dog will be dead by the end of the summer.' She eyed the scrawny hound with disgust as it lolled in a corner of the kennel. No doubt its innards were as infested as its hair if the open sores were anything to go by.

'I found this one hiding,' said Hoel, his blue eyes lingering on the hound in question. 'His name's Merlin and he's supposed to have bitten the old lord's son badly.'

Maude grinned. 'Obviously a dog with sense, then.'

Hoel bent down to scratch his neck affectionately. 'Alys, the laundress, said that he survived because he used to hide from him. If Gant ever went too close, Merlin would snarl and Gant would run away. Said it was possessed and no one would touch it after that.'

Maude sighed, suddenly feeling something of a kindred spirit to the dog. 'That sounds very familiar.'

She was making a tour of the rest of the keep at the insistence of de Rohan so that she knew every part of the place. The outbuildings were run-down and dirty and the inside rooms were little different. There was a lot of work to be done and it would seem that William de Rohan had very little idea about how to tackle it.

Hoel and Thorston had stayed in the stable for the night as she had insisted that they would be vital to her role as protector. De Rohan had not dissented, much to her surprise, and the boys were pleased. The stables were in better condition, largely because Gant had taken greater pride in his mounts than anything else. A couple of stablehands eyed them with barely concealed suspicion before raking out the hay that littered the floor. Maude was clearly some-one to be avoided at all costs.

Maude could not help noticing how everyone seemed to jump to the man's slightest command. It was not odd in itself, of course, save that de Rohan was one of the King's new men. Such favourites were not always offered the re-spect and loyalty shown towards the inherited aristocracy, and so the puzzle about de Rohan continued.

Small black particles of ash floated in the early-morning breeze. The blackened thatch on the blacksmith's hut still smoked from the fire the night before and the smell seemed to permeate their very skin. Despite the mess, Maude judged the repairs would not take too long. The adjoining armourer's hut was largely untouched and work there was not affected.

The two remaining huts were used to store food and grain. When Thorston opened the first door, they could hear the scattering of tiny claws. Peering through the rising dust, he was certain he saw rats. With a shudder, he slammed it shut. It was a relief to hear the cry for breakfast.

'I don't much like the look of that lot,' muttered Hoel indignantly. 'They keep watching us as if we're about to steal something.'

Privately Maude agreed with him, but attempted to eat her lumpy porridge and ignored the sneering eyes of de Rohan's entourage. 'We're just different. Once they get used to us, they'll forget all about us.'

Thorston just raised expressive blond brows. 'Doubt that,' he murmured with his mouth full. 'They've got noth-ing to do. Like as not they'll get bolder.'

The three of them were huddled together on one of the lower tables breaking their fast in the hall. From their places on the top table before the fire, de Rohan and his crowd surveyed the lesser mortals. They partook of the same lumpy porridge, slabs of stale bread moistened with honey and several dishes of dried-looking fish. No one looked to be enjoying the meal. Maude gave up the struggle to swallow such leaden and unappetising fare, but Hoel and Thorston seemed oblivious to its deficiencies and carried on.

It wasn't just the nobles who were causing a problem, though. The servants were noticeably reticent to come anywhere near her. When they did, they would not look her in the eyes and nor would they perform any task for Maude. Basically, she was being ignored.

'You're to come to the bailey when you've finished.' Riddell's sullen voice broke her train of thought. 'Lord de Rohan wishes you to see the men training and offer any suggestions.' It was clear from his tone that Riddell did not approve of any such action.

With a sense of release, Maude followed him to the steps outside. A soft, warm wind ruffled her hair and it offered a welcome relief from the smoky atmosphere in the hall.

'Well, Maude? What do you think of my acquisition?' De Rohan had crept up on her without a sound.

A slight stiffening of her back was the only sign that she had heard the question. For a moment or two she let her eyes rove across the shabby bailey and then out across the fields to the green land beyond. 'It's a pretty place, here. The potential is there if you look for it.'

He stood close to her in companionable silence. 'What would you do with it?' he asked after a while.

Maude smiled up at him then. 'Sheep, my lord. I think you need some sheep.' Shifting to a slightly different position, Maude pointed to the hills in the distance. 'If you put them out to grass over there, you'd make a profit from the clip. You'd need some good weavers, of course.'

De Rohan looked a little stunned by her suggestion, but in his favour he recovered quickly. 'You have experience of such things?' He seemed genuinely interested.

She shook her head with a wry smile. 'We worked for someone who does last year. Raymond of Stannleigh. I'm sure he would give you advice, should you wish it.' Maude reached out to touch his cloak. 'His stuff was as good as this.'

He ignored her words. 'Apart from the sheep, then?'

She shrugged, retracting her hand. 'The keep, the people, the animals, are all badly neglected. There's much to be done here.'

'Did you know them? The Gant family, I mean?'

A small shiver passed over Maude as she looked up at him quickly. He was still standing very close, and he was watching her with that observant look about his eyes. Maude blinked rapidly. 'Well, yes. That is to say, the sons rather than the father.' Honesty as far as possible was the only solution. Once he found out she was capable of lies, the man would never trust her.

'Sons? I thought Hugh Gant had only one son?' He frowned, trying to sift through the threads of remembered information.

'Aye, that's true enough now. There was an older brother who drowned in the river.' He would never know how much it cost her to say that without stumbling over the words. Not so long ago she would have cried.

'I didn't know that.' With a flourish of his arm, de Rohan indicated that he wished to walk with her for a bit. They descended the steps and skirted round the bailey puddles, ostensibly watching the twelve men there practising their swordstrokes. 'It doesn't really matter, though, since I intend to move on as quickly as I can.'

Although he affected a casual posture, Maude could almost feel the stiffness in his body. 'Move on? I don't understand.' Beyond the courtier-like expression, she caught a glimpse of something far sharper and more clearly defined.

'Why, Maude, I thought I told you? I intend to marry an heiress with a large amount of land and considerable personal charm.' His dark hair glinted in the sunlight and Maude was reminded of how handsome he was.

The silence between them lengthened as Maude considered his words. There was nothing unusual in his ambition, but it did give some substance to the man beneath the simple façade. So her initial appraisal of de Rohan had been correct. William de Rohan was no simple courtier, he was a man who wanted something more than being the King's man.

'Have you a candidate in mind?' she enquired, curious.

William hesitated for a moment, considering the question seriously. 'There are three strong candidates who appear to return my interest and I shall be attending to their invitations over the next few weeks.' The smile disappeared as suddenly as it had come. 'I hope you will not take this amiss, Maude, but I want nothing to happen to spoil my plans. Do you understand?'

This was as close to a threat as he was likely to make. 'Aye, my lord. Perfectly.'

Suddenly, he slung an iron-hard arm over her shoulders. 'Good. Then I think we shall get along well, Maude.'

He steered her towards the palisade gate and nodded to the guard. Outside the keep walls, Maude felt at once a sense of freedom as well as vulnerability. Somewhere in the distance a soldier barked out an order and several chickens squawked loudly. De Rohan caught the sounds and looked back at the keep. 'I'm the King's man and as such am worth a significant sum of silver.' His tone was almost flippant. 'Enemies are never far away, even in an isolated place such as this.'

'Hence those two yesterday?'

His dark head nodded in response. 'A pity they both died,' he added quietly.

'I didn't know they had.' Had she detected a hardening of his voice?

'Why, yes. Did I not say? The one you shot broke his neck as he fell. The other drowned.'

Maude shivered and he must have felt it under his arm. De Rohan looked down at her quizzically.

'Do you have any idea who they were?' she asked quickly.

'None. I was hoping you might be able to answer that. The only clue is this.' He held up a battered silver mark that had been worn as some sort of pendant. 'It was recovered from one of the men. Have you seen it before?'

Reaching out for the mark, Maude's fingers touched de Rohan's. Neither was prepared for the shock that ran between them and they jumped apart as if burned. Recovering quickly from the embarrassment, Maude shook her head. 'No, but I can make enquiries.'

'Of course.' He put the coin back in his waist bag. 'Now. Enough of this. Come see my men and tell me what you think.'

When they reached the bailey, de Rohan's men were sweating like pigs in the warm sunshine as they persevered with their weapons. Several of de Rohan's guests were watching at the top of the keep steps, including Piers de Vere. There was no sign of Gundreda.

Maude shook her head. 'A shambles, my lord.' It wasn't really true, but there was room for improvement.

De Rohan stood there, imitating her despair. 'Do you know, Maude, I said only the same to FitzCount the other day.' He smiled at her. 'I'm sure they would be better with green cloaks, don't you? It would all look so much nicer.'

Maude gaped at him, completely disbelieving what she had just heard. 'Er...no, my lord. Not really.'

Bewildered, she watched him call Riddell over and place his own cloak over the unfortunate man. 'Well? What do you think?' He was looking at her in all sincerity, awaiting her thoughts on green cloaks versus brown ones. Riddell's black eyes were piercing into her, clearly holding her responsible for all of this nonsense.

'Well, actually, my lord, I think it might be better if your men dispensed with their cloaks altogether.' Maude held her tongue with admirable restraint. 'It's too hot for them to fight in.' From the corner of her eye, Maude could see several of the men frown at each other. It was as if his behaviour was completely beyond their comprehension. Were that true, then her supposition about de Rohan was correct. He was definitely pretending to be something he wasn't.

She smiled at him. It was a smile that lit up her entire face and one which certainly took de Rohan aback with its force. 'In fact, my lord, I think I have the perfect remedy for sloppy, workshy men such as these.'

'You do?' he said, looking at her somewhat warily.

She grabbed him by the hand, ignoring the heat of contact between them, and led him to the centre of the bailey. 'Aye. You shall show them how it's done, my lord.' Maude beamed up at him innocently, brows raised.

That wiped the smile off his face. Sheepishly, de Rohan glanced at the interested faces of his men. 'But, Maude, I know nothing about it.'

'Ah, my lord. You might surprise yourself, you know. Surprises can be so exhilarating, don't you think?' She was going to enjoy this immensely.

* * *

'By the Face of Lucca, Brian, that woman is not going to live much longer.' William eased himself carefully down on to the bed, his face contorted in pain.

FitzCount grinned as he sat down at his side. 'Best performance I've ever seen. If I didn't know you could handle a sword, man, I'd really think you were totally inept.'

William closed his eyes and leaned his head back against the wall. 'She's a witch. The priest was right.'

Wordlessly, FitzCount passed him a goblet of wine.

'There isn't a part of my body she hasn't whacked with her sword,' he complained, scowling into the goblet. 'Just so that she could show the men how not to do it.' He gulped down a mouthful of the liquid and grimaced. 'What's this?' he demanded irritably. 'River water?'

On familiar territory, FitzCount took the goblet from his hand. 'Very likely.'

'She made me look like a complete fool!'

FitzCount nodded. 'She did at that. Certainly had us all convinced.'

William peered at his friend from under his brows. 'Even de Vere?'

Scratching the remains of some old food stains from his tunic, FitzCount pondered the question. 'Looked that way. He smiled a lot.'

'Oh, well then. If he smiled, it must have been convincing.' William folded his arms across his chest and stared at the other end of the room mutinously.

Raucous laughter filled the room. 'Good God, man. She's actually got to you!' FitzCount's plain face crumpled into disbelief.

William ignored FitzCount's adolescent teasing. 'Can you believe that the girl actually suggested that I become a sheep farmer? The question is,' he said scathingly, 'where's she got to now? God knows what damage she could do, let loose around the keep.'

His laughter subsiding, FitzCount straightened up. 'Ah. In fact, I do know where she is. With any luck, Maude is trying to instigate some improvements in your domestic arrangements. Young Thomas has gone with her to keep an eye on her.'

Curiosity got the better of him as FitzCount knew it would. 'What domestic arrangements?'

'Precisely. Has it not occurred to you that we could eat a little better than we do, or have our clothes washed with greater regularity or even,' he added with a wicked gleam to his eye, 'have the floors swept?'

William stared at his friend, taken aback by this sudden interest on the part of his friend. 'No,' he said blankly.

Rubbing his neck with his hand, FitzCount shook his head. 'Well, it didn't to me either. But it did to Maude, and she felt it part of her duty to deal with such matters.'

The two men stared at one another. De Rohan finally shook his head and reached out for the goblet of wine again. Perhaps it was a case of better the devil you know.

'My lord!' Thomas's round, red face came through the door. 'It's Maude!' The boy had been running.

De Rohan leaned back against the wall, eyes closed. 'What is it with Maude, Thomas?'

The rest of his loping body came into sight as he stood before the bed. 'She got them to do some cleaning in the hall. The women from the village, I mean,' he stammered quickly. 'Everything was all right until one of the women fell over and hurt herself.'

De Rohan and FitzCount frowned in confusion.

'It's the priest, see. He says it's all Maude's fault and that the woman will die. The women have gone mad down there.'

Sighing in disgust, William got gingerly to his feet. 'I suppose I shall have to rescue the little witch then,' he muttered. 'But it would serve her right if I left her to them.' He shoved his sword into its sheath and speared FitzCount with a weary look. 'Coming?'

Maude did not think she would be so pleased to see de Rohan's cheerful face quite so quickly. As it was, her pleasure was short-lived. Beneath that easygoing smile, she sensed his hidden irritation.

The priest was standing amongst the group of women, reeling off a list of her sins and the likely outcome of having her in the keep. One of their number was moaning loudly, gripping a cloth to a large bump on her head. All around them lay the brooms and cloths the women had been using to clean. Piles of filth and reeds were scattered far and wide. The place was a complete mess.

'Maude, is there a problem?' De Rohan's pleasant enquiry earned him a tight smile. Thomas and FitzCount followed behind him.

'Nothing but a small domestic dispute, my lord.'

'She's the daughter of the devil,' railed the priest again. 'Having her stay here will bring death and destruction. Heed my words.' The cold, thin face of Father Michael stared at her across the table.

Maude could feel the colour drain from her. 'I am no such thing,' she argued flatly. 'The woman tripped and hit her head on the bench. It was an accident.' Despite the confident tone of her voice, Maude did not feel at all at ease. These were complete strangers and she was alone. Philippe was not here. She swallowed hard and looked at de Rohan, wondering suddenly if he would take his revenge for her earlier activities in the bailey.

'If anything, it was my fault,' announced de Rohan, causing all heads to turn to him. 'Had I made the necessary arrangements earlier, the poor woman might not have tripped.' He bent down to hand her to her feet and smiled brilliantly. 'Here.' He offered her two silver marks which the woman took with alacrity. 'I'm sure you'll be fine in a day or two. See the old woman.'

His concern earned him a toothless grin from the victim as she staggered out of the hall. Maude could feel the tension slide from her.

The priest turned to face him. 'She'll bring death here, my lord. The evil is all around her.'

'Hmm,' replied de Rohan. 'I feel honour bound to give the girl a chance. The King is most keen to see us all do our Christian duty, Father, and I would not wish to displease him.'

Father Michael could say no more in the face of such an argument. Any hint of dissent could be construed as treason these days, and the King's spies were everywhere.

'Come, Maude.' De Rohan held his hand out to her. 'I think we have much to discuss.'

One dark brow was raised in question as they stared at each other over the tables. She smiled at him then. 'Aye, my lord. I think we have.'

Well, they were just about even now.

# Chapter Six

FitzCount drank deeply of his ale before wiping his mouth on his sleeve. 'I'm for hunting, this morning, de Rohan. What say you?' He reached for the jug to refill his leather cup. With one arm supporting him against the wall, Brian FitzCount stood before the fire in the hall, clearly bored with the lack of activity.

'An excellent opportunity to assess Maude's hunting skills,' came the languid reply. De Rohan looked up at her without warning from his seat by FitzCount and she was almost flustered by the intensity in his dark eyes. Obviously a good night's rest had still not restored his charm.

Piers de Vere sat back and surveyed Maude with a certain amount of distaste. So far he had said nothing to her, despite his kindness to her at the archery competition. His hard eyes flitted from face to face and finally came to rest on his wife. 'I would prefer it if my wife remained within the keep, de Rohan. She is still unsettled, aren't you, my dear?'

Gundreda managed a weak smile. 'I fear so. Needlework is as much as I could manage today, my lord.' Her lovely skin was pale and patchy and it looked as though she had been weeping. 'Now that your solar has been made more comfortable, I should very much like to spend my time there, if I may?' She was also as nervous as a fawn.

'By all means. Thomas can stay with you.' De Rohan smiled at her kindly, ignoring Thomas's outraged look of protest.

Gundreda shook her head quickly. 'Oh, no. Please don't. I would much prefer to be alone.'

Her hands had begun to flutter again as an indication of her welling emotions and the men about her looked a little edgy. Maude had watched her often, noting the delicate, feminine movements Gundreda made, but seeing also the effect they had on the men. As far as her husband was concerned, they appeared to trouble him not one bit, aside from him developing a rather dangerous-looking half-smile.

Maude had not yet decided whether Piers de Vere was just excessively pleasant or evil to the core. Judging by the cold shivers his presence gave her, she came down generally on the latter. As for de Rohan, he genuinely appeared unmoved by such ruses—Maude was quite sure that was what they were—but usually contrived to seem concerned. So much for that as a method of attraction!

The more Maude watched her, the more she realised that none of the men was truly taken in by Gundreda's act. It was some comfort that even the most beautiful and feminine women failed in their objectives. Just what Gundreda de Vere's objectives were, though, she was at a loss to know.

The forest close to the keep was not too dense, which was just as well since any attackers would have less cover. It also meant that any game that they disturbed would have a greater chance of escape as it could see the men coming. The hunting party finally numbered ten, with several soldiers, Maude and Thorston for protection. Hoel had been left behind to see to the kennels and find out any information he could from the servants.

The beaters shouted out the strange cries that agitated the forest wildlife and made the hearts of the hunters pound with excitement. Maude and Thorston carried their spears, with bows, arrows and knives placed strategically about their bodies. Hunting could be a precarious business, so Maude had insisted that de Rohan wore a hard, riveted hauberk for protection.

Despite the fact that the morning was well advanced, little sun penetrated much of the forest and the damp mist still clung beneath the branches. The sounds of the beaters echoed around them as Maude and Thorston trudged ahead of the main party, leading their horses by the reins. For a while, it was easy enough to forget what she was doing there and just lose herself in the task at hand.

As they entered a gloomy clearing, Maude suddenly felt the hairs on the nape of her neck stiffen and she gripped her spear tighter. She motioned to Thorston and the party behind them to stop. In the silence hovered an air of anticipation, a foreboding that no hunter could ignore. Then, in a burst of sound, a beast came crashing through the undergrowth towards them. Instinct told her it was a large stag, but Maude did not wish to take any chances. A quick glance over her shoulder confirmed that Thorston had his arrow already in the nock. De Rohan and FitzCount remained unmoving in the shelter of some trees. Bracing herself, she stepped into the path of the animal with her spear aimed ahead.

They saw each other at the same moment. Within a heartbeat the stag changed direction and dived gracefully into the mist again. Behind them, FitzCount yelled to the rest of the men to follow him. Maude and Thorston mounted quickly. The chase began in earnest.

Mile after mile they hurtled through the trees, ever deeper into the forest. The beaters had been left far behind when they finally drew to a halt in a large clearing. Several arrows had pierced the creature's sweat-covered hide, and now, weak from loss of blood and exhaustion, it stood panting by a fallen tree trunk. Its glassy eyes stared blankly at the men who surrounded it and Maude felt a pang of guilt for the coming death of such a magnificent animal.

'He's yours, de Rohan.' FitzCount's voice carried across the clearing.

William de Rohan stared down at the stricken stag for a moment before smiling at his friend. 'I would be most grateful if you could do the deed, FitzCount. It deserves a clean death at least.'

FitzCount nodded curtly before launching his spear into the stag's heart. It crumpled into the green bracken with little more than a soft snort. The rest of the men dismounted and crowded around the twitching body, but Maude noticed that de Rohan remained in his saddle, barely watching them. 'Do you not join the others, my lord?' she asked, moving her horse alongside of his. 'It was a fine creature.'

Somewhat preoccupied, de Rohan blinked at her. 'I confess, Maude, I am happier away from the blood and the smell of death. My skill with spears and arrows is as lamentable as my swordstroke.' Carefully, he flicked some dirt from his cloak and rearranged the folds. His confession of such weakness did not seem to affect him in any way at all.

'Have you so little experience, then, my lord? I had heard the King was very fond of hunting.' Lark shifted uncomfortably in such close proximity to de Rohan's stallion and Maude leaned forward to pat her gently.

'A hopeless case,' he replied evasively. 'FitzCount is always amazed that I have managed to last so long.'

She considered his words. 'You've known him a long time, haven't you?' Her eyes strayed to the proud FitzCount who was standing by his stag, inviting the others to admire his aim.

'FitzCount? Always, it seems like. Henry took us under his wing when we were both very small. He's more like a brother.'

'Do you have any family at all?' She knew this was a bold question and probably one she shouldn't ask, but she was just a little curious. After all, it was important to find out as much about the man as possible.

De Rohan stiffened and his eyes glittered in the gloom of the forest. 'Am I a peasant, do you mean?' He looked away from her then, breathing deeply of the earthy, moist air. 'That's usually what most people want to know.'

'No,' Maude replied guardedly, 'that wasn't exactly what I meant. Philippe used to say that families can be an irritating source of trouble when someone is in danger. It has often been my experience.'

The ghost of a smile flickered across his face. 'I had forgotten what an experienced woman you are, Maude.'

That brought their conversation on to an entirely different footing and an inconvenient flush to her cheeks. 'My brother would often discuss his work with me,' she snapped indignantly.

'Ah. The missing Philippe.'

'He is not missing,' she said defensively. 'He's on a mission.'

William de Rohan studied Maude's expression for a while and then leaned forward on his horse. 'I think you lie to me, Maude, and you will find out firsthand what I do with liars. My dungeon is not a pleasant place to spend some time.' He reached out to pluck a leaf from her braid.

'Why should I lie?' Maude braved his touch with a gritted jaw.

Straightening, de Rohan shrugged his shoulders. 'I have no idea, Maude, but I will discover the truth about you.'

So, he had suspected something about her, but at least he knew nothing of fact. She would have to be very careful. Maude dismounted quickly.

Once the stag was tied securely on to a pole, the party declared itself keen to hunt more. After a fairly copious amount of rough wine and oat cakes had been downed, they set off back in the direction of the keep. Spirits were high, although Maude noticed that the normally lively Sir William was somewhat subdued.

An ear-splitting shriek suddenly halted the easygoing banter. It echoed, rising above the tree-level and was unmistakably human.

'By the Face of Lucca!' breathed Maude. 'What's happened?' Without waiting for an answer, she ordered Thorston to remain with de Rohan and the rest of the party whilst she took some soldiers to the source of the cry. At a rough count, there were five men missing, including Piers de Vere.

Not more than one hundred paces ahead of them, they found the man. He was a scout, but from the look of him, Maude doubted he would work again. Blood was seeping from a dreadful wound that ran practically the length of his entire right leg. Quickly, Maude pulled her cloak from her shoulders and laid it over him. His lips were colourless and his face a stark white. Gently, one of the other soldiers placed a reassuring hand on his shoulder and spoke quietly to him in the Breton tongue.

On closer examination, Maude could see that the wound was most likely fatal. By the look of it, a boar's tusk had ripped the flesh. Blood was pumping on to the bracken beneath him and the man was beginning to shake. A reed-like wail drifted from his lips. There was little she could do to save him, but she would do what she could to make him comfortable at least.

Suddenly an unwelcome vision of the priest swam before her and Maude grimly reached for a strip of linen from her waist bag. If the man died, all hell would surely break loose in the keep. She wrapped the linen firmly round the wound in an effort to staunch the blood. It wouldn't be enough, though, and from the silence about her, all the soldiers knew it, too.

'What's happened?' William de Rohan's voice cut through their thoughts.

Maude looked up to find him standing by her, staring at the man on the ground. 'A boar, by the looks of it. Can't be far away.' She returned to her task of binding the wound close to the soft skin of his groin.

De Rohan moved to the man's shoulders and knelt down at his side. The words he spoke were in the Breton tongue, low and comforting. With difficulty, the wounded man turned to him and managed a reply that caused the whole group to smile broadly at Maude.

'What did he say?' she asked, glancing up at the man's now grey-tinged face before turning back to de Rohan.

Their eyes held. 'He said you have a gentle touch and that if you were to move your hand a little higher, he would die a happy man.'

Cheeks flaming, Maude snatched her hands back to her sides and gave them all a quelling look. She had no time to dwell on the Breton sense of humour. The boar had to be found before it did more damage. 'Ask him if he wounded the boar.' Maude had finished with his leg and stood up. Her hands, tunic and breeches were soaked in blood.

After several exchanges, de Rohan nodded to the man and stood up to join Maude. 'It took him by surprise as he was looking at some tracks. He managed to get a dagger in its side before it went off over there.' He pointed to a thick clump of impenetrable undergrowth.

'Get him sent back to the keep and have them give him syrup of poppies. I'll see to him later. My lord,' she added as a humiliating afterthought.

A glimmer of a smile crossed de Rohan's face. 'Rest easy, Maude. I have every intention of doing your bidding this time.'

Turning quickly to his men, he barked out her orders in his guttural Breton tongue. He sounded very much like the warrior she suspected him of being. His completely hopeless efforts at the sword practice the day before had convinced her he knew exactly what he was doing. She smiled a little at the memory.

'You were supposed to stay with Thorston and the others,' she remonstrated, scanning the line of undergrowth. 'This is a dangerous time, my lord.'

'I pay you to be my protector, Maude. No one else.' He was standing very close so that she could smell the wine he had drunk earlier. The strange silence of the old forest enveloped them, wrapping its enchanted fingers about them, protecting them from the outside world. The men had gone and they were completely alone. Without knowing why, Maude turned to face him and found his lips just above her own. With a sigh, de Rohan pulled her body to his and kissed her.

Heat coursed through her blood as his lips fitted firmly on to hers. The smell of the blood, the wine and the rich, dark earth of the forest mingled with William de Rohan's own scent. Maude was aware of his growing stubble against her skin as he gently coaxed a response from her. His hands

were hot against her tunic as they held her tightly to him.
For no more than a few seconds, she felt a sudden surge
of energy between them as both were lost in the moment.
It was a heady experience that her body was clamouring to
progress.

Willing herself to remember that he was a very experienced courtier who suspected her of intrigue, Maude drew
back from him. It was one of the hardest things she had
ever done.

'Hunting is a very dangerous sport, Maude de Vaillant,'
he murmured, pushing her braids back over her shoulders.
'Have you no fear for yourself?'

They were still pressed together, thigh to thigh, hip to
hip, but strangely Maude did not feel embarrassment and
neither, it would seem, did he. After all, he probably did
this all the time. She raised her chin and eyed him levelly.
'I rely on instinct, my lord. It has always served me well.'

He laughed suddenly, wrapping his arms around her and
giving her an affectionate squeeze. 'By the Face of Lucca,
Maude de Vaillant, you stir my blood. I think you've bewitched me.'

She pushed him away, confused. 'That is a foolish thing
to say, and a dangerous one.'

'The girl is right, de Rohan. You'd best guard that tongue
of yours in case such dangerous declarations reach the
King's ears.'

They had been so absorbed in each other that neither had
heard de Vere approach them. Startled suddenly, they both
turned to him. Maude had no idea how long he had been
watching them, but it did occur to her that de Rohan had.
Was his kiss deliberate, then?

De Rohan was the first to recover. He slapped Maude
playfully on her behind before bending down to retrieve
the knife she had dropped. He grinned and winked at her

as he slipped it in her hand. 'Just words, de Vere. They meant nothing.' He advanced with his courtier's swagger towards de Vere. 'I was merely taking advantage of the… ah…break in the proceedings.'

'So I saw,' came the superior reply. De Vere moved from the shadow of the tree to stare around him, almost, thought Maude, as if he were looking for something. His eyes were cold and hostile, chilling her deep into the bone. 'But you should take care where you drink your fill, de Rohan. These are dangerous times.'

Before anything more could be said, a high-pitched squealing accompanied by a heavy thrashing about the undergrowth erupted suddenly. All three whirled round to find a small boar hurtling at high speed towards them. Seizing her spear, Maude took two steps towards the oncoming animal. Every nerve in her body was taut as she stared in horror at the wild, mad and very dangerous beast. Its small red eyes were fixed on her as its hooves sped across the clearing. Streaks of blood where the scout had wounded it were visible down one side, but it was impossible to know how much damage he had done to it.

It was a battle to the death. Time and time again, the boar charged Maude. Each time it passed her, she drove her spear into the weak point in the shoulders. The spearhead did no more than skitter off the tough hide, but as it surged past her once more, the deadly tusks ripped through her breeches. Maude felt nothing, but she could see a black stain spread quickly about her calf. Turning on her again, the boar launched itself at her, the light of death in its wild eyes. Gritting her teeth against fear, Maude aimed her spear low and prayed to God that she survived.

It was enough. With a terrifying shriek that was neither animal nor yet human, the boar impaled itself on her spear.

It bucked and writhed with the death throes before collapsing in the mud.

Maude sank to the ground no more than a few feet away, listening to its last grunts and closed her eyes. Pain caused her to grimace. From a distance she could hear a sudden, awful squeal of pain and then silence.

'Maude.' Strong arms pulled her up and when she opened her eyes, she found William de Rohan's face before hers.

'It's not safe.' She pushed him away. 'The boar could rouse even now. You must—'

'It's dead,' he interrupted.

Ignoring the throbbing pain in her leg, Maude hauled herself to her feet. The boar lay still, a second spear lodged through its neck. Piers de Vere seemed to have vanished.

'That was foolish, my lord.' Maude looked at William with a rueful smile, tinged somewhat by the pain she felt in her leg. 'But I am most grateful for your intervention.'

That brought a smile to his lips and Maude was not at all sure whether it was pain that caused her heart to almost stop or him. Her reaction to the man was extremely unfortunate, but it was not one she wished to examine for the moment.

'I thought you were about to relinquish your position in my household, Maude, and I have little desire to adjust to another such protector. We had just started to make some progress, I thought.'

'*I* thought you didn't trust me, my lord.' She nodded to the boar. 'That was a very accurate shot for someone who is completely inept, don't you think?'

'A lucky shot, most likely born of total fear, Maude.' He glanced at the boar. 'Your courage is quite breathtaking, you know.'

The smile and the humour were gone and as Maude

looked at him, she saw he meant what he said. 'That's what you pay me for,' she said quickly, averting her eyes. Sitting down, she examined her leg wound. It was no more that a light gash and, with a little care, it would not trouble her greatly. She had been lucky.

A shout from the edge of the clearing reminded them that they were not alone. 'Reinforcements,' mumbled de Rohan. 'De Vere took his time.'

By the time they reached the gates of the keep, the afternoon sun was beginning to sink. Maude heaved a sigh of relief as she slipped off her horse to stand beside de Rohan. Her mouth was as dry as dust and her leg was throbbing abominably.

'You can let me past now, my lord,' she murmured as de Rohan issued orders about the injured man. 'I must see to him.'

'Be quiet for once, girl.' His voice had lost its customary affable tone and she wondered what had caused his loss of humour this time. 'You'll follow my orders for a change.'

'But—'

'Maude de Vaillant, if you do not cease arguing with me, I shall dock a silver mark from your pay!' He glared at her, almost daring her to challenge him, but years of dealing with Philippe and Bronwen had taught her well. Maude subsided into irritated silence. 'That's better.'

With considerable ease, he then bent and swept her up in his arms.

'By the Face of Lucca,' she managed to say through gritted teeth, 'what do you think you are doing? Put me down.' He completely ignored her and Maude could not help but feel extremely foolish. After all, was she not meant to be the guard and protector? The experienced tracker and hunter? And here she was, lying in the arms of her lord like some swooning young girl. It wasn't as if her wound was anything serious.

Before they reached the doors to the keep, an angry voice stopped them in their tracks. 'You were warned, my lord. God is punishing you for your defiance.'

Maude's heart almost leapt into her mouth as she recognised the voice.

De Rohan whirled around to face the accuser. 'About what, Father?' Gone was the anger and the tight lips. William de Rohan had transformed once again into his personable self, although Maude could feel his grip on her tighten a little.

The pale, gaunt face of Father Michael stared at her stonily without blinking. The priest was entirely capable of whipping the people into an angry frenzy if he so chose—after all, he had done it before. He was a very powerful man.

'Maude de Vaillant brings danger to you and to us all.' The accusation boomed across the courtyard, bold and unrelenting. Soldiers, villagers and nobles alike shifted uncomfortably, glancing quickly in her direction.

'Why, Father,' de Rohan declared lightly, 'you must have been misinformed. Maude was injured protecting de Vere and me from a boar. Is that not so, de Vere?'

All eyes turned on Piers de Vere who was standing quietly by his horse. His cheeks were faintly pink from the exercise, but his eyes remained cold and unyielding. There was a subtle hesitation as a smile formed on his thin lips.

'What I *heard*, de Rohan, was you declaring yourself bewitched by the girl. What I *saw* was you kill the boar to protect her.' De Vere dropped the reins of his horse into the hands of a waiting servant and walked forward to stand at the priest's side.

'Since the girl appeared at this keep, my wife has been

attacked by ruffians, a scout lays half-dead and a boar nearly rips us to pieces. I believe the girl has brought danger here. I intend to leave this place forthwith.' He lay his hand on the priest's bony shoulder. 'You warned us, Father, and you were right.'

De Vere fixed his eyes on de Rohan, a soft, deadly smile on his lips. 'Perhaps not what you wished to hear, de Rohan, but that is my opinion.'

The knot of people in the bailey stared at them, transfixed.

De Rohan smiled oddly. 'So that's the way of things? I'd be grateful if you would say a prayer of thanks for my life, Father. The King would be pleased to hear of it, I know. He takes my well-being most seriously.'

'I wouldn't be too sure about that,' challenged de Vere. 'Your defiance over the girl isn't the only one, is it? I've heard Bertolini is preparing to investigate.'

De Rohan's face paled a little, despite his dark-coloured skin, but there was no change to his pleasant expression. Silently he turned and pushed open the wooden doors to the hall.

'You can put me down now,' Maude murmured as he pushed open the door to his private solar.

He ignored her and gently placed her on her pallet. 'You need tending, clean clothes and wine. Not necessarily in that order,' he said, straightening. Crossing the room, he picked up a flask of wine and poured her a cup.

The strong wine burned a trail from her throat down to her stomach and Maude found her whole body beginning to relax. Another sip gave her a light-headed feeling of well-being. De Rohan stood by the fire, brooding as he stared at the flames. She decided it would be best to leave him to his own thoughts.

'Was he right, Maude? Do you bring danger to this keep?' He whirled round, trapping her with his gaze.

Her cheeks flamed, but she could not bring herself to deny the accusation. After all, those things had happened. And what of Geoffrey Gant? He wanted to oust de Rohan from the estate. 'That was not my intention.' She felt ice-cold despite the warmth of the fire and the wine. Nor could her agreement with Geoffrey Gant be ignored. 'I would not be your bodyguard and I would not be able to earn your money if it were so.' Her blood was pounding so hard that she thought it might burst through her skin.

He sighed heavily with what sounded like disappointment but said nothing. Eventually he moved back to the wine flask and poured himself a cup. 'So,' he said quietly, 'it is the money, then?'

In fact, it was less of a question than a statement spoken to himself. 'Of course. Did you think it wasn't?' Far better indeed to let him think her motives were based on greed. It seemed somehow more honourable, though knowing him now a little more, she felt ashamed of herself. Ashamed that she would use an innocent man as she had without knowing the full story. Ashamed because she knew Philippe would be disgusted with her for allowing *him* to be used by a man like Gant.

'I had thought...' began de Rohan. 'Well, it doesn't really matter.' He waved away the end of his explanation with his hand.

'Who is Bertolini?' Maude asked suddenly. He seemed important to both de Rohan and de Vere.

De Rohan smiled ruefully into his cup before tossing the liquid down his throat in one. 'My destruction or my salvation, I would think.'

# Chapter Seven

'The Breton scout is dead and this woman is responsible.'
The voice of the priest echoed across the bailey, drawing
the attention of everyone there.

Maude stopped in her tracks and braced herself for another verbal onslaught. Slowly she turned to face her accuser and the narrowed eyes of his audience. The priest
stood by the gates, tall and thin, his grey eyes glinting with
triumph.

'He died of his wounds,' she said slowly, her voice
strained. Every one of those faces turned towards her
seemed to be accusing her of murder, which was exactly
what the priest wanted them to think. No doubt in his mind,
and that of Geoffrey Gant, that she was the daughter of the
devil.

'Sir William says she saved him, but the devil works in
strange ways. Do not listen to the woman, for she will trap
you with her evil ways. Three men died here years ago
because of her jealousy. How many more men must die?'
His harsh voice had risen as the priest found his mark. One
by one the people looked away from her, crossing themselves reverently, before hurrying on to their tasks. Their
priest had spoken and none was likely to gainsay him.

Despite the warmth of the morning, Maude felt a shiver of cold. Since the Breton scout had slipped into a fever and lost his grip on life last night, she had been waiting for the finger to be pointed irrevocably at her. Unwittingly, however, she had dragged William de Rohan down with her and, whatever his shortcomings, he did not deserve to be accused of consorting with the devil's daughter.

Her own wound had already begun to heal thanks to Eadith's foul-smelling poultices of moss and the juice of wild garlic. In the four days since the accident, the angry red of the gash had begun to reduce and, although still painful, Maude was able to go about her duties.

Despite her problems with the villagers, Maude had managed to persuade FitzCount to tackle the problem of the deplorable state of the keep. Under her expert tutelage, FitzCount had galvanised the village women into action. The hall and all other rooms in the keep had been cleaned and whitewashed vigorously, the rushes had been changed and even the puddles in the bailey had been cleared. Altogether Maude had been quite pleased with the changes, but she had no idea what Sir William thought of them.

Since the hunt, she had seen little of Sir William; he had been busy entertaining those guests who had not left with Sir Piers and Lady Gundreda. Eadith had informed her, as she sat with her the next day, that William wished her to stay in his solar until she was completely recovered. Clearly, Eadith thought this most odd since she spent most of the day shaking her head and clicking her tongue at every opportunity. In the brief moments when the old woman left her alone, Maude allowed her thoughts to dwell on de Rohan.

At best, she decided, he was an ambitious man with a conscience. His dealings with her had been, until the hunt, straightforward and honest. In the clearing, he had done nothing more than kiss her—as many other nobles were wont to do with their servants—for no other reason than to fill in time. It had been pleasant, very pleasant indeed, but of no earth-shattering importance, after all. He had said nothing about it since. A nagging voice in her head reminded her, however, that de Rohan was the King's man and perfectly capable of playing a dangerous game with the lives of anyone he considered expendable.

She limped on towards the kitchens. Since the disastrous cleaning episode in the hall with the women, Maude had been reticent about dealing with the servants. FitzCount had been a reluctant hero in this, but even he drew the line when it came to the cook. Apparently, he was the ferryman's brother and a most foul-tempered maggot. The quality of the food deteriorated daily, though, and Maude knew that someone had to say something or they would be struck by dropsy. Bronwen had often attributed such attacks to tainted meat and Maude had no cause to doubt her word.

As soon as she entered the doorway, the noise died magically away. Maude found herself the object of about thirty pairs of frightened eyes and one pair that bore nothing other than arrogant contempt.

'Leofric,' she addressed the cook, 'I would speak with you privately.' Her words were met with a superior sneer.

'I'm not going anywhere with you. The priest has warned us often enough of your evil ways and I have no desire to die just yet.' The cook's fat face smiled maliciously. His meaty hands wiped his tunic slowly and deliberately with more than a hint of a threat.

'Then I will say what I have to before everyone, although I did feel it to be a private matter.' Maude's voice remained steady, despite the atmosphere in the kitchen being one of pure hostility. 'The state of the kitchen is a disgrace,' she began speaking calmly. 'There have been three boys badly burned in the last two days.'

'It's not my fault they can't look out for themselves,' grumbled the cook, glaring at Maude. 'They're always getting in the way.'

'There are too many people working here,' she replied evenly. Maude noticed that several pairs of eyes were now fixed on the cook.

'How else can I serve so many people? The old lord never had so many guests. It's not my fault. You're the one who's brought the keep such bad luck, not me. There was no problem with the old lord.' His flabby chin raised in a defiant challenge.

'What you serve up isn't fit for Sir William's table anyway,' Maude countered, ignoring his affronted stare. 'I want the kitchens cleaned up and some decent, plain food that Sir William can actually eat. If things have not improved by the end of the week, then I shall be forced to find someone who can do the job.'

The man's face had turned bright scarlet and Maude could see that he was about to explode in anger. Without another word, she left the kitchen and hoped that her warning would be enough.


Hoel was lying back in the hay with his dog, Merlin, lolling over his knees. Both boy and dog had their eyes closed as Hoel gently scratched the dog behind his ears.

'I suppose you are planning to do some work?' Maude enquired quietly.

Boy and dog opened one curious eye apiece and each levelled that reproachful eye at her. 'We've been working hard,' protested Hoel. 'Merlin's been ratting in the stores.' He pushed himself up on to one elbow and patted Merlin proudly. 'He's killed ten so far today.' The dog offered Hoel a lick of support.

Maude smiled and sat down beside them on the hay, scrutinising Merlin's hair with narrowed eyes. He appeared to be relatively clean, so she ventured a pat on his back. 'If he's that good, I might send him into the kitchen then. It looks as though there could be a large rat or two there.'

Hoel looked across at her sharply. They were relatively safe in the stables—few of the servants or the priest ventured there. 'Aye, I've heard a few things about that cook.'

'Oh?' Maude tilted her head towards him. 'Like what?'

'Well, I know he's the ferryman's brother, but he's been far more troublesome than he ever used to be. It seems that his daughter's gone missing. Says she's gone to visit his sister, but no one's ever known him to mention a sister before.' Hoel's thin shoulders shrugged. 'Just thought you might be interested.'

'Aye, I am.' Maude smiled at him. 'Are your sources reliable, do you think?'

For the first time Hoel's cheeks turned suspiciously pink and he studied Merlin's right ear with great interest. 'It's Alys. The laundress.'

Maude remembered a small, dumpy woman with stringy blonde hair and a kind face. 'How have you managed to get her to talk, then? She doesn't look as if she has a loose tongue?' If anything, the woman was monosyllabic, but then Maude was used to being treated with dumb silence.

Hoel was silent for a while, just stroking Merlin. 'She says I remind her of her son. He died a few years ago.' His fingers rubbed over the silky ear of the dog. 'It's nice talking to her, but it's supposed to be a secret. She doesn't want anyone to know.' Sensing her scrutiny, his eyes flickered up. 'Don't know why, though. I've done nothing wrong.'

There was a drawn-out silence, interrupted only by the contented sounds coming from the dog.

'Well,' said Maude finally, 'do as she wishes. It can do no harm.' She smiled as she saw the faintest look of relief on Hoel's face. 'Anything else?'

The halo of brown curls shook. 'Only that Merlin got very excited this morning in the shed. There was nothing there, but he was going mad. It wasn't for the rats,' he said defensively, reaching for the dog. 'Was it, boy?'

Merlin's tail thumped heavily on the hay for several minutes. 'There were these on the floor, but I don't suppose they mean much?' His hand dug deep into the pouch at his belt. Two filthy, battered coins lay in his palm.

Maude picked them up and examined them. They were the same as the one de Rohan had showed her before. 'Which hut did you say?' she asked.

'The one closest to the gate.' Hoel looked at her curiously, alerted by the expression on her face. 'Are they important, then?'

'It might be nothing at all—it probably isn't anything, but all the same, we need to watch the place carefully. Has anyone been there recently?'

'Apart from the cook and the kitchen boys? No, I don't...'

'What?' Maude watched the memory blossom on his face. 'What do you remember?'

He shook his head. 'It was that woman. Lady de Vere. The day you all went hunting and she wanted to stay here on her own. She went out for a walk and I saw her near the store hut.' He grinned. 'She nearly jumped out of her skin when she saw me and the dog. It was as if we'd caught her doing something right bad.'

'There was no one else about?' This was a real puzzle. 'No.'

More unexplained puzzles. How on earth could Gundreda de Vere be connected in any way with Geoffrey Gant? It just didn't seem possible. 'And the men who kidnapped Lady de Vere? Have you heard anything about that?'

The boy shook his head. 'No one claims to know anything about them, but the moment I start asking questions, they all go silent. It's really odd.'

Maude heaved a deeply exasperated sigh. That would be Gant's doing, she supposed, although how he would have managed to arrange her abduction was hard to imagine. Maybe the priest was right and the keep was gripped by evil after all. There were plenty of the old pagan stones lying in the fields close by. 'Well,' she said thoughtfully, 'you'd best keep trying. Someone might say something. One day.'

A light shift in the air disturbed them and they turned their heads.

'Plotting?'

Speechless for a moment, Maude could feel the colour in her cheeks burn. 'No, my lord. Just thinking.'

Quietly, de Rohan shut the stable door and advanced towards them. He looked set to go riding, although Maude couldn't help but think that the cloak and gloves might be a little too hot for the warm May sunshine. 'And what were you thinking, exactly?'

Despite their coolness of the past few days, de Rohan appeared quite cheerful. He sat down next to them on the hay and leaned forward to pet Merlin. Sensible to the honour, the dog wagged his tail enthusiastically.

'Why it is that the villagers and servants will say nothing about Lady de Vere's abduction? Someone must have seen something,' she said, avoiding his eyes.

Hoel shifted uncomfortably. 'Maude asked me to find out

as much as I could,' he explained as if to a child. 'I've
found out nothing so far.'

The dark eyes rested first on Hoel and then on Maude.
She was certain she could see shadows lurking there, but
she met his penetrating stare with composure.

'I had no idea the King's spies infested even my own
keep,' he said in mock amusement, leaning over to pull
several bits of hay from Maude's tunic. 'Is there anything
I should know, do you think?'

Maude wondered how much of their conversation he had
heard before he came in. She opened her hand and showed
him the coins.

'Just like the last one,' he murmured, all mockery gone.
'Tell me, then.'

Hoel explained the events whilst de Rohan listened care-
fully and asked him questions. There was no trace of the
King's courtier now—de Rohan was far more than that.
The question was, puzzled Maude, what was he?

When all questions had been asked, de Rohan finally
stood up, brushing the hay from his cloak. 'I came to ask
you if you would ride with me, Maude. There are some
people I must deal with and I might well be in need of
your protection.'

Their small party rode alongside the river towards the
outcasts' encampment. There was no noise from the inhabitants; unless you knew it was there, you could easily miss
it. De Rohan knew where it was exactly and drew his horse
to a standstill close to the fire. Several of the children appeared from nowhere and clustered around Alfred and
Hulda, fear in their eyes.

Alfred stepped forward. 'Good day, my lord,' he said
amiably enough as de Rohan and FitzCount dismounted.

Maude followed their suit and stood close by. There was not even a flicker of acknowledgement in Alfred's eyes.

William de Rohan beamed at him, his dark eyes taking in at a glance how things stood. 'Good morning, my friend. As you see, I have decided that it is time to discuss the matter of your settlement on my land.'

The two men stood face to face, their eyes fixed on each other. Of similar height and age, they weighed each other up.

With folded arms, Alfred challenged de Rohan. 'We have nowhere else to go, my lord. This has been our home for the last year.'

Anxious faces stared up at them and Maude felt most uncomfortable. FitzCount shifted position slightly.

De Rohan stared around him. The settlement was hidden from view by the undergrowth and truthfully the only objection he could have was the smell.

'My villagers have made several complaints about you causing this abominable smell. It seems to me that you have done little to improve the situation, despite being here for so long.' De Rohan stepped back to look at the bedraggled gaggle of peasants. Most were in a sorry state, with ripped, filthy clothing and thin limbs.

Alfred's lips tightened. 'We have nowhere to go, my lord, and no means to improve our lot here. Yet we would stay if you would let us.'

Maude could see de Rohan's eyes rove over the children. Most were very small for their age and pitifully thin. The dirt could almost be scraped off with a knife.

'How do you eat?' he asked eventually.

'Fish, berries, the odd rabbit.'

De Rohan sighed heavily as if considering a problem of enormous proportions and turned to address his friend.

'FitzCount, do you think I should allow them free right of settlement here?'

FitzCount shook his head. 'The fewer mouths to feed the better, my lord. Once you allow this lot to remain, there'll be others.'

De Rohan said nothing but began to saunter around the makeshift huts. 'Your name?' he asked suddenly, turning to Alfred.

'Alfred, my lord. This is my wife, Hulda.' His arm drew the thin woman to his side. Strands of her brown hair hung over her eyes but Maude could see the worry there. She gripped the baby more tightly to her hip.

'And the children. Are they all yours?' De Rohan's calm gaze moved over the wide-eyed girls with polite interest.

Alfred shook his head. 'Two of the older girls are mine and two of the younger ones. And the baby. The rest are orphans or outcasts.' Alfred hesitated for a moment before allowing his honest blue eyes to look de Rohan squarely in the face. 'There's also a lad fishing over there, but he's doing no harm.'

'Except thieving your fish,' mumbled FitzCount, clearly bored. He ignored the two children who sidled up to him, their matted hair sticking out in all directions. Fearlessly they stretched out their dirt-encrusted hands and grabbed at the brightly embroidered edging on his tunic. One of the older girls rushed up to them and whisked them both away, clearly fearing FitzCount's wrath.

'Are you an outlaw?' De Rohan's dark eyes stared at the Englishman without blinking.

Alfred shook his head. 'My master was hung for treason. His land was laid waste and was overrun with brigands and the like. I hoped to find work round here...' He did not finish the thought but merely shrugged his shoulders.

'Quite.' De Rohan turned to face Maude and FitzCount,

leaving Alfred and his family standing uncertainly before their only possessions.

'My lord, I wonder if these people could be of some use to you. Throwing them off your land, although understandable, might not be the best use of your...er...resources.' Maude flushed under the surprised gaze of the two men.

A stunned silence ensued whilst de Rohan and FitzCount absorbed her words.

She took a deep breath. 'Well, what I mean is that perhaps Alfred could be more useful to you outside the palisade than within.' From the quizzical looks the two men were giving each other Maude could see that they didn't understand, and she wasn't yet sure that she had the plan firmly thought out, but she had to do something for these people. They meant no harm to anyone. 'Alfred is probably more aware of what goes on in the forest than many others,' she began explaining. 'He's likely to recognise a stranger and notice any activities that seem a bit odd.'

A slow smile grew over de Rohan's handsome face. 'A most interesting idea, Maude. He is to spy for me, do you mean? It might work, providing, of course, he is not already part of the opposition?' It was very hard to tell whether he was just putting forward a different view of the situation or prodding her for information.

Alfred, although not part of the conversation, had clearly been able to follow the gist. 'I'm no brigand, my lord, if that's what you mean.' His outraged tone was convincing. 'If I'd wanted to be an outlaw, I've had plenty of chances. Food and shelter would have come my way with much less effort on my part.'

He took a pace or two closer. 'If it's loyalty you want, though, I'll give it to you for a chance to build my own place here. I've no wish to be cooped up in those hovels the villagers live in.'

Tilting his head to one side, de Rohan frowned at him in question. 'And why should I believe you?' The gentle tone he had used until this point had been replaced by a far sharper edge.

'I've some things from one of them attackers the girl shot the other day.'

After a moment's silence, de Rohan's lips formed the briefest of smiles. 'You interest me greatly, Alfred. Why did you not mention this before?'

'I knew you'd be coming soon,' he said humbly, lifting his jaw a little. 'It was important to have something to bargain with.'

Maude gaped at the man. She had underestimated his courage greatly.

'Very well.' De Rohan's eyes glinted in the sunshine and Maude had the impression he was actually enjoying himself. 'You have my word. Now show me what you have.'

From the depths of his belt bag, Alfred pulled a battered silver mark. A thin strip of leather dangled from a crudely made hole. He handed it to de Rohan.

'Is this meant to mean something to me?' De Rohan examined it casually, tossing it about in his hand.

'Aye. It should. The men who follow Geoffrey Gant all wear these. I've seen them often enough when they come sniffing round the edges of your land.'

A snort of disbelief came from FitzCount. 'Anyone could say that, man.'

Maude stepped closer and peered more carefully at the mark. It was the same as all the others. She turned to Alfred. 'Where did you find it?'

The Englishman lifted his jaw in the direction of the river. 'The water throws most things up by the sharp bend. They get caught in the reeds and low-lying branches. That's where the boy found it.'

De Rohan's fingers closed around the mark. 'I had no notion that Gant was in the area.'

Alfred rubbed his beard slowly. 'I've seen him several times of late. Nasty piece of work with evil on his mind. He'll be wanting his land back, I expect.'

De Rohan and FitzCount exchanged sombre looks. 'Are you not afraid of being here alone?'

Alfred transferred his honest gaze to de Rohan. 'Well, if I'm to be truthful, I'd rather take my chances in the forest here than be penned in with that sorry lot who live in the village. I'd be ashamed to bring my brats up amongst such cowards.'

De Rohan nodded. 'Build your huts, then, and send word of any strangers.'

The dour expression on Alfred's face was replaced by a broad grin. 'Aye, my lord. You'll not be sorry.'

De Rohan stared directly at Maude. 'Let's hope not.'


Little stirred under the warm glare of the afternoon sun. Maude sat stiffly by the river bank, her back firmly turned towards it, looking out across the flat plain below the keep. Butterflies fluttered above the long grass and the hum of the bees filled her thoughts. Eventually succumbing to the heat, she closed her eyes, trying hard to avoid the sound and smell of the river. In a distant part of her mind, Maude thought she could be happy here if it weren't for the river and its memories.

Behind her, Hoel and some of the village children chattered companionably as they dangled their feet in the cold water. Several of the men splashed noisily in the water itself. They had commandeered the ferry from Osric and had tied it carefully so that it floated in the middle of the river. Some of the more courageous dived in, shouting and taunting the rest with their bravery.

Knots of women had gathered from the keep and the village to stare openly at the frolics of the men. The air danced with their giggling and saucy enticements and the men, in their turn, played to their audience. Most had yielded to the heat and removed their tunics and chemises, allowing their white skin to blush in the sun's rays.

William de Rohan was one exception, preferring to lounge idly with FitzCount under the shade of a tree. Their conversation was desultory, no more than that of old friends. Ignoring the nagging voice of her own curiosity, Maude turned her back on them and allowed the two men some privacy. There would be time enough to find out his plans.

From the far side of the river, they were observed by the ever-watchful eyes of Osric. Short and thickset, his broody presence was the only dark cloud on the horizon. A fog of unpleasant irritation hung over the man permanently and few people went near him by choice. He was no more than a cheating bully and the other villagers were afraid of him.

Suddenly, completely without warning, Maude felt her feet and arms grabbed and was hauled effortlessly into the air. Thomas the squire and Riddell grinned at her with demonic delight. This was their chance for revenge and there was no escape.

'Please,' whispered Maude in fear, 'don't. I beg you.' She knew what they would do.

'Just a bit of fun, lady,' sneered Thomas, his pasty face flushed with the sun and the effort.

Maude kicked with greater strength but to no avail. They moved quickly to the edge of the river. 'Please, I'm afraid of the water.'

'Your turn, my lady,' laughed Riddell, his eyes shining with eager anticipation. 'Time for a bit of cooling off.'

She screamed then with the fear of three years. Three

years of sheer terror, of nightmares, of sudden memories. Freezing, black water and a tangle of limbs and reeds and mud. She was crying, begging, trying to escape. Somewhere, a long way off, she could hear a terrible wail. Shouting and splashing. And then nothing as the hands let go of her. Maude felt cool air rush over her and then the dreadful cold as she hit the river. Her heart was thundering in the silence of the river's womb. Icy fingers gripped her, pulled her, tore at her. Suddenly they threw her into the air and dragged her, spluttering, to the bank.

'By the Face of Lucca, Maude! What is it? Are you hurt, girl?' William de Rohan's streaming face stared at her from above. His thick hair was plastered to his skull and his lashes looked as though they had been glued together with water. That much she registered before she twisted her hands into his hair and hung on to his solid body for dear life.

With another, slightly milder oath, William picked her up and struggled on to the river bank. He wore nothing but his breeches and Maude could feel the cold skin of his chest through her wet tunic. He squelched a short distance before placing her carefully on the ground. Prising her fingers from his hair, he pulled her close to him.

'You're safe,' he said more gently, pressing her head into his chest. His arms encircled her and pulled the rest of her into the protective safety of his body.

The sobbing and the shivering just would not stop, no matter how hard she tried. Mentally, Maude knew what was happening and what she should do, but her body would not follow her instructions. A warm cloak was placed over her shoulders and she could hear William murmur gentle sounds into her hair. Voices came closer and then went away again. They were alone with the sound of the river.

Nothing happened for a while and her compulsion to cry

eventually subsided. Maude surfaced to find her arms clasped tightly around William and her forehead buried in his neck. Solid, warm and safe. With the dawning realisation of her inexplicable lack of control, however, came her horrified embarrassment. Maude snatched her arms away from him.

'I'm sorry,' she sniffed, unable to look at him yet, desperately wiping her runny nose with her soggy sleeve.

Strong arms tightened around her. 'It doesn't matter,' he said. 'Just close your eyes.'

'I can't,' she muttered incoherently. 'I remember then.'

'Ah, I see.' After a moment his hand began to stroke her hair; as it touched her spine, he rubbed gently, easing the tension there. 'Does that help?'

She nodded. It felt good to have someone touch her, even if it was a man she barely knew. They sat for some time, alone, silent and oddly close. The only thing she could hear was the sound of William's breathing and it was comforting in its own way.

Smiling tentatively, Maude pushed herself back to look at him. 'Thank you,' she said carefully, 'although I thought I was the one who was supposed to be protecting you.'

He smiled back. Not his courtier's smile. One of his own. 'I won't say anything if you don't,' he offered in amusement. 'It's quite a change of character, you know. Not many people are aware that I am possessed of such depth. I would be grateful if you would leave them in their ignorance.' The words were lightly spoken, but Maude heard the edge to his voice—surely not embarrassment?

Flushing a little, she pushed back some of her hair and glanced anxiously towards the river. It was deserted now. 'Wh-where is everyone?' she stammered.

'They've all gone.' He paused and looked at her carefully. There was no trace of humour in his eyes. 'Can you tell me now?'

Sighing, Maude lay back, warming herself in the sun. The river seemed much further away. The danger was past.

'It's the water. The river, I mean. Three years ago, I was here with two of my brothers. They knew the Gant brothers.' Maude stared into the blue sky, remembering as if it was yesterday. 'It all happened so quickly. We were out in a boat, fishing. Everything was peaceful. Quiet. Suddenly the boat overturned. When I surfaced there was no sign of my brothers or of Henry Gant. We searched for hours, but there was no trace.'

The tears she had shed over the years no longer welled up, but the pain was as bad now as it had ever been. 'Geoffrey Gant blamed me. He said I had put the curse of the devil on them, but I had done nothing. I had thought...' Her voice trailed off.

'What? What did you think, Maude?' He moved closer again, his fingers resting lightly on her arm.

She hesitated and then finally spoke the thought she had kept hidden for three years. 'Geoffrey Gant did it because he wanted to be the heir, but he blamed me and everyone believed him. That's why the priest is like that.'

'Then it must have been hard coming here? You must have had a very good reason?' he said quietly. He turned her face to look at him full on.

'Aye.' Maude was the first to look away.

'I had not realised your desire for money was really so great.'

Maude flushed at that and this was the time for her to tell him, but she could not. 'Clearly you were wrong.' She sat up suddenly, wondering how she could get away from him. It was all too much.

De Rohan turned, allowing the sun to warm his back.

Maude noticed that his skin was a rich brown. It was very soft and touchable. 'I feel the same way about blood.'

She stared at his back in amazement. 'Why?'

He examined a daisy in front of him. 'My father was betrayed by a woman and was killed by her jealous husband. He bled to death in my arms when I was seven years old.'

The muscles in his back were strong and beautifully crafted by hours of strenuous work. As he moved, they rippled. Maude watched him in fascination as he mulled over his past. He had many secrets, she was certain.

'It's not something you ever get over, no matter how much death you see,' he added bleakly, pulling the petals from the daisy. 'I've had little faith in the honour of women these past twenty years either.'

'No,' she said. 'I can see why you wouldn't.' She heard the warning. 'Which makes it all the more difficult to understand why you chose me as your bodyguard?'

There was a momentary silence whilst William considered the question. 'By the Face of Lucca, I have no idea, girl,' he replied in the end. 'Though I think your black eye played some part.'

'You felt sorry for me?' she flared at him.

He laughed at her expression of outrage. 'No. I wouldn't say that. It was, I think, admiration of your courage. That and the look in your eyes. You do have such expressive eyes, you know.'

Well, it was quite a compliment in the end and Maude decided to accept it for what it was. She sighed and lay back in the grass alongside him. 'Aren't you lonely here, without all those courtiers around?' Maude asked eventually.

De Rohan considered the thought for a moment or two. 'No. I think I prefer the peace and the quiet. As for company, I find that I am coping quite admirably.' He glanced in Maude's direction with a humorous twitch of his lips. 'But to that end, I have a plan which may change the situation.'

'Oh?' Perhaps this was something she could tell Gant.

'We travel to Robert Woodleigh's keep next week. His daughter is an heiress of some standing and quite a beauty, I believe. You will accompany me, of course.'

Somewhat stunned by this, Maude stared at him. 'Douce Woodleigh?'

'Aye. It seems that my ambitions are to be realised, Maude. The road has been a long and rather arduous one.'

'Well, then,' she murmured, 'I hope that this is what you want, my lord.'

De Rohan turned to her and grinned. 'My thanks, Maude.'

In the silence that followed, they both allowed themselves a moment or two with the ghosts of their past. For good or bad, they had crossed a barrier and they could never go back.

# Chapter Eight

The young guard at the gate eyed her suspiciously and Maude summoned up her most careworn expression. Despite what de Rohan thought, she was quite an expert at fooling most people.

'Lord de Rohan has a desire for fresh venison at his table tonight, so I've to see to it.' Wearing her filthy hunting breeches and cloak and with her bow and quiver slung carelessly over her shoulders, Maude certainly looked as though she was about to go hunting. She hoped the fear gripping her innards would not betray her. For greater effect she shrugged her shoulders. 'You know how it is,' she added. 'It's impossible to please some people.'

The guard responded with a grudging smile. 'Aye, and I'll wager that if I checked with Riddell I'd get a tongue lashing for even daring to question it. Especially at this time of the morning.' He scratched at the uneven growth of stubble on his face. 'Be gone then. And good luck.'

Just as Maude had smiled in as conspiratorial a fashion as she could, his hand suddenly shot out and grabbed her arm. Freezing, she looked up at him blankly. 'Any chance of a spare rabbit, I'd be grateful,' he murmured and sidled even closer. Maude hardly dared to breathe with relief.

'There's a young wench in the village who's caught my eye and a small present might give her a bit more encouragement.' He winked and tapped at his nose in what Maude supposed was a sign of conspiracy.

She raised her brows. 'Oh, er…aye…if I get the chance.'

The early morning mist clung still to the trees and the dips in the valley and offered protection from anyone watching her. The silence was broken only by the calls of the birds and the flowing of the river. Maude shivered, but not just because of the cold. She had at last been summoned to meet with Geoffrey Gant.

Last night, after the evening meal had been cleared away, Maude had listened to William de Rohan entertain his household with his singing. The man's voice was attractive, she admitted, but it was the songs that had affected her most. Haunting music and the strange tongue of his native Brittany had wound their way around her heart. Maude was not the only one. Every person in the hall had listened to de Rohan in rapt silence.

Most of the men understood the words, but it was nevertheless rare for hardened soldiers to sit through such entertainment without a certain amount of distraction. Not one dice rolled whilst he strummed the lute and sang of thwarted love and treachery, battles and the fine line men walked between life and death. Well, at least she supposed that those were the themes, since those were the pictures conjured in her head.

Maude had watched him intently as he smiled at each of his female servants. There was no doubt that their hearts all beat faster as the wretched man had gazed at them with love and pain etched on his face. It was a performance she had never expected to see and it was a revelation. William de Rohan was a master at allowing people to see in him what they wanted to see. The women were completely entranced by him and no doubt had he asked it of them, they would have fulfilled any request he might make.

The more Maude thought about it, the more perplexed she became by the nature of the man. Renowned as he was for his skills as a lover, he had so far shown little interest in bedding any woman in the keep, to the best of her knowledge. There had been no gossip amongst the servants—they were usually the first to pick up on any pursuit, no matter how fleeting. For a man who had reputedly been exiled from the court because of the King's jealousy, de Rohan was behaving with remarkable restraint.

Several cups of strong wine later, Maude had been pondering the problem as she headed towards the store huts to check them. It had, in fact, become a habit of hers to check all the outbuildings as a matter of course. The guards were used to seeing her on her rounds and ignored her. As soon as she had descended the steps of the keep and had crossed the bailey, she thought she heard a noise. It came from the same store hut that Hoel had found the coins in. Cautiously pushing the door ajar, Maude found herself dragged into the dark and a calloused hand clamped over her mouth. She could see nothing of her attacker. He was powerfully built, although not tall, and had hands that could snap her neck if necessary. Struggling would have been futile.

'Hold your tongue, girl. I've a message for you.' The voice was rough and urgent in her ear and Maude had no doubt that the man would do all he had to in order to stay alive. She stilled. 'That's more like it. Now, you listen to me, and you and that brother of yours will remain unharmed. D'you understand, girl?'

Maude nodded as best she could, cursing her lack of attention. Had she drunk less, she might have had her wits about her and at least had more chance of discovering the identity of the messenger.

'Gant wants to see you. Same place as before at daybreak tomorrow. If you tell anyone, your handsome brother will die.' The words were hissed into her ear as a piece of cloth was tied around her eyes. A second later, she was thrown to the ground.

By the time Maude had pulled the cloth from her eyes, the messenger was gone. Whoever he was, he was quick and light on his feet for she had heard no sounds. On closer examination, the cloth revealed no clues whatsoever, so she folded it carefully and put it into her waist pouch.

Sleep was long in coming that night, and when eventually Maude closed her eyes, she dreamed of battles, Geoffrey Gant and a handsome Breton warrior hurling his spear directly into her enemy's heart. Clearly she had drunk too much.

The meeting place was no more than a mile or so from the keep and Maude took great care to see she was not followed. Her path tacked in different directions and she frequently backtracked. So far as she could tell, she was alone, but none the less she didn't want to take any chances. When the forest began to thin out a little, Maude was able to hear the sound of the river. Cautiously, she made her way to the same log she had sat on just three weeks earlier.

'You're late.' Gant emerged from the undergrowth shaking the dew and the dirt from his cloak.

'I wanted to be sure I wasn't followed.' Maude stared at him with cold distaste. 'Where is my brother?' Her eyes searched the forest edge, but she knew he would not have been brought this time.

'Safe—for now.' Gant stood back to survey her and a self-satisfied smile spread over his puffy face. 'I have to say, Maude, that your sojourn with de Rohan is not improving your looks.' A pudgy finger reached out to poke at her yellowed eye.

Maude shook him away, unable to bear the thought of him touching her in any way. 'I've done what you wanted so far. What now?'

Her irritable demand was met with a broad smile. Gant turned his back on her and began to stare at the river. 'According to my reports, you seem to be getting on well. Better than I had hoped, in fact.'

'De Rohan trusts no one,' she stated quietly. 'Especially not women. It will take some time to—'

'I don't have the time and neither does your brother,' retaliated Gant, turning suddenly. His eyes had that strange look she had seen before. 'Tell me his plans.'

She was trapped. 'He doesn't trust me yet,' she repeated. 'De Rohan isn't quite the fool he appears.'

The cold blue eyes didn't leave Maude's face. 'Nor am I, Lady de Vaillant. No matter what you think.'

The man was standing close to her and Maude had a sudden urge to run away as far as she could, but she could not abandon Philippe. Gritting her teeth, she shrugged her shoulders. 'Very well. He plans to visit Douce Woodleigh next week. I shall be his guard.'

The startled call of disturbed birds caught their attention for a moment. Gant's eyes followed their flight before coming to rest once more on Maude. 'Your co-operation is most helpful, my lady.' He stretched his thick neck as he pondered the situation.

'And what would you have me do?' Maude said through bloodless lips.

Gant laughed mirthlessly. 'The least you know the better. After all, didn't you say de Rohan wasn't as stupid as he appears?' His lips slid into an abstracted smile. 'I'll tell you more when I'm ready.'

Maude said nothing as she turned to go. A sick dread flooded her stomach at the thought of betraying de Rohan. She owed him no real loyalty, but she had given the man her word. A de Vaillant never broke a promise and that had been her father's main precept. With a heavy heart she headed back into the forest.

William sat back on his pallet with his hands behind his head and leaned against the wall. He sighed heavily.

'Did you have her followed?'

FitzCount nodded silently. 'It was difficult since she was as nervous as a fawn. She met Gant some distance from here, but apparently she wasn't happy about it.' He ran his fingers through his hair and sat down on a stool in front of the fire. 'The guard said she was hunting on your behalf.'

William reached out to pick up his cup of wine. 'How did she know where to go, do you think?'

Rubbing his stiff neck, FitzCount leaned towards the flames. Despite the good weather, the keep was bitterly cold and he regretted leaving the milder climate of the south. 'The lad said she was as white as snow when she came back to the solar last night. Maybe something happened then?'

'Damnable woman.' Placing his cup on the floor, William dry-washed his face. 'Why is she mixed up with Geoffrey Gant?'

'At a guess, I'd say it has something to do with this keep. Most likely he wants it back and you said she's known him for years.' FitzCount stretched out before the fire, allowing the warmth to seep through his aching limbs.

Casting a baleful eye over his surroundings, de Rohan shook his head. 'He's welcome to the place if he wants it so badly. Although...' he peered a little more closely

'…things do appear to have improved somewhat since you took over our domestic arrangements, Brian.'

Frowning, Brian FitzCount gulped more wine down and then wiped his mouth with his sleeve. 'You can thank Lady de Vaillant for that,' he said with a touch of asperity. 'She's been on my back until it's right. Seems keen to keep you comfortable, apparently.'

De Rohan smiled privately at FitzCount's querulous tone. 'It's only another ploy to get me to trust her.'

'Aye, but in the meanwhile we're eating the best we have for years. I'd forgotten what decent bread tastes like. Fewer fleas about, too,' he added cheerfully. 'Simpler to forget about those heiresses and marry young Maude, if you ask me. Pretty little thing without the bruises and mud, most likely.'

William just raised his brow and swigged back more wine. Hauling himself to his feet, he joined FitzCount by the fire. 'Maude de Vaillant is about as easy to deal with as a trapped wolf. Life with her would not be simple,' he pointed out with a wry smile.

'But comfortable,' added FitzCount. 'And you like her.'

William shrugged. 'There's a world of difference between liking and marrying, man. I *like* you for some reason, but I'm not planning to marry you.'

'I may have missed my mark, William, but at a guess you haven't been staring at me with lust-filled eyes this past week either?' FitzCount sighed into his cup. 'You don't usually have this much trouble seducing women.'

Flushing a little, William grinned. 'Seducing? Truthfully, Brian, I think it would be like bedding my own squire.' He stared at the flames, contemplating the puzzle of Maude de Vaillant. 'She looks at me sometimes with those dark eyes of hers and it's as if she can see straight through me. It's a humbling experience,' he added, sipping from his cup.

'Whenever I think about tumbling one of the servants instead, she's watching me with one of those knowing looks of hers. She's a damned nuisance, either way.'

Slinging a comforting arm over de Rohan's hunched shoulders, FitzCount laughed. 'You're the one who'll be damned until you bed her. Best do it soon. Abstinence doesn't suit you, as I'm finding to my cost. You're like a wounded bear.'

William dropped his chin into the cup of his hand and sighed wanly. 'After what she said yesterday, I'm certain Maude is not part of de Vere's ring. Gant has some hold over her and her brother's mixed up in it somewhere. It's entirely possible, of course, that de Vere is controlling Gant for his own purposes. Maude is in the middle of everything.'

FitzCount stood up and stretched his legs. 'De Vere's a clever man and he's up to his neck in it. I'll wager he's pulling lots of strings in this part of the kingdom. Gant's just another tool.'

'But an important one. What worries me is that de Vere's involved Bertolini. Once the King starts to doubt, it could be serious.' William reached forward to push more wood into the fire. 'Bertolini is after glory and he won't hesitate to disfavour me if it's in his best interests.'

'Aye, but he's a fair man, William. We'll have to trust him.' FitzCount pursed his lips. 'Now, man, tell me about this visit to Woodleigh's keep next week.'

William examined another stick of wood before tossing it into the fire. 'He's involved and he's using his daughter as bait. We'll just have to see. I'll wager de Vere will have something planned for me.'

FitzCount rubbed his beard. 'Aye? Well, a bit of action might liven the place up.'

Dr Rohan grimaced before slapping his friend on the

back. 'If I remember correctly, you were the one in need of a quiet life with a comfortable widow.'

'I never said I wanted to die of boredom,' countered Brian. 'Besides, I'm doing this for you. Think of the rewards, man. A rich heiress and lands full of sheep.'

'You're right,' William sighed, but wondered why the dream he had lusted after for so long somehow didn't quite fire his heart as it usually did. There had been moments of late when he had quite enjoyed being himself without going through the pretence of his habitual court manner.

The gong calling the keep to break fast invaded his thoughts. 'Come,' he murmured to FitzCount, 'I can smell the fresh bread from here.'

Maude disliked venison at the best of times, but her stomach heaved at the sight of the meat on her trencher. It was a reminder of her treachery and it weighed heavily on her heart. She nibbled at a manchet of bread and watched the top table covertly.

De Rohan sat silently staring into his goblet of wine. Occasionally FitzCount would say something that brought a flicker of a smile to his lips, but he was clearly not going to be roused from his poor humour. His preoccupation made her nervous. Did he know about her?

The mood in the hall was sombre now that all guests had departed with de Rohan's impending visit to Woodleigh's keep. It was not long before the men drifted back to their quarters or set up dicing tables some distance from their lord. FitzCount gave up the struggle and deserted him for the company of one of the serving wenches. It was not often that de Rohan was alone, so she decided to approach him to find out more information. After all, the more she knew, the more she could plan. Perhaps there was some way she could save both her brother and de Rohan. She picked up her wine cup and approached him.

'Was the venison not to your liking, my lord?'

De Rohan's eyes blinked up at her and made her feel most uncomfortable. After a moment or two, he nodded to the bench beside him. 'Aye, I'd heard you were up early to hunt it for me. A special order, I believe? Your concern for my comforts is most gratifying, Maude.'

Avoiding his eyes, Maude sat down. 'It was the least I could do after you saved me yesterday.'

That drew a soft laugh. 'I could hardly let my bodyguard drown, could I? But I appreciate the gift. My thanks.' His hand reached out to lift her chin, forcing her to look him in the eye. 'You are recovered fully, I hope?'

A deep blush flooded her cheeks as she looked into his eyes and remembered what had happened. He had held her, half-naked, in his arms in broad daylight and murmured gentle words into her hair. His skin had been soft and chilled, smelling faintly of lavender and man. No, she didn't think she would ever recover. It had caused her one sleepless night so far, and no doubt it would cause more. 'Fully,' she replied quietly. A change in the topic of conversation was necessary to divert him. 'You seemed thoughtful tonight, my lord. Is aught amiss?'

He shook his head and frowned. 'A man is entitled to keep his own company sometimes.'

This slightly irritable side to the man was new and it brought a smile to her lips. He sounded exactly like her brother when things were not going his way. She remembered how he had stared at FitzCount and the wench as they left, so it might be that he was simply feeling the effects of deprivation. Bolder now that she was on familiar ground, Maude decided to help him. 'Aye, of course. It occurred to me, though, that you might be in need of distraction, since your own company seems somewhat lowering.'

That little speech caught his attention and those haunting dark eyes levelled themselves on her in open question. 'Are you offering yourself as a means of distraction, Maude?'

There was a humorous edge to the question which she did not much care for, but ignored it, anyway. Philippe was like to say such things and she knew from past experience that taking offence at such gibes was a recipe for disaster. 'Not perhaps quite in the way you meant, my lord.' Maude sipped at her wine, certain now of his attention. 'Philippe would often bemoan the lack of suitable female company.'

De Rohan's thick brows shot up. 'I'm not sure that this is the sort of conversation I should be having with you.'

He had, she thought, turned a slightly pinker shade than before and was looking nervously round to see who was listening. Maude gave him a withering look. 'Do you think I have no notion of such things, my lord? I had nine brothers and 'tis not likely that these matters—'

'Enough!' De Rohan interrupted her by slamming his fist on the table. Everyone in the hall went silent, watching to see what would happen next. He sat forward, his handsome face just a finger away from hers. 'I would have you change the subject, Maude, or I will not be responsible for my actions.'

'Well, anyway,' continued Maude unabashed, 'Philippe thought the only remedy under such circumstances was chess.'

'Chess?' Completely bewildered now, de Rohan could only repeat her suggestion.

'Aye. Do you play?' she asked innocently. His reactions were diverting, she thought.

'Of course,' he snapped, gaining his wits at last. 'Do you?'

'Certainly. There were few worthwhile wenches at our keep,' Maude explained, schooling her features into a bland smile.

Her words left him momentarily speechless. Draining his goblet, de Rohan poured himself another and bade his grinning squire leave the flask. 'Fetch the chess board,' he commanded irritably. 'If I ever come across that brother of yours, I'll have much to say to him. It's going to be a short game, lady.'

Maude just sighed and smiled at him. She decided she much preferred this side of him. It was far more interesting.

By the end of the first game, Maude was certain she had his undivided attention. Whatever the concern causing his irritation was, it seemed to have diminished somewhat.

'You play well, Maude.' De Rohan was sitting forward now and concentrating. He lifted his eyes to hers. The frown was gone. 'You played often, I take it?'

She smiled. 'Aye, I told you, there weren't…'

'Enough suitable wenches. Aye, I remember that,' he finished for her. 'But the company of other ladies? You must have wanted that?'

The chess piece in her hand stilled as she thought back. 'It doesn't really matter, my lord. That's how things were for me. Nothing can change the past.'

He eyed her carefully. 'You might find you enjoy the company of Lady Woodleigh. Her father assures me that Douce is a delightful girl.'

Maude grinned at him. 'I might.' He had clearly not met Douce. 'Tell me, my lord—what exactly do you hope to find in these heiresses?'

'Why?' De Rohan's smile vanished and all of a sudden a light-hearted conversation became something more.

She shrugged her shoulders. 'It interests me to know

what sort of a wife you would look for. Maybe I have knowledge of others that would be suitable.'

Sighing, de Rohan stared at her. 'I would want a young, beautiful, charmingly sweet and very biddable girl who would look to me for her every need. One who would give me no trouble,' he added rather darkly. 'And her clothes would have to be compatible with mine, of course.'

The chess piece hovered over the board. 'Of course. And you think Douce Woodleigh might suit?' Maude placed the piece deftly on the board with an irritatingly smug expression on her face. 'Check. My lord.'

By the time they set off for the Woodleigh keep, Maude and de Rohan had spent several evenings in each other's company playing chess. It had become their nightly ritual and often some of the men would gather round them to watch. Maude thought it was a very pleasant end to the day, although it reminded her greatly of Philippe. Afterwards, she would sometimes persuade him to sing his Breton songs and listen dreamily to his melodious voice.

It was in many ways a comfortable arrangement and Maude found herself looking forward to night-time when the tables were cleared and she and de Rohan would pit their wits against each other. They were evenly matched once de Rohan had realised that she was not just a simple opponent. It was a small step forwards in their relationship but, nevertheless, Maude could not help but feel their bonds growing stronger. Increasingly she worried about Gant and his plans for de Rohan.

De Rohan was also somewhat reticent about discussing his plans for his visit to the Woodleigh keep. Her occasional comments about Douce Woodleigh seemed to have dampened his outward interest in her and he changed the subject every time she tried to bring it up. More and more,

Maude would look up to find a worrying expression on de Rohan's face. He would mask it quickly and turn away, but she had seen it and could not forget it.

The morning they were due to leave for the Woodleigh keep was bright and warm. As the party mounted their horses in the bailey, Maude surveyed the neat, tidy court-yard with immense satisfaction. She had certainly done a good job. De Rohan's keep was far more hospitable now.

FitzCount and de Rohan were standing to one side, dis-cussing the route to take as Maude approached them.

'My lord, I have a plan.' She rushed up to him, pink and slightly breathless. 'About the journey. It might be a good idea to split the group in two.'

Both men stared at her in silence. 'And why should we do that?' FitzCount demanded suspiciously.

William remained silent, awaiting her explanation. The expression on his face was inscrutable.

'It occurred to me that this journey would be the ideal time for any attack, either on you or on the keep.'

'Aye. That much we have managed to think out for our-selves,' snapped FitzCount irritably. 'I have no wish to keep the horses waiting to hear this, so if you've fin-ished…?'

De Rohan lifted his hand to silence his friend. 'I wish to hear what Maude has to say, Brian.'

'I take it that you will leave enough men under Riddell to cope with an attack here, then?'

'Aye, Riddell knows what to do,' came the unpromising reply. De Rohan flicked at his cloak to remove some dust.

'Well, then, if we split into two groups, any attackers would find it harder to locate you.'

'Or would find it easier to attack than one large group,' added FitzCount with a sneer.

'It would be easier for my lord to escape if his attackers followed the wrong group.' Her eyes rested on de Rohan's green cloak. 'Were you to relinquish your cloak to a man of similar size and appearance to yourself, my lord, it may be that any attackers would automatically assume him to be you. Your cloak is, after all, very distinctive.'

De Rohan raked his fingers through his hair and his dark eyes crinkled as a smile formed on his lips. 'I like this plan, Maude. We should try it, Brian, don't you think?'

A look passed between them that Maude could not interpret before FitzCount glared at the two of them. 'I think you are losing your wits, man. The girl thinks up some idiotic scheme and you fall in with it without thinking it through.' He scratched his beard. 'It's your decision, but I recommend staying together in a reasonable force. It's too dangerous any other way.'

Raising his brows at such strength of feeling, de Rohan turned to Maude. 'He has a point, but I think your plan shows distinct possibilities. I am, after all, keen to arrive in one piece.'

FitzCount snorted his disapproval. 'Very well, William. But do not say I did not warn you.'

The first group left with as much ostentation as they could muster. FitzCount was accompanied by one of the soldiers swathed in de Rohan's magnificent cloak as well as a heavy guard. Swords and rivets shone in the morning sunlight as they made their way down to the river, making their cheerful shouts of farewell. De Rohan's double put on an impressive performance, much to the amusement of the man himself.

Maude and a soberly dressed de Rohan waited with Thorston until the others were well out of sight. When Maude deemed the time right, they slipped unobtrusively from the palisade and headed in the opposite direction to the Woodleigh keep. To any prying eyes, they were just hunters setting off for a day's work.

Estimating the journey to the north-east would take them several hours, Maude had taken enough food and drink to last for much longer in case of extreme emergencies. At first they headed east towards the long hills under cover of the forest. For the first time in weeks, Maude felt as if she were on safe ground. If Gant were to attack now, she was sure that de Rohan could escape. None the less, her eyes and ears were sharp to every sound. They stopped frequently so that Maude could venture forward alone to see if all was safe.

After one such foray late in the morning, Maude returned to find de Rohan and Thorston sitting on a tree log. Clearly de Rohan deemed it necessary to rest and she was not unwilling. The sun was high and, although the forest gave them shade, it was warm.

'Have you seen or heard anything?' De Rohan turned to Maude as she fetched the water flask from her horse.

She hesitated before shaking her head. 'Not so far. We must bear north now and pick up the river. The terrain will give us less protection so we must be more careful.' She tossed her head back and drank freely of the water before passing the flask to Thorston.

'It's too quiet here,' said Thorston suddenly. 'You feel it, don't you?' He looked up at Maude enquiringly.

A shiver passed through her as she thought of Gant and Philippe. 'The sooner we leave this place the better I'll feel,' she said quietly. 'There's an odd atmosphere.'

De Rohan looked from one to the other and sighed. 'All your forests are strange. The priest was telling me about some of the old legends.' He shook his head. 'There are times when being the victim of court gossip is far easier to deal with. Can I hope for a rest further on?' There was a boyish tone to his voice that caused a flicker of a smile on Maude's face.

'Think of the future, my lord. There's a rich heiress at the end of it all.'

De Rohan glanced up, all trace of the courtier gone. 'Aye,' he said quietly. 'This trip and this heiress are important to me, Maude. Don't give me cause to regret bringing you.'

Maude and Thorston looked at each other and then gathered their weapons together. De Rohan carried a sword too, at Maude's insistence, although he was not pleased since it spoiled the line of his cloak. She mounted and then looked at him. 'Perhaps you would wish to know a little more about Douce, my lord?' she asked.

De Rohan tightened his lips. 'Why do I feel you're going to tell me anyway?'

'A most noble-minded lady of strong principles, my lord.' Maude stared straight ahead.

'You do not care for the lady much, I take it?' he asked unperturbed.

She shrugged her shoulders and pushed her braids back over her shoulders. 'She never did care much for me. We had little to do with each other, really. She is certainly pretty to look at, though.'

That wrought a laugh from de Rohan. 'You don't say those words with any enthusiasm, Maude. Perhaps it would be best if we dropped the subject before I decide to turn back.'

If de Rohan was at all nervous, he was certainly not showing it. The screams that came from behind changed his equanimity. The three of them stopped dead and Maude's blood ran cold. 'By the Face of Lucca!' she whispered. 'It's an attack.'

Turning to Thorston and de Rohan, she grabbed their

reins. 'Take your lord up river as fast as you can,' she commanded. 'The Woodleigh keep is only another hour or so hard ride. Stop for no one.'

Thorston nodded his head and waited for de Rohan's sign. De Rohan, however, appeared reluctant to leave. 'I pay *you* to protect me, Maude,' he said grimly. 'Do you desert me?' His eyes did not leave her face.

'My guess is that the plan worked, my lord. I shall see if my lord FitzCount is in need of help and then follow behind you. I may be able to find something of use to you.' Pulling the bow from her shoulder, she patted his horse's neck. 'Now go, or my plans will be undone.'

Maude's heart was in her mouth as she watched the two of them disappear into the forest. With any luck, FitzCount would have taken at least one captive to interrogate and she would then be able to locate Philippe. Nervously she urged Lark forward towards the noise.

She found them but ten minutes' distance from where they had rested. There was no sign of the attackers, save for a good number of arrows and spears protruding from the trees like hedgehogs. FitzCount was shouting at some soldiers to gather up the supply carts and see to the wounded.

As soon as he saw Maude, his eyes narrowed. 'Where is he?' he almost hissed at her.

Calmly, Maude dismounted. 'Safe. Thorston took him on ahead.'

'You would leave him unprotected?' He gaped at her with an open mouth.

Maude ignored his question. 'Did you take any prisoners?' She stared at the two bodies slung up against a log.

'No.'

Disappointment mingled with relief flooded through her. De Rohan was safe, but what would become of Philippe now?

# Chapter Nine

Maude cursed as the rain poured down on them. By the time Maude and FitzCount arrived at Woodleigh's keep two very long hours after the attack, they were soaked to the bone. Her braids hung like rats' tails and she was in no good humour. The heavy baggage wain had become bogged down frequently in the muddy tracks and she found herself railing at de Rohan for his exquisite taste in fine garments. As he had explained earlier during the journey, he had not known what to bring with him, so he had brought everything!

Woodleigh's immense keep towered over a lush green valley that stretched out towards rolling hills. The hardy sheep fared well there, despite the poor weather, and it was well known in the area that Robert Woodleigh had been pleased with his increasing revenues. Competition for the hand of his daughter was likely to be intense.

That William de Rohan was interested in Douce Woodleigh was no great surprise. The young heiress had countless suitors since any future husband would be heir to a considerable amount of land and resources. It was the thought of de Rohan and the very dour Douce Woodleigh that drew a wry smile from her lips.

As they thundered through the gates of the keep, FitzCount demanded news of de Rohan. The guards obliged by informing them that de Rohan and his man had arrived an hour earlier and were currently enjoying the hospitality of the lord and his daughter.

FitzCount saw to the baggage and his men whilst Maude made her way across the bailey to the stables. Lark was as wet as Maude and a few moments to herself in the peace and quiet of the stables would be welcome. She needed time to think.

'It pleases me greatly to see you in such good health, Maude.' William had apparently followed her and, incredible though it was, he must have been waiting for her. She could hear the dry amusement in his voice since her appearance most definitely left a great deal to be desired. His attitude irritated her beyond measure.

'By the Face of Lucca! Do you have to creep up on me like that?' she exploded, pushing her sopping wet braids over her shoulder. She turned to face him.

Ignoring her outburst as well as her lack of address, de Rohan simply smiled at her as his eyes took in her bedraggled state. 'You really must stop using such language, Maude. It might have a bad effect on me and the men.' He reached out to brush some raindrops from her face. His hands were warm and gentle and it reminded her of when he had done the same for the lovely Gundreda de Vere that first night in his chamber.

'Actually,' he continued without the smile, 'I was concerned for your safety. Were anything to happen to you, it struck me that I would no doubt have to explain to the invincible Philippe. He will appear one day, I take it?'

If possible, de Rohan looked even more entrancing. He had apparently bathed, changed and clearly felt at ease in his new surroundings. Wordlessly Maude bent down to pick up a twist of hay and began to dry Lark with vigourous strokes. Had he guessed about Philippe, then? Her throat was suddenly very constricted.

'There was no need to worry, my lord. As you see, there was no further trouble and Philippe is unlikely to appear in any case. He is presently involved in a secret undertaking which will last some time.' She cleared her throat and changed the subject. 'I take it that the remainder of your journey was uneventful?'

Maude could feel him standing patiently behind her as she worked on her horse, but she could not bring herself to look at him.

'Aye. Your plan was most effective.'

Her hands stilled. 'This time, anyway.'

'All the more reason for me to be concerned about the safety of my bodyguard, don't you think?'

She risked a glance over her shoulder at him. Leaning casually against the stable wall, William de Rohan did not have the air of a concerned man. His relaxed attitude only served to confuse her. 'Gratifying though it is, my lord, your concern is unnecessary. You pay me, after all.' She threw the wet hay down and patted Lark on the neck.

'Aye,' he said eventually. 'That's true.' Pushing himself away from the wall, he began to brush the dirt from his cloak. 'Tell me, though. Was it Gant who attacked?'

Maude held her breath. 'It's very possible. He's a determined man. I have learned that to my cost.'

Lark whickered nervously and both of them looked around. There was nothing there save the rain, but Maude glanced at de Rohan in question. He shook his head. 'It's nothing.' He ventured towards the stable door and peered out. With a sigh, he closed it again and turned to Maude. 'Where do you think Gant is most likely to be hiding out?'

It was a question Maude had puzzled over long and hard.

'I don't know, but he would need somewhere safe and iso-lated. There are several abandoned villages round here that have long been reclaimed by the forest. He could be hiding in an old Saxon settlement quite comfortably. No one would know since few people venture into the forest these days.'

'I see. And Woodleigh would not necessarily know, then, if Gant were hiding in the area?' His eyes fastened on hers and she found she could not look away.

Shrugging her shoulders, Maude shivered. 'I am not well acquainted with Robert Woodleigh, but he has always struck me as being a very careful, cautious man. He sends patrols out regularly. On the look out for fortune hunters, most likely,' she added with a raised brow.

His answering smile caused her to shiver even more. 'I am merely in search of a comfortable life, Maude. Nothing more.'

Grudgingly, Maude smiled. 'Aye, my lord, but there must be a less dangerous way of going about it?'

'Actually, Maude, I'm beginning to find this dangerous life rather appealing. It's entirely possible that I might find a comfortable life rather tame now.'

Maude looked at his beautiful garments and smiled wryly. 'I suppose, my lord, that anything is possible.'

He laughed and pulled her to him. With infinite care, he placed his hands around her face and dropped a gentle kiss on her forehead. 'Maude, I think I shall miss you greatly when you aren't here. You are the most entertaining wench I have ever come across. Perhaps I should consider em-ploying you on a permanent basis?'

Close as they were, Maude felt absolutely no compunc-tion to pull away from him. It did indeed feel good to be held by William de Rohan, even though he was doing this because he wanted something of her or because it was part of his plan to charm her for some reason. Knowing that didn't seem to make much difference, Maude realised. She liked it very much. Blushing slightly, Maude sighed. 'I doubt that Douce Woodleigh would agree with you, my lord. A female bodyguard is perhaps not most brides' ideal.'

His sigh echoed hers as he withdrew a little from her. 'Aye, I fear you may be right, Maude.' He grinned. 'Talking of Douce, you must clean yourself up before entering the hall. I gather she is most particular about cleanliness and appearance. A very good sign, don't you think?' His hands brushed his cloak with more than a little pride. 'Her good opinion is vital and I would not have you shame me, Maude. Do try your best, at least.'

Maude snorted in disgust as she stalked from the stables. William de Rohan was nothing more than a vain popinjay and he fully deserved marriage with Douce Woodleigh.

Clearly her best was not good enough. Maude could feel Douce Woodleigh's accusing eyes on her, even though she was half-hidden by several large soldiers. The hall was decked out magnificently in bright wall-hangings and hundreds of wax candles. Despite the number of people joining in the feast in de Rohan's honour, the hall remained cool thanks to the open windows. The floors were clean and sweet-smelling and there was not a hound in sight. Maude could not fault Douce's skills as a housekeeper.

The girl in question bore down on Maude with indecent haste. Those cold grey eyes swept contemptuously over her makeshift appearance. Maude glanced up at Douce and sighed. She had always attributed her ethereally pale skin to the hours of devotion practised in the dark, stone church. Her piety was as well known as her quiet loveliness, but Maude was convinced that the girl had a heart of stone.

She had never seen her smile, let alone laugh, and Douce had always insisted on behaving with a maturity far beyond her years. Now sixteen, she was acting like an elderly matron with her priest close at hand. What use would she have, then, of a tall, well-built husband with a handsome face and an excess of charm?

'You are Maude de Vaillant, are you not?'

Close to, Douce's pale skin was almost translucent and the blue veins shone through. Her large grey eyes glittered in the candlelight.

'Aye. You know I am,' she said uncertainly, misliking the tight-lipped expression on the girl's face.

'I thought I recognised you.' Douce glanced quickly over her shoulder to the priest, who hung behind her rather in the way of a vulture feeding on carrion.

Maude inclined her head, remembering de Rohan's entreaty. 'It has been a long time,' she allowed.

The cold eyes continued to survey her mercilessly. 'Your reputation goes before you, Lady de Vaillant. As you see, this is a God-fearing keep and I expect certain proprieties to be maintained.'

Maude stiffened, wondering what indignities the girl could heap on her now. 'Rest at ease, my lady. I have no wish to cause any offence.' Folding her arms across her chest, Maude softened the sharpness of her voice with a brief smile. 'I am here only as a protector to William de Rohan and will carry out my duty as best I can. If there is a problem, I am sure we can come to some solution.'

Douce lifted her chin a little and stared down at her. 'It is a question of your appearance. I will have no woman dressed in breeches at my table. It is a most brazen and distressing act that serves no purpose other than to attract the attention of men. We have heard of what you are, Maude de Vaillant, and will have none of your ways here.'

Douce Woodleigh might be lovely to behold, but she was as charmless and as cold as a statue. No matter how irritating William might be, all of his charm, his cheerfulness and his grace would be completely wasted on her. Maude smiled tightly at her. 'It was considered by Lord de Rohan to be the most sensible form of dress and I am sorry that you do not approve.' She shrugged lightly. 'Unfortunately, I do not possess any other clothes, my lady.'

The icy light of battle was in Douce's eyes. 'That will not be a problem. There are several gowns belonging to my maids that you can choose from. If you wish to remain in this keep, then you must change immediately.'

Flushing with anger and humiliation, Maude had to bite her tongue to keep herself from saying what she felt. Across the crowded room, Maude could see William smiling at her, encouraging her to please the lady, although he could not have heard a word of the conversation. He probably thought, as others would, that Douce was merely bestowing her goodness on an undeserving wretch. Still, she had promised she would not shame him before the Woodleighs. A grimace was all she could manage. 'As you wish, my lady. If you would show me the way?'

The gown was serviceable, if not a little tight and faded. Originally a dark green, the dress was now a lighter shade that seemed to suit Maude. In a rather strange way, it felt good to feel like a woman again as she followed the lines of her body with her hands. Maude decided that it must have belonged to Douce at one stage because it was made of soft wool and had obviously been shortened. The long shift she had borrowed was also of fine linen, so her skin was not likely to rub against the material.

As a parting touch, Douce had insisted that Maude wore her hair long, in the manner of unwed girls. Maude suspected that had more to do with humiliating an unmarried nineteen-year-old than maintaining standards of propriety. Nevertheless, she agreed to whatever Douce required of her.

It was worth it all to see the look on William's face. At first, he found it hard to keep his eyes from her. 'Maude,' he declared. 'Is that you? Truly? Do you know that you no longer look like my squire?' This last was said with a certain edge to it, but Maude ignored him. Perhaps the man had had too much to drink?

'It would help,' she hissed grumpily, 'if you said nothing at all. My lord.'

He smiled at her and handed her a goblet of wine, bending his head down towards her in an intimate gesture. 'You're right, Maude,' he murmured softly. 'I might get carried away again and then where would we be?'

All of a sudden, it was as if they were the only people in that crowded hall. William towered above her, his handsome face smiling down at her, shielding her from the gaze of anyone else. Maude felt ridiculously small, but oddly protected by his gesture—as she knew it was—and smiled up at him. The air between them was heavy with unspoken words and thoughts. Maude could feel herself swaying towards him and wondered what on earth would happen if she…

'De Rohan.' A rather delicate, particular voice broke the spell between them. Sir Robert Woodleigh approached them, his narrow face pained and distant as if he expected them to commit a most heinous crime before his very eyes. And so they might have, Maude remembered with a hectic flush, if he hadn't interrupted them.

'So pleased you arrived without too much difficulty. There was an attack of some sort, I hear.' Sparse brown brows lifted over slanting blue eyes. 'Outlaws are a problem these days, to be sure. I hope you will take it up with

the King when you next see him? Come take your seat by
me.'

Tall and almost painfully thin, like his daughter, Sir Robert picked his way through the crowd and indicated to de
Rohan where he should sit. Detached now from Maude, de
Rohan seemed to resume his normal outgoing cheerfulness
and set about charming anything that was put before him.

Everything, apparently, except Douce Woodleigh. She
sat silently next to him, inclining her head regally and with
such delicacy towards de Rohan that Maude decided she
must have swallowed something foul. From her seat at a
lower table, Maude found herself avidly watching those
first tentative steps in their relationship. It was not a promising start.

Soberly dressed compared to de Rohan, Douce could
barely bring herself to answer him or to smile at him. When
she deigned to look in de Rohan's general direction, she
merely offered him a reluctant twitch of her lips. Nothing
he could do seemed to have any outward effect on the
superior attitude of Douce Woodleigh. Even when he offered her the choicest morsels from his trencher, they were
politely refused. The girl ate practically nothing, Maude
noted with asperity. He would probably feel at ease with
that, at least!

William de Rohan acted as a true courtier. He smiled,
laughed, told jokes and anecdotes about the King and court
life. All about him, elderly matrons giggled and blushed
like young girls. Douce just pursed her lips and stared
ahead, occasionally nodding or placing her thin fingers delicately over the gold cross at her neck. The ever-present
priest stood behind her, his head bowed in prayer throughout the interminable meal. It seemed like hours before the
tables were cleared in readiness for the songs. At least they
could enjoy that. No doubt de Rohan could be entreated to

sing too. She doubted very much he would want to miss displaying his talent before an heiress of Douce's standing. If anything could touch her heart it would be that, and de Rohan knew it.

'Tell me, Lady Woodleigh, what you do to amuse yourself?' His dark eyes smiled down at her, gentle and adoring without being too forward. Maude smiled to herself. He had used that particular ruse to great effect on many occasions before.

Douce stiffened even more, if that were possible. 'I pray and sew, my lord. I find I have little need for other diversions.' Her severe expression was not encouraging.

De Rohan persisted. 'Do you ride? Your estates are magnificent.'

At the mention of her estates, Douce Woodleigh raised her chin and looked down at him as if he were no more than the lowest serving boy. 'I am perfectly adept at most feminine pursuits. There is no question as to my competence at anything.'

William glanced over at Maude, then, sensing her eyes on him. There was an odd gleam in his eyes. 'Do you play chess?'

Douce looked as though he had made the most improper suggestion possible. Gasping, she clutched at her throat. 'Most certainly not. That is for men and soldiers. A lady would not consider such a game.' Her cold eyes glanced quickly in Maude's direction and it was perfectly clear to all who were listening exactly who she had in mind.

He blinked. 'Of course. A foolish thought, no more.' Schooling his features, William affected a hazy smile and turned his attention to the more nervous Robert Woodleigh.

'You'll forgive me, my lord, but I fear it is time for us to retire.'

Woodleigh blinked hard and even Douce looked rather perplexed by this bald statement. 'Us?' he queried.

De Rohan nodded in Maude's direction. 'My bodyguard, my squire and I. If Maude does not get a good night's sleep, her temper in the morning can be most trying. I'm sure you understand.'

The entire hall gaped in shock at his words. Maude was no exception. Crimson from head to toe, she glared at him. Ignoring them all, William stood and raised his hand imperiously in Maude's direction. 'Come, Maude. We shall rise early in order to attend mass with Lady Woodleigh.'

If Woodleigh or his daughter were about to say anything, those words certainly took the wind from their sails. Maude followed her lord quickly, unwilling to find out what gossip would be unleashed by his words.

'Where are we going?' she hissed at his retreating back.

He turned suddenly to open a door to a small room off the hall. Plain and functional, it boasted three mattresses and some blankets. A fire of sorts flickered in the grate.

'Have you gone mad?' she queried.

'Most likely,' he muttered as he closed the door behind him. 'But I could stand it no longer. There are limits to my patience. Being entertaining can be hard work. Being polite in the face of such arrogance is beyond even my skills.' He sat down on one of the mattresses and stretched out full length with a decidedly disgruntled look on his face.

Uncertain as to what to do, Maude stood by the fire. 'Well, I thought you were most charming.' For some unearthly reason she found herself wanting to give him some support. After all, she knew how much effort he had put in.

He raised his head slightly and squinted at her. 'Another jest, Maude? Why cannot I see your smile?'

She smiled, enjoying his light-hearted bantering. The

past week or so had been most instructive on that particular front. It had become part of their conversation to gently poke fun at each other without causing any offence and Maude had come to like it greatly. It was not the sort of thing she had ever indulged in at home. 'No jest. Were I a wealthy heiress, my lord, I am sure I would make you an offer forthwith.'

A deep sigh rose from the bed. He had his eyes closed. 'Another proposition, Maude?'

'Well,' Maude said slowly, going over to the mattress next to de Rohan. 'I do play chess, but that is rather a drawback apparently.' She sat down and stretched out alongside him. The mattress was comfortable and it had been a long hard day.

Suddenly, William levered himself on to his elbows and turned to face her. His smile was gone and he studied her in silent contemplation. 'Were you a wealthy heiress, I think I would—'

Whatever he would do was interrupted by the arrival of Thomas. Without speaking, he stomped to the third mattress and plonked himself down.

William sighed again and smiled at the boy. 'Ah, Thomas. Just in time. Did Thorston give you any information?'

Thomas nodded. 'He said there was much you should see to the west of the keep. A short ride towards the river.' His white, pasty face gleamed in the flickering firelight. 'Will there be anything else?' His eyes slid over to where Maude was lying. He glowered at her, clearly indignant that she was taking his rightful place.

De Rohan shook his head. 'Maude and I shall be up early. We shall require hot water and some bread first thing.'

'Aye, my lord.'

De Rohan tugged at Maude's hair. 'Take off the gown, Maude. I wish you to wear it tomorrow since it will suit our purposes well enough.'

Gulping, Maude frowned at him, more interested in his plans for the next day than her modesty. 'It will? How?'

De Rohan sank back onto his mattress. 'Trust me. Now do as I say, or shall I be forced to dock another mark?'

'Another?' she asked askance. Unfortunately, she found herself addressing his back. Her question would clearly have to wait.

The morning, in contrast to Maude's temper, was bright and fresh. A light wind appeared to have blown the rain-clouds to the north, leaving soft blue skies and the smell of clean earth. Maude glared at de Rohan.

'I give up, my lord. This particular journey of discovery is beyond me. Please explain to me why we rose at such a godforsaken time to have a look around Robert Wood-leigh's estates? I'm sure the Woodleighs themselves would be only too proud to take you on a tour. It is, after all, the purpose of this trip.'

De Rohan leaned forward in the saddle to look at her carefully. 'Maude, we really must do something about that abominable temper of yours first thing in the morning. However did Philippe deal with it?'

Washed and dressed in hunting attire, William almost glowed with vitality and good humour. His dark hair curled a little round his shoulders and his face had been barbered with extreme care. Distractedly, Maude noticed there were no nicks on his chin. Thomas must have aided his toilette. There was something the boy could do well, at least. 'Let's leave Philippe out of this,' she muttered, allowing Lark to pull on the rein. They were sat on their horses, a short distance from the Woodleigh keep, close to the edge of the forest.

De Rohan had roused her from her dreams just as dawn was breaking, refusing to tell her the purpose of their outing. He had dispatched the even grumpier Thomas with a message for FitzCount and chivvied Maude into getting dressed quickly. They had saddled up their horses and ridden through the gate, leaving a bemused guard in their wake.

'Well, if I really must tell you,' he said, staring out over the forest, 'we are going to see if we can locate Gant's hideout in the forest. The sooner he is despatched, the safer we will be. Won't we?'

It did make perfect sense, of course, but he did not know about Philippe. Any trouble would mean danger for him. 'Aye, but we must go carefully.' She looked at him, all humour dispelled. 'Gant is dangerous and there's no telling what he's really up to.'

There was a hint of a smile. 'Ah, Maude, I think I have an idea.' He stared at her, his dark eyes resting on her face.

'You do?' Her voice was almost a whisper. What now?

'Aye,' he said, avoiding the question. 'For now, we'll just observe. Nothing more. Besides, if my plan works, we'll not be alone for long.'

The man was a complete mystery. 'No wonder the King was keen to rid himself of you,' she muttered darkly. 'It must be very quiet at court.' With a sigh, she urged Lark on and headed into the forest. She could hear de Rohan laugh behind her.

The sweetness of the early morning soon brushed away any bad humours and Maude began to enjoy herself. Tall trees lined their path westwards of the keep, the horses' hooves sinking into the muddy ground. At once earthy and strange, the spirit of the forest embraced them and drew them deeper in. The only sounds were those of the forest creatures and the birds. As the sun rose, specks of light filtered through the canopy of leaves overhead, dancing in an odd cadence all around them.

Apparently William had sent Thorston on a secret scouting mission shortly after they had arrived and the boy had found several clues which might lead to their attackers. Such information only confirmed Maude's belief that William was far more than a courtier claiming the hand of an heiress. What did confuse her, though, was the fact that he trusted her with this information. He had already said she had lied to him and he would find out the truth and yet here he was, riding with her into the jaws of his enemy. It did not make sense at all.

Without warning, William suddenly motioned to her to dismount. Silently, they slid from their saddles and tied their horses to a low-lying branch.

'Ahead,' he whispered in her ear. 'I think we may have found something.'

They moved carefully forward to the edge of a clearing. Maude clutched at her long skirts, inwardly cursing Douce for hampering her freedom, and pulled her knife from around her waist. There was a strange feeling about this place, disturbed and disquieting. She soon saw why.

Ahead lay the abandoned village of Saxon settlers, the huts overgrown with weeds, creepers and grass. Bronwen had often said that the souls of the dead inhabitants would linger in their dwellings, breathing death on intruders. A deep chill gripped her innards. Whatever the truth, Maude could not stop her apprehension.

On the far side of the clearing, she could see three horses tied up outside a hut. A thin line of smoke drifted from a hole in the roof. Her eyes darted around but she could see no one outside.

'What do you think?' William stood so close to her that they touched.

She took a deep breath. 'I think we need to bring FitzCount and some men. It's not safe. There may be more.'

De Rohan said nothing for a moment, his dark eyes narrowed and scanning the huts. He nodded and then looked at her. 'Come, then. I have no great desire to start a career as a hero.'

They had reached the horses when trouble struck. Bronwen would have said it was the souls of the dead having their revenge, thought Maude. Whatever it was, it was very inconvenient. Two solidly built men emerged from behind the trees, swords in hand and death in their eyes. She reached for her sword.

'Get your sword out,' she hissed to de Rohan who seemed to have been struck to stone. 'This is no time to play the innocent courtier.'

She couldn't see his face since she was watching the two men approach them, but she could sense his smile.

'I pay you to do this, Maude,' came the grim reply. 'I have a yen to see your true worth.'

She exhaled in despair. 'Well, at least get your sword out and *look* as if you might know what to do with it. Stay by the tree,' she added. She wondered if he was wearing his hauberk under his tunic, but was not hopeful. No doubt it interfered with the fall of the cloth.

Heart hammering, Maude gripped her sword and faced the men with grim determination. Her skirts would hamper her greatly and the men were large and strong-looking. Nevertheless, she would fight to the death to protect de Rohan. Moving a little away from him, she swung the first blow. Finesse and grace had their places in swordfights, but this was not the time. Maude abandoned such notions and slashed and thrust at the men with all her strength. At least de Rohan had the intelligence to move around the tree as they did, staying behind Maude at all times.

The man on the left was younger and weaker in the arm. The second he left his weak side uncovered, Maude thrust her sword into his ribs. He crumpled in a heap at her feet. The second, seeing his chance, threw himself at her as she pulled her sword from the first. Maude was too quick and whipped the weapon upwards and outwards in a savage movement that caught him a nasty blow on his shoulder. Enraged now, her opponent growled and renewed his onslaught. Heavy blows rained down on her and Maude could feel herself tiring. Strong and skilled as she was, this was one fight she was not going to win without resorting to trickery.

She could feel the sweat trickling down her brow as she thrust time and time again, desperately looking for a chance to move. Suddenly, as the man bore down on her again, her feet got caught up in her skirts and she fell full length on to the ground with a heavy thud. Her sword skittered away from her hand. Maude stared up at the face of her enemy, frozen with terror.

He toppled over her and landed just to one side. Blood poured over both of them. Winded and frightened, Maude opened her eyes. Apart from the inert body on top of her, she was still alive. De Rohan suddenly appeared.

'Not dead yet, then?' he asked, echoing the phrase he had used the first day they met.

She stared at him, open-mouthed, and then at the man. There was a knife protruding from his back. The jewelled hilt glittered as it caught the light. 'You killed him?' she whispered in disbelief. 'You threw your knife?'

William was kneeling down at her side, staring at her blood-covered bodice. All colour seemed to drain from his face and Maude remembered his aversion to blood. 'William,' she said quietly, shaking his arm. 'William, pull him off me. We must go.'

His eyes were fixed on a battered silver mark around the man's neck. With a quick jerk of his arm, William snapped it off. He dragged the man away and pulled his knife from the body. Maude hauled herself to her feet. 'Come,' she repeated urgently. 'We must go.'

He turned to her then and looked at her. 'Are you hurt?' he asked.

Confused at such an odd question at such a time, she shook her head. 'No, but—'

'Good. Then shut up.' He glared at her fiercely before pulling her hard against him and kissing her with a strength and a passion she did not know he possessed. This was no courtier's kiss, that much she did know.

The flame that had burned before ignited between them, consuming all coherent thought. Their mouths opened for each other and their hands clutched at each other's shaking body. Relief at still being alive and fear of death tore through her as she sought comfort against him. Maude entwined her fingers within his thick hair and pulled him tighter against her.

His body responded with unmistakable urgency. Lowering her gently to the ground, William broke the kiss to cup her face with his fingers. Silently he looked at her before kissing her. This time it was different. Gentle and tender, his tongue traced a delicate line over her lips before moving to the soft, sensitive skin below her ear. Maude gasped and arched back with the pleasure it gave her. As his lips nuzzled at her neck, William's fingers pulled at the laces of her gown and sought her breasts. Cold fingers against hot, swelling flesh wrenched a soft sigh from her. There was nothing in Maude's mind other than the pleasure

and the dull, throbbing ache that was building deep within
her.

'So, de Rohan. This is the nature of your early-morning
ride?'

Shock, confusion and disappointment swept through her
as Maude heard Robert Woodleigh's cold voice somewhere
above them. Her body ached as William pulled away from
her and gently levered himself up. With amazing presence
of mind, he retied the laces of her gown and pulled Maude
to her feet. The extent of her humiliation was not complete
until she saw about ten of Woodleigh's patrol ranged about
them, interest written on all their faces. Douce Woodleigh
emerged from amongst them and urged her horse forward
to stand before Maude and William.

If ever there was a time for swooning, Maude thought,
this would be it.

## Chapter Ten

The dead bodies should have been evidence enough. Robert stared down at William as though he had committed some dreadful crime. All colour had drained from the man's face.

'What happened?' His voice was quiet and slightly panic-stricken.

William dusted down his cloak, the suggestion of a smile hovering on his lips. 'A little local difficulty with some outlaws, I believe. Maude was able to dispatch them efficiently. There is no need to worry.'

This last was said as he watched Woodleigh's eyes flicker across the clearing for signs of further attack before coming to rest coldly on Maude. 'They appear to be alone, though we should perhaps investigate the area. Just to be sure,' continued de Rohan.

Maude looked at him, wondering why he didn't mention the horses and the smoke in the hut nearby, but his face remained calm and unperturbed. He was certainly far more relaxed than she was. Deeming it wise to remain as insignificant as possible, Maude fixed her eyes on the ground.

There was a charged silence as Woodleigh considered this suggestion. 'Why exactly were you here, de Rohan?'

he said finally. His tone was almost accusatory, thought
Maude, but William seemed not to notice. It was hardly
the reaction of a host to an honoured guest who had barely
survived a vicious attack. But then, of course, he was not
likely to be endeared to a potential son-by-marriage who
was caught *in flagrante delicto* with a woman of very du-
bious reputation.

He shrugged. 'Oh,' he said vaguely. 'You know how
these things often are, my lord?' He gestured towards the
trees. 'I had a desire to see the estate. The King bade me
see the full extent of it, after all.' His eyes glittered in the
shadows as he offered Woodleigh a magnificent smile.

The silence of the forest hung about them like a cloak,
disturbed only by the soft morning breeze and the birdsong.
Caught up in the tension between the two men, Woodleigh's soldiers remained in their saddles, quiet and watchful.

'I'll send some men to look around,' came the strained
reply. He beckoned to one of his guards and ordered out a
small patrol. 'There have been several incidents recently,
connected, no doubt, with the attack on your way here. It
may be that you've stumbled on something of a nest. What
exactly did you see?' Woodleigh leaned forward in his saddle to stare at de Rohan. His scrawny neck was working
almost convulsively, and Maude noticed his fingers shaking.

'Nothing,' replied de Rohan. 'We were just riding, when
these two ruffians set upon us. I have to say, Woodleigh,
that I'm not impressed by your patrols. I fear that my cloak
is ruined.' He frowned in the general direction of the soldiers.

Despite the seriously humiliating situation, Maude felt a
dreadful need to laugh. Stifling the urge, she finally managed to raise her eyes to the silent and somewhat forgotten

Douce Woodleigh. Douce, it would seem, had not forgotten her.

Although her face betrayed very little of her true feelings, her eyes were large and luminous with suppressed anger. Pale and effacing, Douce maintained an icy veneer of detachment, but Maude could tell that the girl was furious. There was only the slightest hint of a blush on her cheeks, but it was enough.

'We must send up a prayer of thanks that you were not injured or hurt in any way, my lord,' she said with tight-lipped coolness. 'You were most fortunate.'

William stepped forward and took the reins of her horse. 'Your concern is most touching, my lady.' Again, the brilliant smile, but it had little effect on Douce Woodleigh. If anything, Maude decided, she had become even more pallid and stiff. Perhaps it was not so surprising in view of what Douce had witnessed between them. She would have to tread warily.

'I am sure you wish to return to the keep to recover from such an ordeal.' Douce carefully avoided looking at Maude. 'I shall send my servants to tend you the moment you arrive. Later, perhaps, we can attend mass as you suggested?'

William bowed his head in acceptance of her command. 'Your arrangements are more than welcome.' He looked up, capturing her cold eyes with his gaze. 'Just one more thing, though. Lady de Vaillant is in need of a bath and another gown. Could I perhaps prevail on you to see to her needs?'

Maude gulped. It was the first time that William had ever referred to her by her title. Indeed, she had not known if he had ever been aware what it was.

Douce's gaze transferred to Maude. It was as if cold darts had been shot into her heart. 'I shall, of course, do my Christian duty,' came the brittle reply. Douce surveyed them both with faint disgust before impatiently snatching her reins back from William. 'I shall ride on ahead to make the necessary arrangements. I trust you will follow shortly.'

William watched her stiff back for several moments, deep in thought. Maude looked up at Robert Woodleigh.

'Will you have these bodies brought back to the keep, then?' She was glad to hear that her voice sounded normal, at least.

His sparse brows rose in question. 'Why should I do that? They're hardly worthy of a proper burial. The wolves or some such creatures will take them.' Pressing his thin lips tightly together, Robert Woodleigh looked like a frightened man.

'They may be identified.'

Woodleigh merely shook his head. 'The peasants round here are so thick with the outlaws that nothing will happen. They'd be too afeared.'

He glanced quickly at de Rohan, but he was absorbed in the restoration of his garments. 'Were I you, Lady de Vaillant, I would be far more judicious about your conduct on or around my estate.' He breathed in slowly, considering the situation further.

'My daughter may have little choice in her marriage arrangements, but I do not wish to see her humiliated before all and sundry.' His hand swept towards the soldiers with contempt. 'Your reputation for evil is well known and rumours that you have bewitched de Rohan are already in circulation. Go carefully, Maude de Vaillant.'

'I am paid to protect de Rohan,' she replied quickly. She had no wish to antagonise him, though. 'There was no malice intended. It was just…' Maude blushed furiously '…it was the shock, I believe.'

Woodleigh gave her a withering look and rode back towards his men. Maude and William tramped over to their horses. There was a faint smile on his lips.

'You knew they would come, didn't you?' she accused, turning on him suddenly. Her hand stayed his arm. 'Tell me the truth.' It was the only thing that made sense. Why else would he let his passions loose whilst there was a hut full of outlaws but a few steps away? She had come to realise that William de Rohan rarely did anything without good reason.

The smile had gone but William didn't look at Maude. His eyes were fixed on the tree-line. 'Aye, I did. Does it matter?'

Maude rounded on him. 'Matter?' she shrieked. 'Of course it matters!' Her voice lowered to a mutter. She felt like battering the man around the head, but resisted since she didn't think Woodleigh would view any further crimes on her part with any favour.

'Most of the county think I'm a witch and keep well away from me. Having Woodleigh and his people see me frolicking in the forest with the King's favoured man aside two dead bodies and within a stone's throw of a nest of outlaws is not likely to improve things. Is it?' She rounded on him, forcing him to look at her.

'You were irritated by the Woodleighs for looking down on you and saw your chance to get your own back, didn't you? You didn't give a damn about me or my feelings, did you?' By this time, Maude's voice had risen alarmingly and she could feel herself precariously near to tears. What on earth was the matter with her? 'By the Face of Lucca, William de Rohan, you're worse than all the rest put together. At least they don't trouble to hide their dislike.'

Pushing him hard away from her, Maude stormed towards her horse. A strong arm grabbed her shoulder, his fingers digging into her flesh. He whirled her around and held her upper arms tightly. His face was white. 'Aye, I wanted to humiliate them and I knew they would be there, but I had not planned…what happened. I did not mean to…anything by it.' He drew a long, quivering breath, schooling his emotions. 'Woodleigh's involved up to his neck in a treasonable plot and I wanted to frighten him.'

'Frighten him!' she countered through clenched teeth. 'You were doing a very good job of frightening me! Why didn't you fight those men with me? I know very well you can use your sword, William de Rohan.' The words had welled up with her deep-seated anger and spilled out without her thinking.

He pulled her to him tightly, holding her eye to eye with him. There were two dark red splotches on his cheeks. 'Because that's your job and there was every chance that Woodleigh would come in the middle of it all. I could not take the risk.'

Jerking herself free, she stood back and slapped him across the face very hard. 'Well, so much for your risks and the job. You can find yourself another bodyguard.' She would have flounced away except that he yanked her arm so that she was facing him again.

'By the Face of Lucca, Maude de Vaillant, I'll do no such thing. I'm paying you to do a job and you'll do it, do you hear?'

They both stared at each other breathlessly, their anger subsiding. Maude could see the vivid print of her hand on his face and was glad that she'd been able to make some impression on him at least. 'You've paid me nothing, so far,' she said more quietly.

His eyes stared down at her, stormy and unquiet. 'I'll pay you in full when I'm ready.'

* * *

FitzCount glanced up at the hunched shoulders and passed a goblet of strong wine to him. 'It may help,' he added.

De Rohan grunted and pulled the cup towards him. 'It might, but I doubt it.' He poured the wine down his throat before placing the goblet noisily on the table. 'I've been in that church for two candle notches. Even my eyelashes are frozen. The woman must be made of stone.'

'Aye, well. Good for the soul, perhaps?' FitzCount raised a coppery brow at de Rohan before draining his own cup. 'Bound to put you back in favour.'

'If anything, the girl looked even more stone-hearted after mass than before. The only way I'd ever be in favour with Lady Woodleigh would be if I were a priest,' he replied darkly.

FitzCount nodded silently and wisely refrained from adding anything which might provoke de Rohan. Pouring another cup of wine for each of them, he changed the subject. 'Woodleigh's scared. I'll wager it's Gant that's in his forest and de Vere's linked in with it all.'

De Rohan fumbled in his belt bag and then carefully placed a small battered mark on the table between them. 'That came from the neck of one of the men who attacked us.'

FitzCount picked it up and examined it. 'It's the same as before.' He shoved it back towards de Rohan. 'If we don't catch them soon, they'll kill you.'

De Rohan sighed into his cup. 'Well, Maude's doing her damnedest to prevent them, I'm pleased to say. We still can't prove that de Vere is involved, though. Who knows what damage he's doing at court meanwhile?'

Frowning, FitzCount rubbed at his beard. 'It's about time

I went to see King Henry. I might be able to find out what's going on there. What about Gundreda?'

The dark brows of de Rohan lifted at that. 'She'll not tell me anything, Brian. Not until she's sure that de Vere is going to lose.'

'I'll set off when we get back, then. Might pay a visit to an old friend while I'm there. She'll be able to tell me what Bertolini's up to.'

De Rohan nodded silently. 'Another of your comfortable widows?'

FitzCount laughed. 'Well, at least I'm predictable. I've heard that you were overly attentive to Maude this morning.'

'It was part of the plan,' replied de Rohan quickly, rubbing absently at his cheek.

'That good, was it?' FitzCount enquired airily.

De Rohan slammed his cup down onto the table. 'Dammit, FitzCount. The girl was covered in blood and I was worried about her, that's all.' He shook his head. 'She just got carried away. You know how these women can be.'

FitzCount tilted his head. 'Carried away? Are we talking about the same Maude, William?' He grinned into his wine cup.

'Well, if she hadn't been wearing that gown, it would never have happened,' came the irritable reply. 'It's been a long time since...' De Rohan sighed heavily, allowing the sentence to remain unfinished. 'She just looked very different, that's all. I'm sure Lady Woodleigh will have seen the error of her ways and Maude will be back in breeches again.'

'Hmm. And what of Lady Woodleigh? Put in your offer for her yet?' FitzCount grinned at him.

De Rohan leaned forward to put his face in his hands. 'I'm damned if I can make her out, Brian.'

'Well, she's lovely, quiet, biddable, religious and still young,' he pointed out. 'Those were your very stipulations as I recall.'

'Aye, she's all those things. The truth of the matter is…' he hesitated and drew closer to FitzCount '…it would be like bedding a cold fish. I'm not sure if I've the stomach for it, Brian.'

FitzCount shook his head. 'Think of the land and the money, man. It would still be an excellent match.' He inhaled deeply and pursed his lips in contemplation. 'Besides, there'd be no need to bed her often. Women like her don't like it, so you'd be free to take your pleasure elsewhere.'

De Rohan gave him a gloomy look. 'Aye, I know it, but somehow I doubt if she'd allow me much pleasure in anything.'

Unable to argue the point, FitzCount said nothing more and pushed the flask of wine towards de Rohan.

'My lord?'

Both men looked up from their contemplation. Thomas stood uncertainly before them, his thin brown hair damp with sweat.

'You look as if you've actually been running,' pointed out de Rohan. 'Nothing serious to merit such unusual exertion, I hope?'

Thomas shrugged, oblivious to the sarcasm. 'It's Thorston. He bade me run to get you. Says to hurry. Lady Woodleigh is in the stable with Maude and he's worried.' He grimaced before adding, 'Don't know why, though. Lady Woodleigh would hardly be able to do much to Maude, would she?'

A thousand reasons ran through de Rohan's mind as to why Thorston would have cause to be worried. He wasn't a boy given to panic and Douce had clearly been upset by what she had seen that morning. There had been something cold and hard in those eyes when she actually looked him in the eye. He also remembered telling Maude not to spoil things for him, and honour-bound as she was, Maude would not wish to do anything that would endanger his plans. Guilt flooded through him as he stood up.

'Most likely she just wants to give the girl a bath and Maude is trying to get out of it.' He sighed, masking a confusion of irritation and concern. 'She's very resistant to water, as I recall.'

The warm, musky smell of horses assailed her as Maude entered the stables. Freshly bathed and dressed to her relief in breeches and tunic, Maude had wanted to escape the noisy atmosphere of the keep to spend some time to think on her own.

Comforting initially, the familiar aroma did not entirely dissipate Maude's growing sense of unease. She had no desire to return to de Rohan's chamber or set eyes on the man for quite some time. In fact, she had no idea what she wanted to do. It had all seemed so simple before she met William de Rohan.

Sighing, she made her way to a pile of hay close to Lark's stall and threw herself disconsolately down. Confused memories of the morning rushed through her mind: the sights, the sounds, the smell of fresh blood. Mostly she remembered herself in de Rohan's arms and closed her eyes against the hurt of his words. It didn't matter to him, but it mattered very much to her. For the first time in her life, Maude found herself prey to the vagaries of the heart and she didn't like it one bit. William de Rohan was not for her—he would marry a rich heiress, not a penniless girl of ill repute. Why she should be so interested in him was still a mystery too. He was a vain popinjay who lied constantly and was not likely to survive the barbaric life in the north.

Someone would tire of his antics and put an end to him fairly soon. She, most likely, would not be around to see it.

The stable door creaked open.

'Maude de Vaillant? Are you there?'

Maude stood up slowly, uneasy about the sharp tone in the voice. 'Aye, I'm here.'

Douce approached her, one hand gripped around a small, leather pail, the other behind her back. In the background hovered her faithful priest.

'Skulking about dark corners,' muttered Douce, her eyes boring into Maude and her unconventional attire.

'I have no wish to cause offence in any way,' began Maude. 'I thought it best to stay away from the keep for a while,' she added, her eyes flickering nervously towards the priest.

Douce pressed her lips more firmly together in disapproval. 'At least there are some things we can agree on, then. Let's hope there are other areas of agreement.'

Maude tilted her head in question. 'Such as?'

'Such as leaving William de Rohan alone.' Douce took a few steps closer to Maude. 'He may not be my equal, but he brings with him the King's favour. That much I do deserve.' The words were uttered with a bitter hiss. All her lovely features were contorted with dislike and Maude suddenly felt very worried. She was alone with this girl and her priest and was helplessly bound by her word to de Rohan that she would do nothing to spoil his interest in the Woodleigh estate.

Eyeing the shaking pail, Maude cleared her throat. 'This morning...it was not what it seemed. Lord de Rohan was merely offering me comfort. The shock...'

A strange smile lit up Douce's face as Maude's words trailed off. 'Comfort? Shock? Were you a good, honest

woman you would never have been alone with the man.
The truth is that you are an evil woman. I must rid you of
the spirits possessing your soul, Maude de Vaillant. You
will not come between me and my true mission.'

Maude gulped as the situation deteriorated before her
eyes. 'Mission? What do you mean?'

Douce surveyed her with dispassionate eyes. 'My mission is to bring greater piety to the King's court through
William de Rohan. The King is a good man, I know, but
he is surrounded by evil spirits. I shall help him.'

The priest merely nodded his head and began to chant
in Latin.

'But I have no claim on William de Rohan,' Maude denied. 'I mean nothing to him other than as a bodyguard.'

Douce blinked. 'I must rid him of your evil influence,'
she whispered.

For a moment, there was utter silence between them and
then Douce launched the contents of the pail at Maude.

Shocked and drenched, Maude shook herself. 'What is
it?' she spluttered.

'Holy water. My priest approved such a use.'

'Well,' said Maude with more than a touch of asperity,
'now that you have thrown holy water over me, are you
satisfied?' Pushing back strands of her wet hair, she took a
step or two closer to Douce, hoping that she would move
aside and let her pass. The sooner she made her escape, the
better.

'Oh, no,' muttered Douce, her pale face beginning to
flush a little. 'There is more.' She moved her other hand to
halt Maude's progress. It held a willow switch.

Maude stopped and looked at the weapon before turning
her eyes on Douce. As she did so, Douce lifted the switch
to bring it down heavily across Maude's arm. It whipped
through the tunic with stinging ferocity.

Maude's instinct was to grip Douce's wrist to prevent further hurt, but the priest moved forward to stop her. Citing parts of the Bible, he grabbed hold of Maude's hands and yanked them away from his mistress. Douce took hold of one of her hands and between the two of them, they pulled Maude's wrists behind her back. Thus pinioned, Maude was at the mercy of Douce Woodleigh and her priest.

'I shall whip the evil from within you, Maude de Vaillant. I shall whip it until it begs for mercy, but I have none. Evil must be driven away and purged.'

Kicking out, Maude tried desperately to get away. Douce was mad, surely. 'Set me free,' she said through clenched teeth. 'I'm not evil.'

The switch hissed through the air and left a shooting hot pain in its wake over Maude's shoulder. It came down again and again. There was only one person who could help her and his name escaped her lips as the pain took hold.

'William!'

The door opened with a crash as William de Rohan forced his way into the stable. Thorston, FitzCount and Thomas stood behind him with shock written all over their faces. Maude sank to the hay as the priest released his grip on her. Tears rolled silently down her face.

William took one look at her and strode forward. Pulling the switch from Douce's hand, he threw it on the ground. 'Get out of my way,' he roared at Douce and the priest.

Bending down, he gathered Maude into his arms and lifted her against his chest. She cowered against him, holding on tight to the safety and warmth of his body.

'She is evil,' whispered Douce, her beauty and innocence restored. 'She has bewitched you. I was trying to save you.' Douce looked up at him, her eyes huge and pleading.

'Save me?' William hissed. 'You don't even like me. Well, rest assured, Lady Woodleigh, your purity is completely safe. I have no further interest in your father's estate.'

Douce's thin fingers clutched at the cross around her neck. 'But it is my mission. How can I save the court?'

He stopped to stare at her. 'Save the court? From what?'

Douce, realising she had de Rohan's attention, smiled at him. 'Why, from evil, of course. And you are to help me, William. This is God's will.'

William gripped Maude's body tighter. 'No, Lady Woodleigh. I'm afraid I am not your man. You have made me realize how unworthy I am of your hand for so exalted a task.' With admirable grace for a tall man carrying a heavy burden, de Rohan managed a very creditable bow before turning towards the stable door.

'De Rohan? What wickedness has the de Vaillant woman committed now?' Robert Woodleigh appeared before them like a silent spectre. Thin and gaunt, his pallor was grey-tinged and his lips bloodless. For a few seconds, he looked across at his daughter and her priest and then turned his attention back to de Rohan.

'Maude was the victim of your daughter's misplaced sense of justice and religious zeal, my lord.' De Rohan's dark eyes fixed on the face of Woodleigh. 'Unless you wish me to inform the King of such unnatural vices in one so young...' he paused for dramatic effect '...I suggest that you administer a similar punishment to Lady Woodleigh. It might restore her wits.'

Outraged, Robert Woodleigh gasped at his guest. 'I shall do no such thing. Douce is the epitome of virtue. That woman—' he pointed a menacing forefinger at Maude '—is no more than a wicked woman intent on wrongdoing.'

'A whore, Father. She's no more than a camp-follower who brings death and destruction wherever she breathes.' Douce's soft voice broke through the silence and even the normally placid FitzCount looked shocked at the use of such words from a young, gently reared girl.

'She's no more a whore than Lady Woodleigh,' replied William coldly to further gasps of outrage from Douce and her father. 'I'll not have her reputation shattered because of the jealous outpourings of an arrogant girl. We have had enough of your hospitality, Woodleigh. With your permission, I shall order our bags to be packed within the hour.'

Somewhat taken aback by the speed of events, Robert Woodleigh merely blinked and then nodded his head. 'By all means, de Rohan. I could not contemplate your licentious behaviour a minute longer. As soon as your bags are ready, I shall expect you to leave my estate.'

William nodded curtly and then strode through the door to the keep. Despite her pain, Maude could tell from the stiffness of his body that he was very angry.

'I'm sorry,' she whispered when they reached his private chamber. 'I didn't mean to spoil things for you.' The tears that had subsided now welled dangerously in her eyes and Maude could feel her lips wobbling precariously.

William placed her gently on her feet before the fire and took her grubby face in his hand. 'Maude, you foolish girl, it was not your fault. It was mine. I should have known how things were with her.'

Maude sniffed, the tension within her thawing a little. 'You should? How?'

He smiled down at her. 'Ah, Maude. For such an experienced woman, you have very little knowledge.'

'Oh?' bristled Maude. 'And what is that supposed to mean?' Her lips formed a tight line. She was certainly not going to be bound by any code of honour towards William de Rohan.

The smile turned into a cheerful grin. 'By the Face of

Lucca, Maude, I'm glad to see you haven't suffered too much.' Gently he rearranged several errant strands of her hair before putting her from him and surveying her with a critical eye.

Maude frowned. 'It might not look like it from where you're standing, my lord.'

The smile was wiped from his face at that. 'Oh, no! I did not mean that…I was just glad that your spirit was still intact.' He peered at her more closely with genuine concern. 'If you cannot travel today, I will insist we stay another night.'

Maude held up her hand. 'No. I have no wish to stay here. I'd rather go home.'

De Rohan reached out to touch her face. 'Home, Maude? Would that be my keep or—' his arm waved vaguely in a north-westerly direction '—would that be…somewhere over there?'

Flushing hotly at her hastily spoken words, Maude jerked her face away from his touch. 'Home, my lord, is whoever pays me most.'

He laughed. 'I have no idea what I did for entertainment before you arrived, Maude. I'm not at all sure that I can manage without you. Perhaps I should increase your pay? Shall we say two silver marks a week?'

Maude managed a smile. William de Rohan was making things very difficult for her. The sad thing was that she had no idea how she was going to live without him, and she was going to have to do just that. Very soon. 'With all this danger, I think it ought to be three, my lord.' She looked at him steadily. That was what Philippe would have said, most likely.

De Rohan raised his brow. 'Three?' He looked at her speculatively. 'If you can take Geoffrey Gant alive, Maude, I'll give you three hundred marks.' Sighing, he turned away, the tension gone. 'Now, unless you need tending, I suggest you pack your things. I have no wish to remain here longer than absolutely necessary.'

'Yes, my lord.' Maude closed her eyes briefly. How on earth was she going to deal with this?

## Chapter Eleven

'Maude de Vaillant has brought you nothing but trouble since she came. To my mind, we'd do better without her. I'm not the only one, judging by the villagers' mood when we came back.' FitzCount's terse voice cut through the silence of the summer day.

William fixed his friend with a belligerent look. 'She's connected with Gant, I'm certain. He's got her brother, probably, and that's why she showed up when she did. If she'd have wanted to kill me, she'd have done it weeks ago. No, Maude'll bring Gant to me.'

'Ha! More than likely she'll bring your head to him or de Vere. I don't suppose she's wept in your arms and confessed all?' His chestnut destrier stomped uneasily beneath him, unsettled by the tone of FitzCount's voice. FitzCount leaned forward to soothe him, slapping him gently on the neck.

The two men had been surveying the fields and orchards beyond the keep. With the approach of June, the crops were ripening and they could smell the richness of the land. A soft wind from the west tugged at their hair and the sun warmed their skin. De Rohan closed his eyes in contentment.

'No, she hasn't. Not yet,' came his murmured reply. 'But she will.' The ends of his hair floated about his face and he batted them back impatiently.

FitzCount shook his head in despair. 'Well, William, if you must know, the villagers and I seem to be in very exalted company. I received word from one of my sources close to the King this morning. Someone is feeding him with stories of your involvement with evil influences and he's getting nervous. De Vere is right. Bertolini has been alerted.' He hesitated a moment. 'There's a whisper that the failed assassin was you, William.'

William digested this news slowly. 'Does Henry believe it?' His voice was calm, but this was serious news.

'You know the King. He doesn't think straight when it comes to plots. The man trusts no one and my guess is that he'll have you watched, anyway.' He scratched his hair. 'So you see how dangerous Maude de Vaillant is for you? Everyone is suspicious of her. Accidents have happened since she's been here. Henry's religious fervour is almost as great as his greed. He won't like the idea of this girl being here at all. She can only do you harm in his eyes, William.'

FitzCount blinked rapidly before turning to face the fields again. 'If all you want to do is bed her, man, then get it over with and get rid of her. Then we can all have some peace.'

His words brought de Rohan up sharp and he stiffened visibly. 'Bed Maude? Are you witless, Brian? She looks like a peasant most of the time.'

FitzCount looked at him sideways on, not unsympathetically. 'Hmm. Didn't look too much like a peasant in that gown at Woodleigh's, I've heard.' He smiled faintly. 'It's plain enough for the rest of us to see. Can't take your eyes off the girl some days, William.'

'With good reason. I can't know what she's going to do next or what trouble she's going to land in.' He pushed his hair back in exasperation. 'I leave her to go to mass and the next thing I know is she's being attacked by the most pious beauty in the north.' De Rohan gritted his jaw and cast FitzCount a disparaging look. 'Besides, if I get rid of her, who can I play chess with? You present little challenge on that front.'

'Play chess with her, bed her, then send her packing. It's the only way.' FitzCount subsided into silence.

William sighed and stared sightlessly at the land before him. FitzCount didn't know the half of it. He liked the girl. She had a short temper and a sharp tongue that never failed to amuse him. In many ways, he found it intriguing, since most women did no more than bat their lashes at him. At heart, the girl was essentially kind and it was the first time he had felt at ease with another human besides FitzCount for years. Her honesty, too, blazed in her eyes. It did occur to him, though, that he had never seen lust written on Maude de Vaillant's grubby face.

'I think it's about time I took control of the situation, Brian. What say you to a Midsummer Eve fair? If de Vere is going to try anything, that might precipitate the event, do you think?'

FitzCount frowned. 'I don't follow. Why?'

William raised his brows. 'If I were to invite several of the most important Normans in the area, he might consider it an ideal opportunity to disgrace me or attack me.'

'And how would that help, exactly?' FitzCount stared at him as if he were witless.

'We need to draw de Vere in and allow him to think we have no notion of his plans. His arrogance will let him down and he'll make mistakes. Were we to bring Bertolini himself into our plan, that would safeguard our position.'

'Only if Bertolini agrees,' pointed out FitzCount.

William said nothing for a moment, his thoughts taking another turn. 'He will if I mention Gundreda, I think.'

'Gundreda? The man's never shown much interest in women, to my knowledge.' FitzCount's surprise showed in his wide-open eyes. 'Always thought the man… Ah, well. And how did you come by this particular bit of information?' Curiosity drew him closer to de Rohan.

'The King mentioned that Bertolini had asked about her once, but he was negotiating with de Vere for her hand at the time. Gundreda's love of money and power was well known and the King thought it best to reject the offer out of hand. It was also more convenient to have her marry de Vere.'

'So that's how the wind blows? If he's still interested, Bertolini could be useful to us, then.' FitzCount rubbed his chin thoughtfully. 'Clever. Providing it all goes to plan, of course.'

William shrugged his shoulders. 'Once Gundreda sees de Vere is under suspicion, my guess is that she'll be helpful.'

FitzCount shook his head. 'Funny. I always thought that you and she might marry one day.'

A strange smile caught on de Rohan's lips. 'Aye, well, I thought so once too, but her greed was more important to her than affection. You know, I never told you this before, but the King gave her the choice of me or de Vere at the time of her marriage. I was penniless and without property. She chose de Vere.'

FitzCount said nothing, digesting the words and the hurt that went with them. 'You loved her, didn't you?' he said eventually. 'If de Vere is caught, you could always marry her. I'm sure the King would be sympathetic.'

De Rohan shook his head. 'No. It's true that I loved her then, but I was young and learned much from the experi-

ence. We would never have been happy, I think.' He smiled
wryly. 'There are several heiresses I can choose from who
would make charming wives and I mean to stick with my
plan, Brian. I'll not get trapped like that again. Bertolini is
welcome to Gundreda.'

FitzCount nodded. 'I'll leave on the morrow and try to
persuade Bertolini to return with me. There'll be no harm
in discussing it with the King, I take it?'

De Rohan shook his head. 'But tread carefully, Brian.
De Vere has friends everywhere.'

'Aye, well, be that as it may, I'll bid you to take care
whilst I'm gone. Try not to do anything foolish, William.'

There was a wealth of hidden meaning in his words but
de Rohan just laughed. 'Maude will protect me, Brian. I
have faith in her, at least.'

FitzCount glowered at him. 'That's what I'm afraid of.'


Hoel pulled the bowstring back and waited for Maude to
give him the word. Concentration was etched on his face
and the tip of this tongue was visible between his lips.

'Now!'

The arrow sped through the air and landed in the hay
figure with a thud. Hoel beamed up at Maude. 'I hit it!'

'Aye. That was a good, solid shot. You've done well.'
Maude grinned down at her pupil and ruffled his brown
hair.

The bailey was relatively quiet at this time of the day
since most of the soldiers were out on patrol. Few people
would be disturbed by their shots, so they had taken their
chances. De Rohan was out with Thorston and some men
to hunt for further clues as to Gant's whereabouts. His re-
fusal to allow Maude to accompany him made her uneasy.
She was to be in charge of the keep, FitzCount having left
for the King's court earlier that day.

As Hoel prepared for another shot, Maude noticed four peasants arrive in the bailey. Well-covered despite the warmth of the day, the men shuffled forward, rolling several caskets of ale. They stacked them in something resembling rows, but they put little effort or care into the work. None looked familiar, but it was Maude's habit to take note of any newcomer. They appeared a drab and sullen bunch who took little interest in what they were doing.

'Do you think Lord de Rohan will be pleased with me?' Hoel's question drew her attention.

'Aye, I'm sure of it. The more bodyguards who can shoot well, the better, as far as he's concerned.'

A yelp of pain cut through the bailey and one of the peasants fell to the ground, rolled up in agony. Dropping the bow, Maude ran to the man, who was still groaning and cursing. His three friends stood watching, their uncertainty shining in their eyes. Maude knelt down and reached out to see what the damage was.

'Don't touch him,' a rough voice growled in her ear.

Maude stopped and looked up. Hard blue eyes stared down at her. 'I might be able to help,' she explained patiently. 'I have some knowledge of these things.'

'Aye. We're sure you have.'

Maude stilled and then stood up. 'What do you mean?'

The man who had spoken before leaned closer. He smelled of sweat and filth and his ugly, pock-marked face was grimy with years of dirt. 'You gave Edric that evil eye of yours, lady. We saw you.'

The man on the ground had stopped moaning and was merely lying on his back, staring at Maude with accusing eyes. The other two men began to move towards her.

'Don't talk nonsense,' Maude answered calmly. 'Your carelessness caused the accident. It had nothing to do with me.' A cold shiver ran through her. Several of the servants had appeared from nowhere and were watching the group with great interest.

'Touched by the devil, like the priest says,' sneered another. 'Don't look so brave now, though.'

Gritting her teeth, Maude looked at the men with the haughtiest look she could muster. They were all much bigger than her, but she still had the authority, albeit of tenuous nature. A quick glance around her, however, confirmed that there were none of de Rohan's men about. Her recent brush with pain at the hands of Douce Woodleigh had knocked the confidence from her and Maude could only swallow loudly.

'There's no one to protect you, lady. De Rohan is not close by, this time.'

Maude took a step back. 'I need no protection since I have done nothing.' There was an audible quiver in her voice and the mood of the crowd began to change.

Several more people had gathered about them, effectively hemming Maude in. There was no escape.

'Take her to the river,' called out a voice. A murmur of assent grew around her. As hands grabbed out to take her, Maude pushed them away.

'Step back, and none of you will suffer,' she said loudly. 'William de Rohan gives me the protection of his name. If I am harmed, then he will seek out the wrongdoers and exact punishment.'

'She's charmed him. De Rohan is in league with the devil's daughter.'

Not liking the direction the crowd was heading, Maude tried to stop them. 'De Rohan is the King's man.'

'Are you sure?' The authoritative voice stunned everyone into silence. The crowd parted before her to reveal the priest who had accused her before. 'No King's man would protect a woman such as this. She killed Geoffrey Gant's brother, two of her own brothers and cursed Gant's father. Maude de Vaillant caused these problems for her own ends. Geoffrey Gant is innocent of any crime and she has made him suffer for his virtue.'

The bailey was silent as the people just stared at the priest. Maude gaped at him, her mind whirling around his accusation. 'His virtue? Why should I do those things?'

'Greed. He would not have you to wife for your evil ways. This is your revenge.' His thin, sour face turned to her. 'Geoffrey Gant recognised you for what you are, but de Rohan is weak and cannot resist women such as you. He has brought this evil woman into our midst and now we must suffer for his actions. It is time to take matters into our own hands.' His voice lashed through the silence with the force of an iron-tipped arrow. The priest snatched up his rosary and held it aloft with Maude in his sights. 'The Lord leaves it to us to rid ourselves of this evil.'

Stunned at the bewildering speed of events, Maude could only stare hopelessly around her. Suddenly a small stone hit Maude on the head.

'Stop!' Hoel's voice rang out loudly. 'Lord de Rohan will have you all flogged. Leave her be.'

The priest smiled menacingly at the thin boy whose arrow was aimed at his heart. 'You see?' he shouted victoriously. 'She has even charmed the outcast boy.'

'No!' Maude's voice carried above the whispering. 'Leave Hoel out of this. He is innocent.' She could feel a warm trickle of blood down her cheek where the stone had hit her. This was increasingly dangerous. 'I'll go with you if you leave the boy alone.'

Eyes feverish with triumph, the priest levelled his cross at Maude. He brandished it menacingly before her face. 'You see how she threatens even now? Good people of the keep, act now and save yourselves before further calamities occur.'

The tension that had built up over the past few minutes now burst in a flood of babble. Maude was jostled and pushed forward towards the gate. Pinching fingers and sharp tools prodded her on and Maude found herself breathlessly yanked down the high mound of the keep, through the village and down to the riverside.

The noise and excitement of the crowd were almost dreamlike and Maude had difficulty in realising the extreme danger she was in. Finally, as she stood by the banks of the fast-running river, the realisation dawned. A cold, sick feeling washed over her as the hysteria of the crowd grew.

'Throw her in and be rid of her,' came the frequent shout.

It was the priest's raised hands that silenced them. 'It shall be done and properly,' he thundered. 'Tie her hands and feet. The Lord wishes her to die in the same manner as her first victims.'

Maude roused herself to protest. 'I am innocent of all he says. If you kill me now, you will all be guilty of murder and the Lord will send far worse.' Her voice wavered but as she grasped for words that might halt this terrifying process, the priest interrupted her in shocked tones.

'Do you hear the threats from this woman? She dares to deny justice by swaying you with her evil.' The cross was brandished once more before Maude's eyes and the shouts and jeers of the crowd grew.

Quickly, the priest muttered some sort of incantation that Maude had never heard before and in that all-too-brief period of respite, Maude closed her eyes and willed William de Rohan to come riding up to save her.

It was a shock to realise that no such luck was in store and that the bank of the river was perilously close. Without further ado, Maude was dragged to the makeshift raft that served as a ferry and hurled to the feet of the ferryman. The man known as Osric had harsh eyes and a mean mouth. There would be no quarter given by him.

Casting her eyes upwards, Maude took her last look at the keep outlined against the blue summer sky and knew that these were her last moments alive. No one could save her now. With some difficulty, she elbowed herself up and managed to stand. If she was going to die, she would do it with the courage of the de Vaillant family.

'Hold!' A loud voice carried to her ears and Maude glanced gratefully about her. Finally she located its source.

Alfred, the outcast, stood several feet from the priest with his bow and arrow poised. The arrow was pointed directly at the priest's throat and the man looked very much as if he would like nothing better than to lodge it there permanently. His dark, greasy hair floated in the breeze and those honest eyes stared directly into the paling face of the priest. 'Release the maid or I'll kill the priest.' There was a controlled anger in his voice that all recognised. One or two of the villagers shuffled uncomfortably.

'Why would you save her?' demanded one gruff villager, clearly confused by events.

'She's done nothing to my knowledge. I'll not have innocent blood spilt for naught.'

Something of his sanity must have reached the crowd since they began to mutter things between them. The priest remained silent, but Maude could tell from the colour of his face that he was greatly afeared. An angry Alfred was indeed a worthy foe!

Alfred addressed the people again. 'I know something of what goes on here and I believe you are greatly worried by what could happen to you if you do not do as you are told. But I tell you now, good people, Maude de Vaillant is not evil. The same men who frighten you have forced you into this for their own purposes. The only ones who will be accused of murder in the end will be you. William de Rohan is a fair man, but if you kill her, he'll not stop to ask questions.' His eyes glittered in the sun as he fixed a look of utmost disgust on the priest.

'The priest is using you. Take heed. He has no mouths to feed come winter. If de Rohan casts you out, as I was, who will feed your children?'

Osric bent forward with his knife and with one yank, split her bonds. Maude started forward before regaining her balance and rubbing her wrists. The faces in the crowd were no more than a blur, but she could feel the hate and the fear among them. The mood was a precarious one, but Maude recognised that she had this one chance and that she wanted to take it.

With her chin held high, she pushed her way through the people and finally stood by Alfred's side. Slowly, the man lowered his bow. 'Get to Hulda, lass. You'll be staying with us until de Rohan comes for you.'

Maude did not wait for further explanations. The walk to the outcast huts was one of the longest she had ever made. At every moment she fully expected to see the crowd burst around the bend, baying once more for her blood. They never came. Within minutes of her arriving at the camp, Alfred appeared. He nodded at the fire in the clearing where a pale-faced Hoel was waiting anxiously with an assortment of thin children. 'Sit you down, lady. You'll be needing some ale.'

Hoel took her arm and squeezed it. 'I'm glad you're safe. Me and Alys were right worried about you.'

'Alys?' enquired Maude shakily. Her mind did not seem to be able to think quite straight.

'The laundress. She told me to get Alfred.' His pale face was smudged and tear-stained, and Maude could not stop from putting her arms about him and drawing him close for a moment or two.

'Well, I'm very glad you did,' she whispered somewhat tearfully. 'I was frightened.'

'You were?' he said with a frown. 'You didn't look it. I thought you were very brave.'

'I was absolutely petrified, but there was nothing much else to do but pray.' She accepted the cup of ale from Alfred with a grateful smile. 'My thanks. For everything.'

Alfred sat down heavily at her side and reached forward for his own cup, warming by the fire. He sipped a little and savoured the sour taste before swallowing. 'Well, I reckon de Rohan will be much in my debt now. It'll be worthwhile.'

'Oh, quite,' said Maude faintly. 'Let's hope so.'

Alfred's stony face was suddenly alight with laughter. 'Oh, he will, girl. I've no doubt about that.' He sobered a little, taking pity on her. 'Still, it was a frightening ordeal for anyone. I'd have done the same whether or not it would have been to my advantage.'

'You would?' Maude glanced round the fire at the thin, grimy faces. Alfred could easily have been killed by the villagers and where would it have left his family?

'I couldn't have had it on my conscience.' He stared into the fire for a while, collecting his thoughts. 'Besides, that old priest is a troublemaker and I reckon Gant's behind all this. He was sniffing around here the other day whilst you were at Woodleigh's. I thought he was up to no good. The villagers are a cowardly bunch and will do anything he says. I suppose it's not really their fault.'

Despite its bitter flavour, the ale was reviving and Maude closed her eyes to allow the pent-up tension to escape. 'I had no idea the people hated me so much they wanted to kill me, though.' Reaching forward, she warmed her frozen hands against the fire. She was glad of it despite the sun.

'Aye, well, a nervous crowd can be whipped up to blood-lust if it's done right.'

'Nervous?'

Alfred fixed his eyes on Maude. 'In your absence, there were quite a few unexplained accidents. Small enough in their own way, but more than usual. No doubt the priest played a part in telling them you were responsible.'

'I have no idea why he's doing this. I've done nothing.'

Glancing up at her grim face, Alfred sighed. 'It doesn't really matter, lass. The priest has his sights on glory and no doubt Gant has promised him something like that.'

Maude said nothing. If Alfred had seen Gant about, she wondered whether he had any idea about her role in all this. 'He's the evil one, not me.'

'Aye, lass. I saw the two of you together. It's fairly clear to me what the story is behind it all.'

'I see.'

He looked at her for a moment in quiet contemplation and then smiled gently. For all his size and strength, Alfred could be no more than ten years her senior, but he had seen far more of life than she ever would. 'Do you?'

Curiosity got the better of her. 'So how come you've said nothing to de Rohan, then? He would reward you well for such information.'

'Aye, he might.' He drank more ale. 'I reckon he knows, though, and it makes no difference to him. He trusts you.'

Maude's blood went ice-cold. 'How do you know that? I've said nothing.'

Alfred smiled. 'You don't need to, lass. There's no harm in you. Anyone could see that.'

Somewhat deflated by this assessment of her character, Maude sighed. 'He's blackmailing me with my brother's life, but I don't know why.' She rubbed at the pink marks on her wrists left by the rope. 'I want to find out what he's planning to do with de Rohan and save my brother. So far, I've found out nothing.'

Alfred threw the dregs of his cup onto the grass and sat back. 'It's all to do with Piers de Vere. Gant is in his pay.'

Stilled by his words, Maude exhaled loudly. 'The shire reeve? Why?'

Alfred shrugged his shoulders. 'Complicated, I reckon, lass. As far as Gant's concerned, it's for the land, aye? He'll be after proving de Rohan a traitor since it's the only way he'll ever get the land back. De Vere is more important, but he wants rid of de Rohan at any cost and is willing to play Gant's games to do it.'

'That must be it! Why haven't you said anything, then?' Maude asked suspiciously.

'I've no proof.'

'Alfred?'

'Aye, lass?'

'What did you do before you were cast out?'

'My lord was the former shire reeve, my lady. Osbert Strang.'

'Osbert Strang? Wasn't he proclaimed traitor with Hugh Gant?'

'Aye, but it was a lie. He was a good, honest man. Someone made him look like a traitor and my guess is de Vere. He'll stop at nothing to have his own way.'

Maude sipped thoughtfully at her ale. 'What happened to Sir Osbert? Did he go to Normandy?'

Alfred shook his head. 'He was hanged, my lady. I promised him I'd find the traitor for him, though. I was the head villager on his estate. We were all cleared off the land when de Vere took it over. I reckon he expected to get the Gant estate, too, but de Rohan gained the King's favour and took it from him.'

Before she could say anything more, a loud clatter of horses and men interrupted them. Alfred sprang to his feet, bow in hand. Hulda was already gathering her brood of thin offspring into the woods.

'Maude!'

William de Rohan strode into the clearing, his sword gripped tightly. Seeing Maude and Alfred in one piece, the anxiety on his face turned to anger. Sheathing his sword with a dexterity and speed Maude could only have guessed at, de Rohan speared her with a thunderous look.

'And what exactly have you done this time, Lady de Vaillant, to rouse the villagers so much?'

Maude was just about to tell him when de Rohan grabbed her by the upper arms and began to shake her violently. 'When will you learn to do as I tell you, woman? I cannot leave you alone for more than five minutes without some dreadful accident, abduction or tragedy striking.' De Rohan then pushed her away from him, but he was obviously warming to the task. His dark skin was flushed and there was a murderous look in his eyes that did not bode at all well.

'You had clear instructions to remain within the bailey gates, but I find you and the boy sitting comfortably at a campfire at some distance from the keep. What were you thinking of?' His voice had risen and he was close to shouting.

Weary of being singled out for such attention, Maude levelled her gaze at him. 'If you could stop shouting, then I can explain. Until you are quiet,' she added repressively, seeing his mouth open to abuse her further, 'I intend to say absolutely nothing.'

De Rohan shut his mouth obligingly enough, but she

misliked the way he continued to look at her. 'And if you make one more move to touch me, William de Rohan, I assure you there will be no question ever of you begetting an heir.'

His lips pursed together tightly and Maude knew some satisfaction at that. He made no further sound nor move in her direction.

'First of all, I did not leave the bailey or the keep voluntarily. This was entirely at the express request of the priest and your villagers.'

'The priest?' De Rohan frowned. 'He has caused you trouble before.' His eyes rested on her in question.

Maude nodded. 'I am in no doubt they would have killed me save for the intervention by Alfred.'

William turned abruptly to Alfred. 'Then you have my profound thanks.'

Gravely, Alfred bowed.

'Riddell.' At the sudden command, the captain urged his horse forward. 'Take Hoel to the keep and have the cook send down fresh meat and good wine to Alfred.' He turned back to Alfred. 'I wish to have private words with the lady, if I may?'

When Alfred had disappeared into one of the huts, de Rohan whirled round to face her. 'Well, Maude. I believe I have much to say to you, and this time, you're going to listen.'

Swallowing loudly, Maude took a step back. She had never seen de Rohan as angry as this. 'I have no wish to listen to you. You can't make me.'

De Rohan grabbed her arm. 'I can, Maude de Vaillant. Make no mistake. Now, you come with me, willing or not.'

Outraged at the man's arrogant orders, Maude glared at him, her hands on her hips. 'I will not.'

William shook his head as if bemoaning a recalcitrant

child. Without warning, Maude found herself picked up and thrown over his shoulders as if she were no more than a sack of oats.

'Put me down,' she hissed into his back.

'When I'm ready,' came the reply, as de Rohan stalked into the forest.

## Chapter Twelve

'By the Face of Lucca,' hissed Maude furiously. 'If you don't put me down, William de Rohan, I shall carry out my threat. You will definitely be the last de Rohan, I promise.'

Maude found herself dumped unceremoniously on a patch of green bracken. De Rohan had carried her without talking for some ten minutes or so. Certainly long enough to make her very angry. Rubbing the tender parts of her backside, Maude rose with as much dignity as she could.

'Now, woman. You were saying?' He stood before her, his arms folded across his chest with a grim expression on his face.

Tossing her dark braids over her shoulders, Maude faced him squarely and with no sense of fear. William de Rohan would not hurt her, she was absolutely certain of it.

'Why have you brought me here?' she flared at him. 'You could just have easily said what you had to at the keep.'

'No, I could not,' he replied firmly. His calm response irritated her no end. She had never seen him in this strange mood before. Taking a step back, she found herself against a tree.

'So, then? What is it you have to say to me?'

He did not answer immediately, but just stared at her as if he were deliberating something of great importance. They were in a clearing some way into the forest and the green canopy overhead allowed dancing beams of sunlight to filter through in places. Crane-flies fluttered in the silent, dusty air and the smell of the green forest caught gently on the breeze. Not far away was the river. They were very much alone.

'Look,' she said, increasingly nervous, 'I've said I was not to blame for what happened today. If it makes you feel any better, I apologise for any distress caused but I did nothing. In fact, I thought I was the one in distress.' Maude clamped her lips together tightly.

Eventually, de Rohan stirred from his silence. 'I am well aware that you are rarely the instigator of the drama, Maude, but I do assure you that I am heartily sick of having to come to your rescue. It can be most wearing to have to guess what disaster will befall you next, and I am convinced you are more trouble to me than the entire keep put together. You are supposed to be protecting me.' As he said this, William moved forward, bringing himself within a finger's distance from Maude's body.

Pressing herself hard against the tree, Maude realised there was no escaping from him. 'It's not my fault,' she began hastily. 'I do my best to protect you, but—'

Her words were effectively cut off by William de Rohan's mouth coming down hard on hers. His hand came to rest on her neck, tilting her face towards him. For a moment, when her resistance stopped, he opened his eyes and released her lips. There was no smile of victory, just a look which bordered on curiosity, before he closed his eyes and bent to her again.

Sighing softly, Maude surrendered to him. It was a

heady, breathless experience that caused her blood to heat and her heart to pound at a most alarming rate. 'Why are you doing this again, William? There is no one watching,' she murmured against his lips. The only reaction she got from him was a tightening of his grip. She tried again. 'William?'

Finally, William raised his head. Whatever he was thinking was not at all clear and Maude just looked at him. 'Well, don't look at me as if that was all my fault,' she muttered. 'You managed that all on your own.'

A self-conscious grin broke his silence. 'Well, it seemed like a most effective method of keeping you quiet, woman.'

'Quiet!' she squeaked in indignation. 'You could have just said.'

He was still no further that a heartbeat from her and was making no effort to place any distance between them. In fact, de Rohan began to pick bits of leaves and twigs from her braids with a resigned smile. 'Aye, you're right, but I did prove something to myself.'

Maude frowned. 'What did you prove?'

His brown eyes, framed by thick, sooty lashes, were hard to ignore. They held her gaze for several moments. 'That my body ignores what my head is telling it.'

She stiffened. 'Oh, and what is your head telling it to do?' As if she didn't know the answer to that!

He raked his hair back in exasperation. 'To leave you alone and concentrate on what I should be doing.'

'I see,' came her tight-lipped response. 'Well, of course, I must apologise for forcing you into doing something so dreadful.' With flaming cheeks, Maude shoved de Rohan away and stalked off into the undergrowth. It had been a bad day so far and there was no sign of any improvement yet. She had no intention of so perfect a being as de Rohan seeing her cry. Dashing her tears away with a dirty sleeve, Maude tramped through bracken, brambles and nettles.

'Maude!'

'Leave me alone.'

'No. You're bound to get yourself into trouble.' His voice carried implacably across the clearing and Maude turned to face him.

The perfect William de Rohan was as dirty and as dishevelled as she was. He was an immensely satisfying sight. Looking at him, Maude could feel the fight drain from her.

With grim determination, de Rohan came to stand before her. 'I never said anything about kissing you being dreadful.' The colour of his face deepened. 'I just said—'

'I heard what you said, you conceited popinjay.' Maude interrupted him to punctuate her words with her finger jabbing into his chest. 'It doesn't take a lot of intelligence to understand the meaning behind the words, either. It's all right to kiss me and to humiliate me, but anything more than that is pure foolishness on your part.'

'Well...' de Rohan looked taken aback '...no, it's not like that exactly.

Maude raised her brows. 'Oh? And what is it like, exactly?'

De Rohan sighed with what sounded like exasperation and cleared his throat. 'If you must know, I was angry.'

Maude watched him carefully. Even with her limited experience, she could tell that his kiss was not rooted in anger. 'Ah. A sort of punishment?'

De Rohan frowned and kicked diffidently at a loose stone by his foot. 'Aye, something like that.'

'Let me see if I have this right. You want to punish me for getting into trouble and forcing you to rescue me. In addition, you don't think you should be bestowing your favours on someone like me, you should be concentrating on a more deserving heiress. Is that it?'

His silent shrug was most eloquent.

'Well,' she said brightly, 'now that we both know how you feel, I'm sure life will be so much easier.'

'Stop it, Maude.' He reached out and took hold of her arm to prevent her from moving. 'Stop it.'

She could not bear to look at him. All the hurt, the pride and the anger within her spilled out. 'Do you think because I dress as I do and hunt instead of sew that I don't feel the same as other women?'

That drew a soft sigh. 'I know very well how you feel, Maude. That's the problem. If you didn't feel so damned good, I wouldn't be so tempted all the time.'

She tried to shake herself free, but his fingers held her. 'Not that again! If you start accusing me of bewitching you once more, your life will be significantly shorter,' she warned him. 'I would be grateful if you would take your hands off me and leave me be.'

He lifted his head. 'Actually, Maude, I can't quite seem to do that.' Without another word, he pulled her tight against his chest and proceeded to kiss her with a thoroughness that left her completely breathless.

She could feel her resolve melting as his kisses deepened and knew that very shortly neither of them could prevent the inevitable. Wrenching herself from him, Maude pushed de Rohan away. 'Is this what happens in court?' she demanded. 'When a maid asks you to leave her alone, you do this?'

De Rohan had the grace to flush. 'No,' he said harshly. 'There's usually no need.'

His pride was hurt! Well, that was the least of her worries, but it did give her an escape from his caresses. 'Do you not think I've had enough of men touching me against my will for one day?' Her chin lifted in defiance and her eyes levelled with his.

William opened his mouth as if to speak, but clearly thought better of it. 'No doubt. Rest assured, Maude, I shall not touch you again unless invited.'

'You'll be having a long wait then, my lord.' Maude turned away from him and began to brush the dirt from her tunic.

'Can you tell me who attacked you?' de Rohan asked after a moment, his voice thankfully reverting to something like normal.

Maude relaxed a little. She far preferred him in his normal mood. Her story was told quickly and with little emotion or embellishment. 'What will you do?' she asked finally.

'A trial,' came the short reply. 'And you'll be there.'

Early the next morning, de Rohan's soldiers gathered the villagers together in the bailey. It was the first time for weeks that the sun had been hidden behind a bank of rather ominous-looking clouds and this had made quite an impression on the people there.

The villagers had shifted uncomfortably in the cooling breeze. Now relatively well-nourished and decently clothed for the most part, the crowd were understandably nervous about this gathering. All would know now what had taken place the day before, and certainly who was involved. They would all be worried about their future, just as Alfred had predicted.

Maude observed them from a shadowy corner near the stables. She had slept badly, partly as a result of the event itself, and partly because of the effect de Rohan's presence was having on her. Nothing seemed right any more and he made her nervous. This confrontation was not likely to improve the villagers' opinion of him.

William strode from the hall and remained at the top of the keep steps. His face was stern but he looked magnificently autocratic. The crowd grew silent and stilled all movement.

'You are no doubt aware of the reason for this gathering,' he said. The tone of his voice matched his expression. 'Were it not for the fact that I have only recently arrived in this part of the country, the repercussions for this latest attack on a woman employed to protect me would have been far graver.'

De Rohan paused to allow the words to sink in. He spoke in the English tongue with a gravity that was clearly understood. The villagers gazed at him in shocked awe. Only the sound of the cattle lowing in the distance broke the awkward silence. 'I was sent here on the King's business,' he continued. The echoes of his voice carried across the bailey without difficulty. 'And anyone who interferes with the King's business must be punished.'

The tension grew as the people realized what might happen. Loyal Breton guards stood before each of the gates. There would be no escape if de Rohan so chose. Mothers gripped their children more tightly and eyes began to glance around nervously. Maude held her breath.

'I offer the main offenders a chance to escape punishment lightly. If they give themselves up, then they will receive only ten lashes of the whip.' De Rohan's statement caused the crowd to catch their breath collectively. 'If not, you will find out firsthand how the King deals with people who cross him.'

Maude could feel her heart beating fast. De Rohan was right, of course. They had almost killed her and unless he took action to prevent another attempt on her life, it would probably happen again. Resolutely repressing her misgivings, Maude straightened herself. She must not show any fear.

Three men reluctantly came forward and stood at the foot of the keep steps. Osric, the priest and another she vaguely remembered glared up at de Rohan with cold eyes. The four men who had caused the situation were nowhere to be seen.

William de Rohan allowed his gaze to travel over the men below him. 'As a man of God, I would have thought you above such actions.' His cold words were addressed to the pinched face of the priest.

The priest stared at him with undisguised malevolence. 'Think what you like, de Rohan. I followed the words of God.'

His words carried across the bailey in silence. De Rohan merely lifted one of his brows. 'I think not, priest. There was no crime proved.'

'And what would you know about the words of God, William de Rohan? You are but a fornicator of women.'

Maude could see nothing but the priest's stiff back and she was glad. The cold tone of his voice was sending shivers through her whole body.

'What I chose to do with willing women is my own concern and has naught to do with the crime we discuss today.' William's voice was firm as he addressed the accused men.

The priest shook his head in denial but said nothing more. Osric and the other man remained silent and tight-lipped.

'Flog them. Ten lashes each.' De Rohan's voice carried across the bailey so that all could hear the warning.

Within minutes, the three men were bound to a post near the bailey gate. Their backs were bared to the onlookers, their hands tied above their heads. Riddell stood behind them, a leather whip in his hands, awaiting the sign from his master.

The clouds were darkening by the minute and Maude could feel the eerie atmosphere which surrounded the keep. No one said a word as de Rohan gave Riddell a brief nod. The whip cracked down with a swish on to the white, thin back of the priest. A red weal was left in its wake before Riddell brought the whip down again. This time the skin was broken. Half-fascinated, half-disgusted, Maude closed her eyes and wished she was somewhere else.

The crowd watched the punishment of all three men in smouldering silence. Their sympathy lay with the men under the whip and their hatred was reserved entirely for de Rohan and Maude. As the men were dragged away, Maude knew that things were going to get far worse.

'I have decided to hold a Midsummer Eve fair here, Maude. What do you think?'

It was a good place, thought Maude as she surveyed the fields. There had often been such events at her own keep and she had always felt that *frisson* of the unknown when one of the old pagan festivals were celebrated. 'A good idea, my lord. It might appease the villagers.'

They were standing on a small promontory, not far from the keep. The shallow valley stretched out before them, dotted with the strange stones that the old inhabitants of the area had erected centuries before. Whenever she visited such places, Maude trod warily, remembering still the childhood tales Bronwen had often told her. They held a strange fascination for her, even now.

'It worries you, doesn't it? The villagers' attitude, I mean.' He looked across at her, his expression guarded.

Maude shrugged. 'I think anyone would be hurt if people tried to kill them.'

'It isn't you, Maude.' He rubbed the back of his neck and stretched it a little. 'The priest is the troublemaker. I believe he draws on their worries and fears and forces them to think you are the root cause of their problems.'

'And I'm not?' She looked at him quizzically.

He smiled. 'No, Maude. I don't think you are the problem at all.'

There was a stillness in the air that was filled with tension between them. Was this de Rohan's way of telling her he trusted her? 'And how are you so sure about that, my lord?'

'For all your experience, Maude, you are still innocent in many ways.' The dark eyes glinted at her. 'You have had many chances to kill me, hurt me or lie with me and you have taken none of them.'

Flushing, Maude sighed heavily. 'Is that why you took me into the forest, then? To see if I would lie with you or kill you?'

'There was always that possibility,' came the grim reply.

'Well, you're very lucky, then,' she said. 'Killing you would have saved me from a lot of aggravation, I'm sure.'

De Rohan laughed. 'Actually, I think I was rather hoping it might have been the former.'

'Were you? It didn't seem like that at the time,' she said with more than a little asperity.

Saying nothing, they made their way down the slope to stop at a grassy tussock where three large standing stones rose majestically from the ground. De Rohan indicated they should dismount and they left their horses to graze quietly whilst they sat down. Maude breathed deeply of the fresh air and closed her eyes.

'Do you think of your home, Maude?'

'Not exactly, my lord.' She opened her eyes to find him watching her intently. 'I was thinking about these stones.'

He tilted his head to one side. 'Tell me about them, then.'

The dark clouds had rolled steadily throughout the day, but they hung low in the sky and Maude could almost smell the storm coming. 'It's a story Bronwen used to tell me when I was little. They came from the time when the people here worshipped more than one god.'

She pointed at the nearest stone. 'This small one represents a beautiful girl, given by her father to a strong warlord as wife. It is said that the father wanted peace for his people and she was sent to his enemy to settle their feud. She had begged her father not to marry her to this man, but he would not listen. The warrior was overjoyed at the sight of his new wife and promised to protect her people as if they were his own. He was a man of his word.'

'I take it then that all was not well for this couple, then?' William's voice broke through her thoughts.

'No,' she continued softly. 'The girl was in love with a harp-player and when her husband found out, his rage was truly terrifying. He summoned an old crone to place a curse on the couple. They were to die within the passing of a day.'

William sighed. 'A tale of crossed lovers. This one, I take it, is the harp-player?'

Maude looked up at the larger of the two stones and nodded. 'They died in an ambush set by her father's enemies as they ran away. That stone over there is the husband and those others his men. Legend has it that when he saw the body of his wife, he was so overcome with grief for what he had done, that he invoked the wrath of the gods. He and his men were turned to stone so that they could protect the inhabitants of the valley forever.'

'Then justice was done.'

Maude shrugged her shoulders. 'It is said that when music is played in these hills, the souls of the lovers are freed for the night.'

'An enchanting story. Perfect for a Midsummer Eve fair. Do you think we can bring them back to life?' He offered her a wry grin.

'What I think is, my lord, that you pretend to have a soft heart underneath all that finery of yours. I take it there is an ulterior motive for the fair?' She gave him an arch look before turning back to look at the stones before her.

'Ah, sometimes I do forget that you are a very astute woman.' He took a sip from the wine skin before wiping his mouth with his sleeve. Looking at the ground in front of him, he spoke slowly. 'But, yes, there is another heiress who is dying to make my acquaintance, I believe.'

Maude could do nothing to stop her heart from lurching at his words. 'Do I know her?'

'Louise de Moresby. She lives further to the north.'

'Oh, yes,' she replied quietly. 'I do know Louise.'

If de Rohan was expecting to hear more of Louise, he was disappointed. Finally he spoke.

'Well, then? Have you nothing to say about Lady de Moresby?'

A vision of the lovely Louise came to mind. There was nothing she could say against the girl, save that she was the one her brother had wanted since he first laid eyes on her. And where was Philippe? She shook her head. 'Nothing bad, anyway. Louise is beautiful, young and biddable. Exactly what you wanted.'

Surprised by Maude's reticence, William looked at her more carefully. Her colour was definitely paler. 'Not possible,' he said gravely. 'I doubt if the woman exists, then.'

Maude managed a quick smile. 'Oh, well, this one does. She would suit you well, I think.'

Increasingly concerned at his protector's quiet voice and lack of colour, William reached to touch her. 'What is it, Maude? What's the matter?' His grip on her wrist tightened as Maude's lips remained closed. 'Tell me.'

Well, he asked after all. It would do no harm to tell him. 'Very well, although I fail to see what difference it will make. My brother has been making calf-eyes at Louise since we worked for her father last year. We were fighting off the unwanted attentions of an over-eager, disappointed suitor.' She glanced up at his unreadable expression and shook her arm free from his grasp. 'I had thought Louise returned his interest but, as he is not rich, I doubt her father will view things from her perspective.'

'I see.'

'Do you?' Maude raised her brows. 'Perhaps it's just as well,' she continued. 'Philippe would have to face up to the fact sooner or later that he could never marry her. You'd be kind to Louise and she's a sweet girl. No doubt she would forget Philippe quickly. It would be for the best.'

De Rohan was silent for such a long time that Maude wondered whether she had said anything to upset him. His expression gave nothing away. 'You are very close to Philippe, aren't you?'

Maude nodded, her eyes trained on the darkening skyline. 'I'd do anything for him. I just wish...' She smiled at him quickly. 'I wish he would hurry back.'

'Do you tire of protecting me?' De Rohan's eyes smiled across at her lazily.

She sighed heavily. 'My lord. I have said this before, but it is perfectly obvious to me that you have no need of any protection whatsoever.'

'Then why do you stay?' He stared across the fields.

'For the money,' she stated flatly.

'Do you know, Maude, that I do not believe a word of

that excuse any more?' De Rohan rolled on to his stomach and eyed Maude with interest. He was so close that she could smell him, almost feel his warmth. It made her feel nervous again.

'Oh?'

'I think you stay because you cannot bear to leave me. Admit it.'

Unexpected as this statement was, Maude could not help from laughing. 'You are being foolish, my lord. You pay me too well.'

He sat up and grinned. 'I do? Well then, Maude de Vaillant, it's time you earned your keep.'

'What now, my lord?'

'Fishing, Maude. We are going to fish.'

Maude looked across at him sharply. There was no trace of humour in her face. 'In the river?'

'No. There's a small, shallow pond that feeds off it. I have a desire to cool myself there.'

Maude looked up at the sky. 'It's going to rain, my lord. Soon.'

He stood up and held his hand out to her. 'Then we must hurry, Maude. We have work to do.'

The dark water of the pond looked cold and uninviting. Fear gripped her. 'I can go no further, my lord.' She eyed the water with a distinct feeling that her stomach was about to rise up to her throat.

William looked at her carefully, nodded and then sat down at her feet in a thick clump of bracken. Hesitantly, Maude did the same. For a while they talked of this and that and then he stood up again and took her hand.

'Come, Maude. Just a little closer. There's no current in the pond.' His voice was kind and gentle, and Maude was reminded of his tone when he dealt with a fractious horse. His hand tugged at hers.

Gritting her teeth and fighting the fear, she took a hesitant step forward. She wanted to show him she was strong.

'Good. Can you make it down to that rock over there? You'll be more comfortable.'

With no more than a brief nod, Maude took several steps forward. When she stopped some way from the rock, he looked down at her with a frown.

'Oh, well. You've probably seen a naked man before.'

So saying, de Rohan unbuckled his belt and removed his boots. He dropped them where he stood.

'What do you mean?' Maude squeaked in alarm. 'And why are you taking your clothes off?'

'Well, I have no wish to ruin perfectly good clothes. It'll be much easier naked. If you can get to that rock, you'll not see what I'm doing, of course. I don't mind, Maude.' He offered her a leer that almost caused her to run to the rock.

'You are a monster, William de Rohan.'

'I suggest you close your eyes, Maude, or you will see for yourself the true state of affairs.' He laughed then.

Outraged at his lack of propriety, Maude sat down on the rock with her eyes tightly shut. Reflecting that her lord had apparently undergone another significant change of heart regarding his concern over his clothes, Maude allowed herself a smile. A sudden shower of cold water broke through her thoughts. 'By the Face of Lucca, William de Rohan! Do not torment me so.'

'You can open your eyes, Maude. You are perfectly safe.'

Experimentally, Maude opened one eye. The only part of him that was visible was his head and his sun-bronzed shoulders. Knowing that he was naked beneath the water caused Maude a moment's weakness. For a while he splashed about, just like a carefree boy. He did not, of course, remotely resemble a boy. She watched, almost mesmerised, as the water swirled over his heavy shoulders and upper arms. Had she really called him a popinjay?

When he started fishing, though, she realised he was well practised. Silent and still, he waited for ages until suddenly he scooped his hands deep into the water and then out again, bringing a shower of water and a shocked fish. It landed close to the edge.

Maude stared at the fish. She would have to go and get it, but it was right by the water. Glancing at de Rohan, there was no way she could ask him to get it. It would have to be her. Quickly, Maude removed her boots and took the five steps necessary to reach the edge of the water. She picked up the fish and tossed it towards the rock.

'Well done, Maude.' The words were spoken quietly but she knew he was truly pleased with her. It had taken courage.

The fear of the water was still there but this had been the first time she had gone so close voluntarily for a very long time. Maude smiled back at him, wistfully thinking that Louise was a lucky girl and partly regretted ignoring his roundabout suggestion that they lie together. There was much about William de Rohan that she admired, but she was finding it increasingly difficult to ignore her growing affection for him.

'I think,' she said softly, 'I would like a game of chess, my lord.'

He smiled back. 'You almost read my mind, Maude,' came his cryptic reply.

## Chapter Thirteen

**M**aude's head had barely touched the hay when a thick hand covered her mouth. Trying desperately to face her attacker, she found herself pulled up against a stinking hauberk. Air was denied her as the hand slid upwards to squash her nose.

'Thought I'd forgotten you, Maude?' The voice that hissed in her ear was sickeningly familiar. 'If you want your brother to live, you'll obey me, do you hear?'

Maude nodded quickly, fearing her head would shatter if she didn't breathe soon. In an instant, she was thrown back into the hay where a large booted foot came to rest menacingly on her chest.

'What do you want now?' she grated as she glared up at the man.

Gant smiled. 'To tell you how pleased I am with your progress, Maude. It has been most entertaining to hear how de Rohan falls from grace because of you.'

Stifling a rapid retort, Maude forced herself to tighten her lips instead. 'Just tell me what you want and then give me Philippe back.' Her fingers were trembling as she pushed her braid behind her shoulders. 'I take it he still lives?'

'Of a fashion.'

In the gloomy light of the stables, Maude could just about make out the smug smile on his face and she longed to tear it from him. But she had to wait.

'And what is that supposed to mean?'

'It means no more than your co-operation lasts, my dear. He's weak now since the food he's given is not likely to sustain a man of his size.'

Maude knew now for certain that Gant intended to kill them both. If either one lived, he could never rely on their continued silence. They only lived because she was useful to him for the time being. She would have to kill Gant first. 'I repeat. What would you have me do?'

The boot on her chest pressed down harder. 'Time is vital now.' Gant lowered his face closer to her so that Maude could smell his sour sweat. 'The King is apparently disposed to hear my petition concerning these lands very shortly. What I want you to do—' his thick fingers curled around her braid and pulled sharply '—is to bring de Rohan to me. I must be certain that you can bring him when I ask it of you. There will be no harm done to either of you. Let's call it a show of faith.'

Despite the pain in her scalp, Maude blinked back the dampness that welled in her eyes. 'Where?'

'The place you found near Woodleigh's keep will be as good as any. Having seen you in action there, I was most impressed by your powers of persuasion, my dear. You have far more talents in that direction than I had supposed.'

Shifting restlessly under his booted foot, Maude surveyed him with grim hatred. 'And when is this meeting to take place?'

The light was poor in the darkened stable but even so, Maude could see Gant smiling to himself. 'Two days hence. I'm certain you'll be able to entice the poor fool again.'

'You'll not hurt my brother. Give me your word.'

Without warning, Gant removed his foot and roughly jerked Maude to her feet. 'I'll not give my word to a witch, Maude de Vaillant.'

His air of arrogant triumph was more than she could bear. 'A witch, is it? Well, then, Geoffrey Gant, be warned. If any harm comes to Philippe or de Rohan, then I promise you, you will die.'

She was not at all sure that Gant would take any heed of such a threat, but it was all she could think of on the spur of the moment. All the same, the sickly smile on his face disappeared.

'I heed none of your threats, girl. Just bring de Rohan to the hut when the sun sets. I'll take care of the rest.'

'We'll be free, then?' Maude persisted, brushing the hay from her tunic.

'I'll free your brother if you bring de Rohan to the village,' confirmed Gant with a return of confidence. He reached out to cup her face in his hand. It felt hot and clammy. 'Perhaps not straight away, but soon after if all goes to plan. From what I hear, you've managed to bewitch de Rohan. Have I not earned your favour for such an opportunity, Maude?'

His leering face loomed closer and Maude shook herself free. 'You misheard,' she hissed and took a step back.

Laughing, Gant allowed her this defiance. He hooked his fingers into his belt and surveyed her. 'I'll warrant de Rohan finds you quite a challenge. You're certainly not his usual kind.'

'William de Rohan has behaved with complete discretion since I have been at the keep,' Maude retorted sharply.

'Gundreda de Vere was ever his favourite. Still sees her privately, I hear.'

Pursing her lips in disapproval, Maude glared at Gant.

'You have my agreement to bring de Rohan to your place at sunset in two days. I expect to see Philippe soon after.'

'Jealous, Maude? Surely not?'

'I have no need of jealousy. De Rohan is no more than an arrogant peacock who is only interested in his own future. My concern is merely for my brother.'

Bored now, Gant took two steps back. 'A pleasing answer, Maude. You're harder than I thought.'

Watching him retreat, Maude stared at him. 'I wish it were true,' she murmured quietly. 'Or I'd have claimed that three hundred marks by now.'

There was nothing hard about Louise de Moresby. The girl was a vision of softness and curls. If anything, she was even more beautiful than Maude had remembered. A delicately structured face, soft smiling lips and glowing blue eyes were surrounded by a halo of honey-brown curls. For such an heiress, a man would sacrifice much. William de Rohan would not even have to do that. She was exactly what he wanted.

William de Rohan stood inside the bailey looking handsome, relaxed and smiling. His dark hair ruffled a little in the breeze and his face had been barbered with extreme care. Clad in an emerald green tunic, black breeches and a jewel-encrusted belt that glistened as he moved, he would be enough to take any girl's breath away.

Maude stood stiffly at his side, watching their meeting with a thumping heart. This was going to be far more difficult than she could ever have imagined.

Sir Thomas aided his daughter to dismount from her palfrey and guided her to stand before her host. 'Sir William, I have the pleasure of introducing my daughter, Louise.'

Louise curtsied gracefully and with a shyness that was charming. 'My lord,' she murmured softly.

William fell to one knee before the girl and gently took hold of her small gloved hands. As he raised her to her feet, he smiled down at her, his eyes twinkling.

'It is a delight to meet you at last, Lady de Moresby. I hope that you find much pleasure here today.'

Maude could feel her throat contract as she watched them together. They were well matched in looks for certain. She missed the compliments William made about her gown, but she noticed how Louise flushed with pleasure at his attention. She was right. Louise de Moresby was the perfect match for William de Rohan.

'Maude? Is that you?' Sir Thomas approached her with a broad smile. His pleasant face was pink with heat and his thin, grey hair plastered to his skull. Of medium height and sturdy frame, he nevertheless commanded respect.

'Aye, my lord.' She grinned at him. 'I am pleased to see you again.'

Louise jerked her head towards Maude, her lovely face paling. 'Maude de Vaillant?' A tentative smile wobbled on her lips and her eyes swept the rest of the crowd assembled before her. Maude returned her smile, wondering what had made Louise act so.

'Well, it's good to see you again, lass,' bellowed her father pleasantly, slapping Maude loudly on her back. 'You're here to give de Rohan succour, I hear? Good. Good.' His smile was genuine and Maude felt her heart thawing a little. It had been some time since she had felt welcomed by anyone.

'Aye, my lord. Nothing that can't be solved.' She looked up at him. 'Did you have any trouble on the way here?'

'No, lass. It's quiet on the roads.' He looked about, much in the same way his daughter had. 'That brother of yours here, too?' His voice had dropped to almost a murmur.

Maude shook his head. 'He's involved elsewhere.'

Sir Thomas nodded gravely and wiped his shining forehead with his sleeve. 'Perhaps it's just as well, then. I'd
not like to get Louise nervous.'

Before Maude could say anything further, William de
Rohan invited the travel-weary group into the keep for re-
freshments. This was to be just a short visit so that Louise,
her father and de Rohan could see whether marriage would
be a suitable step. Maude need only look at the three of
them to know just how suitable they already considered the
arrangement.

Thomas de Moresby was one of the King's trusted men
who had served him well over the years. He would most
likely be a good ally for de Rohan since his word would
mean much to King Henry.


Dinner was a fairly jovial affair and Maude watched de
Rohan take great care to charm not only Louise but her
father as well. Laughter rang out and de Rohan was clearly
enjoying himself immensely. Once the trenchers had been
cleared away, Sir Thomas took William to one side, but
stood close enough for Maude to hear the conversation.

'Well, de Rohan, I'll be truthful.' Thomas de Moresby
eyed William with frank appraisal, his blue eyes blinking
a little with the smoke. 'You'd not have been the first
choice for my daughter, but I like what I see.'

William merely inclined his head.

'Your lands are minimal but of good quality and your
connections with the King are strong,' he continued. 'My
daughter is still young, though, and I'll not have her married to a man she had no liking for.'

William smiled. 'It's rare to find a man who takes such
care of his daughter, Sir Thomas.'

Sir Thomas merely grunted and looked across at Louise
as she chatted to some of the other women. 'I'll tell you

now, de Rohan, that Louise is heartsore for another, but he's nothing to bring to the marriage.' His eyes flickered briefly to Maude and she knew then that he was meaning Philippe. 'I've given the lad until the end of the summer to amass some money, but the chances are he'll not do it and I'm anxious for Louise to wed.'

So that was why Philippe had spent the last year working so hard: he had offered for Louise and been refused.

The prospect of a lovelorn bride held few problems for William de Rohan. 'I am grateful for your advice, my lord. No doubt with time spent together, Louise and I will find that we deal well together. She is utterly charming and quite beautiful. The King will be the one who is heartsore, my lord.'

De Moresby placed his goblet firmly on the table. 'Let's hope you're right about that, de Rohan. I'll bid you come to stay at our keep next week to see if we can come to some arrangement.'

'My pleasure,' said de Rohan with a satisfied smile which plunged Maude into a sea of depression.

Maude could take the laughter and the enjoyment no longer. Grabbing a cup of wine, she slipped back out into the fresh air. What she needed was some time to think.

Maude made her way to the gate and sat outside the palisade, staring out at the land beyond. It was a warm day with the promise of a hot summer to come. The sounds and smells of the keep and its people caused her to smile. She liked it here, very much. Not even the river held the same dread for her. Maude was now able to look at it without feeling sick, at least. It was odd, she thought, how a place could wrap itself around your heart.

Maude sighed. Admit it, she told herself. It isn't just the land. Her heart had also been stolen by its owner. That brought another smile to her lips. A vain popinjay who took

pleasure in baiting her, who used her and who played chess
with her was the most unlikely man to make her heart beat
faster. But he did, and in the most alarming way. She took
a sip of the wine. De Rohan was not for her. He would
marry Louise de Moresby and that would be an end to her
daydreams. Her fate, she was sure, was linked with Geoffrey Gant.

'Maude?'

Maude looked up to see the nervous face of Louise de
Moresby. 'How did you find me?' she asked carefully,
wondering what on earth she could be wanting with her.
They had not spoken much beyond simple pleasantries the
previous year.

Louise smiled sweetly, the glow of youth and beauty
almost painful to Maude's eyes. 'I did not see you and I
have many things to ask you. Do you mind?' She gestured
to the ground that Maude was sitting on.

Maude shook her head. 'Go ahead, although I would
have thought you'd be missed.'

Shrugging, Louise lay back and closed her eyes to bask
in the sun. 'I told them I wished to speak with you for a
while. It's unlikely that de Rohan or my father would stop
me, do you think?'

There was a faint edge to her voice that caught Maude's
attention. Had she imagined it? 'It's not safe, is all I meant,
Louise.'

'Safe? What do you mean?' Louise struggled up on to
her elbows and looked at Maude. 'Is that why you're here?'

'Aye. Lord de Rohan is a most popular man. He invites
all measure of unwanted attention.'

Louise smiled. 'You like him, don't you?'

'De Rohan?' Maude could feel her cheeks flush faintly.
'Well, yes. In a way.'

Louise sat up and ran her fingers casually over the grass. 'He likes you. He said so.'

'Well, he would. He's paying enough for my services.' Maude could hear the fractious tone in her voice but could seemingly do nothing about it. What on earth was de Rohan about by telling her that he liked Maude?

'Is he paying your brother, too?' It was an innocent-sounding question, but Maude knew that it was carefully planned. There was far more to Louise de Moresby than she had imagined.

'No,' she replied flatly. 'He's away elsewhere.'

Disappointment flooded her face. 'Will he be back soon?' The eagerness in her voice was worrying. No wonder Sir Thomas was keen not to mention Philippe in Louise's presence.

'No. It will take him many months.'

For a while the two of them sat in silence, allowing the peace of the day to drift over them. 'Does he ever mention me?' Louise finally asked.

It was a direct question that required a direct answer, but Maude was not at all sure that this was the best course of action. As she hesitated, Louise continued. 'I love him, you know. I wish to marry him, not de Rohan.'

Maude was momentarily stunned by this bald statement. 'De Rohan is a far better choice for you than my brother, you know,' she said gently. 'He has the King's favour and far more than Philippe could ever give you. Besides,' she added for good measure, 'de Rohan will be kind to you. He would make you a good husband.' How on earth did they come to this?

'I don't want a good husband. I want Philippe.' Her eyes were large with unshed tears. 'You cannot understand how awful these past nine months have been, Maude. I've heard little from Philippe, save that he's working to build up a fortune to impress my father.' Her sigh was heartfelt.

Maude studied Louise's anxious face. The girl had shown far more interest and concern for Philippe than she had ever imagined. This was not going at all well. 'You may feel differently in a year's time, Louise. You have nothing to fear from de Rohan and you might find, that given time, he would become dear to you as well.'

'I do not want to marry him. I wish to marry Philippe.' Behind the gentle voice was a determination that she had clearly overlooked.

Gritting her teeth, Maude decided to do what she could for de Rohan and for Philippe. 'Don't wait for Philippe, Louise. I don't believe he is coming back.'

Colour drained from her face and Louise stared at Maude. 'He would never do such a thing—at least, not without telling me.' Her voice was shocked and Maude felt guilt flooding through her. It was for the best, though. For everyone.

'Aye,' she mumbled, unable to look Louise in the eye. 'He said he wanted to see more of life and to…er…live a little more freely. There was nothing here to keep him so he decided to leave.'

For a moment, Louise seemed to crumple a little. 'Will you tell me where he went?'

Taking a shaky breath, Maude patted Louise's hand. 'I don't know. He didn't tell me. Now, come.' She rose and held out her hand to help up the younger girl. 'We should get back to the hall.'

Louise managed a tight smile, but it did not reach her eyes. 'Aye. I'm sure you're right.'

As Maude allowed her to walk ahead of her through the gate, she wondered truly if she had done the right thing.

Deep down, she felt guilty. Maybe if she prayed long enough, the feeling would disappear.

'Well, Alfred? Will you do it?'

Alfred stared sightlessly at the campfire as he savoured his sour ale. The sun was low in the sky as his outcast family prepared themselves for the evening meal. As far as she could see, that consisted of a large pot of thick pottage. Its strong smell drifted in the evening air, causing Maude's stomach to rumble. It had been a long day and she had eaten little. 'Why don't you tell de Rohan?' he said eventually.

Maude had pondered that one for ages. 'There's something odd about Gant's request. If de Rohan hears about it, he'll rush headfirst into whatever trap Gant has laid.'

'And so will we,' pointed out Alfred drily. 'I'll tell you now, girl, I'm not keen on the idea of getting myself killed just to save de Rohan's skin.'

'No. I don't mean you to do that. We'll just scout around to see what we can find out. Gant looked nervous and said his time was running out, though. The King is to look at his claims on de Rohan's lands again.' She sipped at her ale. 'My guess is that he has to show de Rohan is some sort of traitor. That won't work if he finds us instead.'

Scratching his beard, Alfred looked at her sceptically. 'I don't know, Maude. It's dangerous. I've much to lose.' He glanced across at Hulda and the children. 'Gant is dangerous.'

'Aye. I know that to my cost already.' Maude shifted on the log beneath her. 'I just know that he'll kill Philippe, whatever happens to de Rohan. I couldn't bear to lose him, too. He's all I have left.'

The enormity of the pressures on her were beginning to take their toll. All she knew was that the people she loved seemed to die around her and that maybe there was more to the rumours than she had thought. Forcing herself to rouse from her depressing train of thought, Maude sighed. 'What should I do, Alfred? I can't seem to think things through any more.'

A heavy hand on her shoulder gave Maude a squeeze. 'Well, I've a few scores to even of my own, lass. Osbert Strang was a right good man who should never have died. I'll come with you.'

William de Rohan had spent most of the evening and the next morning staring distractedly into space. Even the loyal Riddell had lifted an enquiring brow at Maude in the vain hope of discovering the cause of this strange mood. The cause, she had no doubt, was Louise de Moresby. Occasionally, William would ask her questions about the girl and then subside into restless silence. When the appointed time came, Maude was glad to escape the keep in the guise of hunting with Alfred. At least she could breathe more easily.

The ride took some time and the late afternoon sun was already beginning to fade when they came into sight of Woodleigh's boundaries. Not wishing to advertise their presence, Alfred and Maude dismounted and made their way as silently as they could to the abandoned Saxon village.

The scent of the forest was sharp in Maude's throat as she settled down to survey the huts from the cover of the undergrowth. There was little to see. Were it not for the clear imprints of fresh hooves in the mud around the huts, she could have easily thought she had imagined the whole thing. Hours earlier than the agreed time, they hoped that they would discover something worthwhile before making their way back to de Rohan's keep.

Suddenly, Alfred grabbed at Maude's sleeve. 'I think I can hear something,' he whispered urgently. 'Listen.'

Beyond the rustle of the trees, Maude could make out the sound of voices and horses. She shrank even closer to the ground as the sounds grew louder. 'Woodleigh? What's he doing here?'

The thin figure of Robert Woodleigh emerged from the forest astride a magnificent horse with a gleaming chestnut coat. With him rode two younger men who looked like guards. They drew to a halt outside the largest hut and dismounted. There they stood for some time, clearly waiting for someone.

Maude had grown stiff with the lack of movement and tried to wriggle a little. 'Hush,' hissed Alfred. 'There's someone in the undergrowth over there. Don't draw attention to yourself or we'll be finished.'

'He's here to meet Gant, I suppose,' she whispered, in answer to her own earlier question. 'I knew he was hiding something when he found us here.' She blushed a little as she remembered what Robert Woodleigh had found them doing.

Before Alfred could answer, three arrows sped through the air, thudding into the chests of the waiting men. All of them fell where they stood.

Shocked and silent, Maude could only stare, open-mouthed. Woodleigh and his men had been killed before their very eyes. Alfred's hand stayed her when she would have left her cover and gone to check for herself. 'Stay. They haven't gone yet.'

Sure enough, several men stormed into the clearing, arrows pointing in the direction of the fallen victims. It was purposeless since all three were dead. Geoffrey Gant appeared and went up to Woodleigh's inert body and kicked it for good measure. 'It's safe,' he called. 'Come see.'

He was joined by Piers de Vere. Maude could hardly
believe her eyes. What on earth was the shire reeve doing
at the murder of one of his most important landowners? 'Is
this the trap, do you think?'

Alfred rubbed his eyes. 'Aye. No doubt about it. De Rohan will be accused of his murder. That could be the only
plan they would have.' He crawled a little closer to hear
what the two men were discussing. Finally, he crawled
back. 'He says Philippe is in de Vere's keep and he plans
to kill him as soon as he picks up de Rohan for murder.'

'They are so sure I'll bring him, then?' Maude asked.

Alfred shook his head. 'It won't matter that much. I'm
sure they can fabricate some evidence if necessary. It'll be
easier for them if they find us here, though. We'd best leave
now and warn de Rohan.'

Quickly they slithered backwards, towards their horses.
As they attempted to mount, however, a cold voice stopped
them in their tracks. 'I reckon Lord de Vere'll be most
pleased to find the witch in his grasp.'

They looked up to see a group of three men, outlaws by
their appearance. Maude thought them oddly familiar.
'Who are you?' she hissed. 'What do you want with us?'

The leader stepped forward, baring a mouth with several
teeth missing. His dark hair was matted and dirty, and his
tunic stained. The smell of sweat was powerful, even from
a distance. 'We caught you, lady. You killed Lord Woodleigh and Lord de Vere is going to know of it.' There was
something so familiar about his pock-marked face that
Maude puzzled over it.

'You're the man in the bailey!' she exclaimed. 'You're
the one who caused the villagers to go against me.'

The smug, satisfied smile answered her. 'Aye. I hate
witches, lady. The fewer the better, I say. This time you
won't escape.' He stepped closer.

'Stay!' Alfred's cold voice halted his progress. The dull gleam of his knife caught all eyes. 'Keep away from her. We did nothing and you know it. But let me tell you something.' His eyes narrowed as he surveyed the men contemptuously. 'If she is a witch, you don't think the lady is going to let you escape, do you? She could curse you and your families for eternity.'

There was a shocked silence as the men digested this piece of information. Alfred and Maude made their move then. Two of the men were dispatched quickly by knife. The third ran like a startled rabbit into the undergrowth to get reinforcements.

'Let's go. Quickly.'

'Alfred. De Vere will come for de Rohan, won't he? He'll take him, anyway.'

'Aye, but at least we have a head start.'

Maude shook her head urgently. 'They'll want me first, if they can. Go to Edwin of Silverdale, Alfred. Tell him what's happened and that we need help desperately. He'll come. Head for the coast. It'll take but an hour's ride from here at most.'

Alfred's eyes rested on her. 'Aye. Take care of Hulda and the kids for me. I told Hoel to get them in the keep for the night. Just in case.'

Maude nodded. 'I'll protect them. Now go!'

Lark plunged through the trees and the bracken with little heed for her own safety. Behind them, Maude could hear the posse following. They were closing down on her. Kicking harder, Maude urged Lark to go faster. Her heart was racing as they emerged finally into the open and Lark could run free.

If de Vere and Gant had been following her before, they had suddenly become invisible. Lark almost flew across the countryside, but there was no sign of the men behind. It was a great relief when de Rohan's keep came into view.

William was waiting for her just before the ferry. Riddell and his men were ranged about the river's edge. 'By the Face of Lucca, Maude. Where the hell have you been?' His handsome face was grim with anger as his eyes roved over her.

'There's no time to explain,' she panted. 'Get everyone inside the keep. De Vere is on his way to take you.'

William dismounted and almost pulled Maude from her horse. 'And why is that, Maude?'

Maude stared up at him. 'Because he thinks you killed Robert Woodleigh.'

De Rohan's face was a finger's length from hers. 'And why does he think that? Have you finally betrayed me then, Maude? After all, that's what your act was all about, wasn't it?'

Maude's face drained of colour. 'No. I...'

De Rohan pushed her away and turned to Riddell. 'Take her to the dungeon, Riddell. That'll keep her quiet.'

Maude closed her eyes and prayed that Alfred had managed to get to Edwin in time.

## Chapter Fourteen

De Rohan's dungeon had not undergone any improvement since the last time she had viewed it. The place stank and was cold. Maude sat on the hard bench, her head in her hands. Why wouldn't he listen to her?

After a short while contemplating her bleak future, Maude heard footsteps approaching. William held a flaming torch high over his head to light the way. His expression was grim. 'Well?' he demanded. 'What excuse do you have this time, Maude?'

Instead of standing up with her hands on her hips and telling him exactly what she thought of him, all Maude could do was stare at him. To her horror, her eyes filled with tears and she could no more prevent them from falling than she could breathe. 'I'm sorry,' she whispered after a moment. 'I'm sorry.'

Almost as shocked as she was, William peered at her more closely, clearly convinced he had the wrong prisoner. 'Why are you crying? Is this another ruse?'

Maude shook her head. 'Go away, William. There's nothing more I can say since you're not likely to believe anything, anyway.'

Vexed by this unexpected reply, William's frown deepened. Eventually he fixed the torch to the wall and sat down next to her. He sighed deeply. 'Very well, Maude. Tell me, then. Tell me everything.'

'What's the point?' came the thick reply.

'Aye, well, if I sound harsh it's because I was worried about you and angry.'

'Angry?' Maude turned to look at him. 'Again? What about?' She wiped away her tears with the sleeve of her tunic.

'You never trusted me with the truth, did you? I thought...well, I thought we had come to an understanding of sorts.' He turned his head away from her and stared around the dungeon. 'I knew you were lying when you first arrived, but there was something about you that was honest. I had hoped that you would come to trust me, Maude, but you never did.'

'Oh, William. It was never like that, really.' She sniffed and placed her hand on William's arm. 'The problem is that I rarely trust anyone now. I have been too badly maligned and used in the past to allow myself to appear vulnerable to anyone. I did want to, but the truth is that I hardly know how to trust. Philippe was really the only one I could talk to and his life was in danger.'

De Rohan slumped forward on the bench. 'Tell me,' he said with resignation.

Maude told him everything. 'I know you must think me very wicked, but I do love my brother,' she said finally. 'I couldn't betray him or leave him. I had to try to help him.' Rubbing her aching forehead, Maude stood up and walked to the far wall. She felt bleak and miserable. 'Now I think he'll die, anyway.'

Shaking his head, William stood up too. 'I don't think so. Not yet, anyway. De Vere will try to use him as much as he can.'

'He'll be here soon and that's all my fault. What will you do?'

De Rohan shrugged his shoulders. 'Riddell is organizing the men and the villagers into some semblance of order. We can but hope that Alfred managed to reach your Edwin of Silverdale in time. I think we'll need him.'

'Will you let me help?' She looked at him questioningly. 'I am good at this, you know.'

He smiled briefly. 'Aye, Maude, I'm sure you are. Just don't get yourself into trouble. I believe I'm going to have much on my mind tonight.'

Maude returned the smile. 'I promise, my lord.'

De Rohan merely raised a disbelieving brow and shook his head. 'Come then, Maude. We have a battle to fight.'

'William de Rohan. I seek entrance to your keep.' The voice of Piers de Vere rang out from the base of the village. All the normal late-evening sounds had stilled. The people stood listening intently as they stared down at de Vere's small army. 'I have come to arrest you for the murder of Robert Woodleigh.'

Maude shivered as she felt the first drops of heavy rain. De Rohan stood on the guard's platform overlooking the gate. There was nothing of the King's courtier in him now. The lines of his face were hard and guarded and she saw the sword he carried in his belt without the slightest concern for the line of his cloak. Maude doubted it was for decoration. 'I am innocent of any such crime, de Vere. This is pure fabrication for your own purposes.'

De Vere laughed. 'My purposes? I admit it was not you who committed the deed, de Rohan. It was that witch of yours. You sent her to kill him for you. Do you deny that she is in your pay?'

'No. I do not deny it. Maude de Vaillant is my bodyguard

and no more. She did not kill Woodleigh. It was you and Gant.'

There was a menacing smile on de Vere's face as he looked up at de Rohan. 'There are several witnesses who say that she did, de Rohan. You cannot blame it on anyone else for the King is already grievously worried about your motives.' The rain came down more heavily and Maude could see the rivulets of water pouring down his face.

'Men in your pay, not witnesses, de Vere. The King knows of your treason and wants you for himself. This time you won't escape.'

Maude could tell from the way de Vere sat on his horse that he was unconcerned by de Rohan's threats. He merely turned around and gestured to one of his men. Two people, a man and a woman, were pushed forward to stumble at de Vere's feet. Their hands were tied behind their backs. When they stood up, Maude gave a gasp. 'Philippe and Gundreda!'

There was no change in de Rohan's expression save a hardening of his jaw. Silently he motioned to Maude to come to his side. 'That's your brother, then?'

Maude simply nodded. 'Why has he brought them? Why his wife?'

De Rohan gave her a withering look. 'To bargain with. Gundreda has never mattered to de Vere, she was simply a link with the King. He uses her now because he knows I used to love her.'

'Used to?' Maude's voice was almost a whisper.

'Aye,' came the harsh reply. 'But I don't wish to see her hurt. She does not deserve that.'

'De Rohan! If you and that witch of yours do not come down, then I shall be forced to set my men on your keep. They are ordered to take no prisoners. I have no doubt that de Vaillant and my wife will get badly wounded in the fray.'

There was an audible gasp from the crowd of villagers. One or two of the women began to cry. 'He is despicable,' whispered Maude angrily. 'What man would kill innocent people?'

'De Vere has no scruples. He is protecting himself. I believe he would not hesitate to do exactly what he says he will.' De Rohan's voice was quiet but grim. He turned to look at Maude. 'I shall have to go to him, Maude. I would not have these people endangered.'

Their eyes caught and she smiled at him tentatively. 'Then as your bodyguard I shall go with you.'

'No. You stay here safe.' The softness in his eyes was gone.

'It's what you pay me for,' she argued. 'Besides, he'll kill you and my brother. You need help.'

They stared at each other for several more moments. 'You would die with me, then?' His dark eyes looked deep into Maude's and she knew she was lost.

'Aye. I would, but I have no intention of either of us dying.'

That brought a smile to his face. 'Have you not?'

She shook her head. 'I can assure you, my lord, that I have every intention of keeping you alive. You still have not paid me for my services and I am determined to collect.'

'Ah, I see. And if I told you that I did not possess such a sum?' He raised his brows in question.

'Then I shall have to be paid in kind, my lord.' Maude lifted her chin and challenged him with her eyes. She was pleased to note that the normally self-possessed William de Rohan appeared somewhat shaken by her words. What did it matter what she said now? They would be dead very shortly, anyway.

'In kind?'

Maude reached out and drew his head down to hers. 'Aye, my lord.' She kissed him deeply before gently drawing back.

De Rohan stood there, speechless for at least two heartbeats. 'Maude de Vaillant, you are naught but a brazen witch. If we survive this, I shall show you exactly what men of the court do with such challenges.'

Maude sighed and smiled at him. 'Come, William. We have a battle to fight.'

With a thundering heart, Maude accompanied William to stand before Piers de Vere. The mud was thick around their ankles and the rain made it hard to walk with dignity. Thorston and the archers had been placed strategically so that, if necessary, they could do as much damage to de Vere's army as possible. De Vere seemed unconcerned, his smile widening as they came near.

Philippe's appearance was shocking. He was hardly recognisable as the brother she had last seen six weeks earlier. His face was a swollen mess and it was clear that he had not seen clean water for the duration of his kidnapping. It was obvious that all his strength was taken by the effort of remaining upright and Maude could feel the tears welling in her eyes again.

'Philippe,' she said quietly. 'I'm here now.'

At the sound of her voice, Philippe's dark head moved in Maude's direction. 'Maude?' His voice was cracked and thick with lack of use. Although he turned in her direction, Maude could tell that he could hardly see her, so swollen were his eyes.

Gundreda stared wax-like at William. 'He's a monster, William. I know he'll kill me this time. I beg you to save me. Please?' The pitiful wail in her voice caused Maude to look up at de Vere. His expression had not changed. He was enjoying inflicting pain and suffering on them all.

'You plead more prettily than I could have hoped, my dear,' drawled de Vere. 'I wonder how tempted de Rohan is? Shall we see?' He turned to smile pleasantly at de Rohan. 'The hour grows late, de Rohan, and I am not disposed to initiate a fight. The thought is most fatiguing. Were you and the witch to come to my keep, I would free my wife and de Vaillant here. What do you say?'

De Rohan scanned the rows of men lined up behind de Vere, their faces blank and enduring. The rain lashed around them, soaking their clothes and freezing their bones. 'And you would free both prisoners?' he asked. 'Do it now as an act of faith.' He had laid down the challenge.

The two men stared at each other for some time before de Vere nodded. 'As you wish, de Rohan.'

As his knife sliced through the bonds around his wrists, Philippe suddenly launched himself at Gundreda, throwing her some way along the mud. 'Now, Maude. Now!' he shouted.

Maude needed no further encouragement. She drew her sword at the same time as de Rohan and prepared to defend them to the death. The crowds of soldiers that would have converged on them were just as suddenly held back by the combined efforts of Thorston's archers and the sound, not far away, of shouting behind their lines.

'Edwin!' she breathed. 'He's come!'

There was no more time to dwell on her luck as Maude found herself engaged in swordfights with two determined soldiers. De Rohan himself was fighting expertly with de Vere. His skills were breathtaking, but he had found his match in the shire reeve. The mud sucked at their feet, making their movements ever harder and clumsier. Slipping all the time, Maude managed to pull Philippe and Gundreda to their feet. She handed him her knife.

'Free the woman and get her to the keep,' she hissed.

'No. Give me your sword. You take her,' he argued faintly. He swayed on his feet, the effort of the past few minutes too much.

Riddell's men had entered the lines and were hacking their way to de Rohan. Edwin's men were making fast progress from behind. 'Never mind,' she muttered, unable to argue with him. 'Stay here with me. Use the knife if you have to.'

Philippe grinned. 'Whatever you say, Maude. Just hurry up. I'm starving.' With what she assumed was a grotesque wink, Philippe positioned himself before the wailing Gundreda, knife to the fore.

When Maude looked up to see de Rohan, de Vere had gone. There was no trace of a body and de Rohan was looking around wildly amongst the mêlée. Riddell and his men had reached them and the danger of being taken now had abated. De Rohan turned to Maude.

'Get back to the keep, Maude. Riddell and Edwin of Silverdale can deal with what's left. I have to find de Vere.'

Their eyes held for a moment before Maude nodded. 'God keep you, William. Remember you still owe me payment.'

'Rest assured, Maude. The thought remains at the forefront of my mind.' He smiled at her briefly and reached forward to push back an errant lock of her hair.

It was a difficult walk back to the keep. The mud was deep and treacherous and Philippe was weakening with every step. Eventually they came within feet of the gate to the palisade.

'Maude de Vaillant? You brought this danger upon the keep. I'll not allow entrance to you.' The reedy voice of the priest echoed about them. He stood, thin and gaunt at the gate, his eyes deep and burning. In his hand was a heavy sword.

'Let me in, priest. There are two innocent people who need rest and treatment. You cannot forbid them entrance.' Maude glared at him in disbelief. Several of the villagers stared at the pair of them, uncertain as to what to do.

Maude could see a small knot of de Vere's men break from the main body of men and head in their direction. 'If you don't let us in, we'll be killed.'

'That's the Lord's will, child of the Devil.' The gate slammed shut and they were barred from safety.

Maude turned to face the oncoming men. One of them was de Vere. 'Well, girl. It seems that you are to die, after all.'

Gundreda pushed away from Philippe and ran to grab her husband. 'No, Piers. Don't kill us. I'll do anything you ask.' Her lovely face was contorted with pain and fear, her pretty hair thick with mud and dirt. The once-beautiful gown and cloak were torn and dirtied beyond recognition.

De Vere simply sneered at her. 'You are nothing more than a pawn in my game, Gundreda. I no longer have need of you and it is not possible to let you live. You know too much.' Kicking her back with his foot, de Vere drew his sword.

With a cry, Maude launched herself at him. He was too strong and experienced for her, though, and within a very short space of time, Maude knew she could hold out no longer. When she suddenly slipped and fell heavily in the mud, she waited for the death blow. It never came.

Piers de Vere fell over her and all but drowned her in the mud. He didn't move. Stunned and dizzy, Maude could feel him being lifted from her and being pulled to her feet. She stood, dazed, and looked down at the body by her feet.

Piers de Vere lay with a sword stuck in his back. He was very dead. It all looked most familiar.

'Maude, are you all right?' She was almost shaken to death by de Rohan.

'If you stopped shaking me, I might be able to answer you,' she muttered.

William stopped and pulled her close to him. 'By the Face of Lucca, Maude. I thought he'd kill you for sure.'

'Did you kill him, then?' she asked, her eyes skittering over the body.

He smiled then, pleased with the look of complete astonishment on her face. 'Aye. It's a trick that comes in handy at times.'

'Well,' she said querulously, 'you could have practised it a bit more frequently.'

'No need,' he replied airily. 'That's what you were paid to do.'

'Paid?' Edwin of Silverdale stood before them, his handsome face turned questioningly to Maude. 'I was under the impression given by my wife that you were in Cheshire, Maude. Clearly I was misinformed.'

Handsome still with thick fair hair and shining blue eyes, Edwin could nevertheless constitute a formidable obstacle when necessary. The serious expression on his face did not bode well.

'Edwin, I'm pleased to see you,' said Maude quickly. 'You must have ridden hard. Is Alfred with you?'

'Aye,' he said gravely with a humorous twitch of his lips. 'A good man.' He looked at William, his eyes assessing him with a practised eye. 'You'll be William de Rohan, then? I've heard much of you from my wife.'

The two men exchanged grins before William nodded. 'Aye, well, my reputation is something I must endure, I suppose.'

Maude sighed heavily. 'Especially as it is very far removed from reality.'

Both men just stared at her, before William turned to Edwin. 'I am sorry to prevail upon you once more, but I would be grateful if you could take care of Maude's brother and Gundreda. Riddell will see to the keep and the prisoners. I,' he added darkly, 'have something to discuss with Maude. Privately.'

Edwin stared at him for a moment or two before nodding. 'I see. My men and I will stay the night and I'll take Maude back in the morning.'

Without further words, William stooped to pick up Maude and carried her in to the keep.

'What are you doing, William? Put me down,' she hissed.

'Be quiet, Maude.'

Maude lapsed into confused silence as de Rohan passed the rows of anxious villagers and made his way through the hall to his room. Once there, he dumped her on his bed.

After the noise and horror of the battlefield, the silence of the room echoed in Maude's ears. It was eerie and yet safe. A good fire burned in the grate and a tub of hot water steamed in the corner.

William thrust a cup of warmed wine into her hands. 'Now, drink that and then we'll discuss terms.'

Somewhat taken aback by his decisive actions, Maude obeyed. The wine burned its way down her throat and warmed her stomach. Gradually, the cold and wet ceased to be so overwhelming.

Standing up, Maude walked to the fire where William was waiting. 'What terms?'

He looked at her, his face dirty and rain swept. The firelight added a warm glow to his skin that was very attractive and Maude could feel her heart beat a little faster. 'You said you wished to be paid in kind for your services, Maude. That is what I plan to do tonight.'

'Tonight,' she said faintly. 'But…but…Edwin and my brother are here. Philippe's very ill and I'm very dirty,' she added, a large lump forming in the pit of her stomach. He could not mean this.

'Edwin will see to your brother. I have no other plans for the night, Maude, and I'm anxious to pay you in full.' There was a determined look to his face that caused Maude to gulp.

'And…er…what had you in mind, exactly?'

'Exactly?' He smiled slowly, pulling off his belt. 'I really have no idea. I thought, though, we might start with a bath. I have no intention of bedding you covered in dirt and blood.'

'Oh.' Well, this was what she had demanded of him in a rash moment, but she could not honestly say that she wanted to turn him down. Quite the opposite, in fact. As she stared at him, Maude could only think that, in a few weeks' time, she would be back in her keep and he would be married to Louise de Moresby. What harm would there be in spending one night in his arms?

'Edwin will take care of the keep and your brother. I plan to forget it all for the night, Maude.' He struggled out of his hauberk and stood before her. 'Will you accept the terms, Maude?'

'Have you no money at all?' she asked in a whisper. A faint smile covered her lips.

He shook his head. 'None, I'm afraid.'

'I see. So, my lord, I shall just have to be content with whatever it is you have to offer?' Maude reached to release her hair from her braids.

'Correct, my lady,' came the grave reply. He began to tug at the laces about her throat.

'Well, then. I suppose under the circumstances, I have little choice.' She smiled at him.

The hot water was wonderful and Maude could feel the tension and the apprehension slipping away with the dirt. William had disappeared so that she could relax on her own and she was grateful for his consideration.

The door opened. 'Still there, Maude?'

She flushed, feeling more than a little awkward. He must be very used to this, but she was not. The water slopped over the edges as she sat forward suddenly in an attempt to cover herself a little. 'I'm sorry,' she said. 'I must have been daydreaming.'

He held a wooden platter full of food and a flask of wine. Smiling he placed it carefully before the fire. 'It matters not, Maude. We have all night.'

'No,' Maude said hurriedly. 'I'll get out. You'll want to use the water, too.'

William shook his head. 'I managed to commandeer some water elsewhere.' Indeed his hair was wet, but she hadn't noticed, so great was her nervousness. 'We need to eat and drink first. I'll get you a drying cloth.'

William stood before her with a large cloth that would have wrapped around her several times over. It was soft and sweet-smelling. He draped it carefully over her and gave her a quick smile. Sitting down on the stool before the fire, she looked at William.

'You don't have to do this, you know.' Her voice was quiet and expressionless.

'I don't?' He poured the wine without looking at her, apparently unperturbed by her words. 'I thought we had an agreement?' Passing her a cup, he took a sip and savoured the soft red wine.

Maude cleared her throat. This was very difficult. 'I

know, but it wasn't meant to be like that. I was just teasing you, really.'

William said nothing. 'I always honour my debts, Maude. Are you saying you wish for the money, after all?'

The warmth of the fire and the wine seemed to light a flame deep within her. His handsome face was close to her now and all she had to do was reach out for him. 'No. It's just that…well…' She took a deep breath. 'It's just that I'm not the sort of woman you would willingly lie with.' The words tumbled out in fast succession. 'I know you like beautiful, sweet women who will look lovely and do as you request. I'm none of those things,' she added, staring miserably at the floor. 'It was just a silly thing to say. I don't wish to force you into anything. I have my pride, William.'

The silence between them lengthened until eventually Maude risked a peep at his face. His expression was serious as he stared at her. Finally he placed his cup on the floor and reached for hers. He then pulled her to her feet. 'Actually, Maude, this is what I have been wanting to do to you for the past six weeks. I would have tried, anyway, had you not mentioned payment in kind.' He pulled her hard against him. 'I have no defences, Maude, for you can feel for yourself how much I desire you.'

That was true enough, she realised. Maude's mouth felt dry as she looked into his eyes. 'So, you want to lie with me, then?'

'By the Face of Lucca, Maude. Shut up.' He bent to kiss her. Gentle at first, his mouth captured hers in a long, lingering kiss that set her heart pounding. Gradually his kisses deepened as his tongue sought entrance to her mouth. Responding, Maude sighed and pressed herself against him, her arms wrapped around his neck.

As his lips trailed down her throat, William laced his

fingers through the strands of her hair. 'I like your hair unbound,' he murmured. 'It pleases me greatly.'

'What?' she said uncomprehending. 'But it's an awful black colour.'

He silenced her with another kiss. 'I have wanted to run my fingers through your hair since I first pulled out those twigs and leaves.' His lips continued rendering her incapable of thought.

Whether he meant it or not, Maude was touched that he wished to say such sweet words to her. 'Then I shall have to confess, my lord, that it was your chess playing that won my heart.'

His lips drew back. 'What?' he enquired with mock distress. 'Nothing else? Not my fine green cloak, my handsome face, my favours from the King?'

'Just your chess playing, my lord.'

'Hmm. Then I shall be forced to display my other hitherto-undiscovered talents,' he murmured, kissing the tip of her nose. 'Kiss me again, Maude.'

The humour between them was very quickly dissipated by the passion that suddenly erupted then. He held her so close that she thought she would never breathe again. It didn't matter. Kissing William de Rohan was like tasting honey, but far more exciting.

Maude found that he was right about her discovering more of his talents. His hands began to rove slowly but purposefully over her body, causing her heated skin to shiver with the sin of it. She had no more thoughts of stopping him, for she could no more do that than she could walk away.

In the heat that rose between them, clothes and coverings were becoming rapidly uncomfortable. It was the work of seconds for William to unwrap her drying cloth. 'I have been longing to do this all evening,' he whispered into the soft, white skin of her breasts. His lips brushed over the sensitive flesh again and again until Maude could bear it no longer. Clutching at his head, she pulled him close so that his mouth could fasten over the hard buds of her nipples.

Gasping with pleasure, Maude was aware of a deep throbbing that had begun in the pit of her stomach. The pleasure-pain she had felt before returned to snatch her breath away. An ache of longing consumed her and she found it hard to stand. Sensing her difficulty, William wrenched himself back from her body. Without taking his eyes from her, he undid his own laces and removed his shirt. Maude could do no more than sigh softly. He was so beautiful.

When she would have stepped forward to touch him, he stopped her with a shake of his head. 'I wish you to look at me, Maude, as I wish to look at you.' The rest of his clothes were removed quickly, leaving Maude staring open-mouthed at the sight of William de Rohan's naked body. Beautiful was not enough to describe him. Long-limbed and well made, the white skin of his legs contrasted strongly with the dark skin of his upper body. It was so hard to resist touching him.

William just stood, looking at her, drinking in the sight of her naked body. 'Your skin is like milk. Let me drink of you, Maude.'

This time, his kiss was very gentle as his hands began to stroke her body. Maude did the same to William. Beneath her fingers, she could feel the hard muscle and the heated skin. She closed her eyes and gave herself up to her senses.

Passion took them both as William suddenly lifted Maude into his arms. Her mouth opened under his and they locked in an embrace that set them both on fire. He lowered her on to the bed and looked down at her with heated eyes. 'Do you see what you do to me, Maude?' Gently, he took her hand and guided it to feel the hardness of him. She had done this to William de Rohan? Slowly, she trailed her fingers up his body, over his chest to linger on the rough stubble on his chin.

'Tell me, then,' she whispered, echoing his words earlier that night.

His fingers caressed her and touched her, leaving her shivering with heat and desire. Lower and lower they went until she could finally stand no more. She pulled his forehead to hers. 'Let me die in your arms tonight, William.'

He closed his eyes. 'Aye, but yours will be a long and lingering death, my lady, to atone for all the trouble you have caused me.'

Lowering himself on to her so that she could feel his weight, he then took her face in his hands and kissed her with a tenderness that almost made her cry. He took her quickly then.

Maude watched his face intently as he thrust deep inside her. It was like nothing else she could possibly have imagined. William was lost in the passion as he took her with him into his world of almost unbearable pleasure. Quite without warning, Maude could feel her breathing speeding up and a strange magical pulsing beginning deep within. As she gripped his shoulders, William pulled her hips upwards a little and slammed hard into her. He penetrated her to her very core again and again. She could smell the sweat on him, taste the salt of his skin. A deep moan escaped from her throat as he pushed into her soul and wrenched the response his body was seeking. Wave after wave of convulsions shook her and Maude knew then that she must be dying. Her cries mingled with his as William drove to his own pleasure and they lost themselves together.

'That, my lady, was only part-payment.'

Maude fell asleep with a drowsy smile on her lips. She doubted she would live long enough to collect full payment.

# Chapter Fifteen

William shifted slightly to pull the blanket over Maude's nakedness. He regretted it since Maude's body was one that was most arousing, but he had no wish for her to get cold. He smiled to himself, remembering their shared passion. It had been so unexpectedly satisfying, so all-consuming that even now his body was craving further demonstrations. The darkness of the night had given way to the soft grey of early morning. Outside he could hear the call of the birds and the sounds of the village waking to another day.

Gently, he pushed away a lock of hair that had drifted over her face. Maude opened her eyes.

'Those northern lordlings of yours are fools.' He smiled at her before lowering his lips for a soft kiss. Fighting against the impulse to rouse her, he pulled back. He saw the disappointment in her lovely dark eyes and steeled himself to ignore it. Affection could play no part in his life. What did he think he was doing anyway? Practically betrothed to an heiress that men would die for, his long-cherished dreams were on the point of realisation. Why, then, was he lying in bed with a penniless woman who lived in breeches? Why, then, was he feeling so at peace when it was a situation that could ruin his plans?

Maude touched his face tenderly. 'I think perhaps it is best that way, William. But I feel honour-bound to tell you that your reputation does not do you justice.'

Amazingly, William could feel a flush of embarrassment flood his cheeks. Why did she make him feel like some nervous youth? He yielded to the temptation and began to stroke the opal-sheened skin above the blanket. It was soft and tempting. Her drowsiness was being replaced with a greater awareness now and William could feel her skin shiver as he stroked it. Trying to distract his own baser thoughts, William concentrated on words.

'Do you know, Maude, that there is a side to you which is lacking in respect?' He sighed dramatically.

'Respect, my lord?' Maude struggled up on to one elbow. 'Perhaps you had best teach me, then?'

He groaned inwardly. He was losing the battle rapidly, particularly as the blanket that covered her had slipped. 'Respect would perhaps be too much to hope for,' he murmured. 'Maybe a simple act of submission?' Despite the coolness of the room, her skin felt like a living flame as she pressed herself upon him. 'By the Face of Lucca, Maude, you feel so good.'

Her tongue traced a line along his stubbly jaw. 'Your language leaves much to be desired, my lord. I think it best if you keep quiet before you teach me any bad habits.'

Conversation between them died as the passion took hold of them. This time their union was faster with little place for the intricacies of lovemaking that he usually employed at court. William's reaction to Maude de Vaillant was so strong and so unexpected that he gave himself up completely to her. This time, he was involved with his body and his mind. He was no longer playing the courtier's role—this was the true man.

In the silence that follows great pleasure, William could

feel his heart almost bursting with the pain and the exhilaration of it all. With Maude, there was no need for pretence since she expected nothing of him save himself. 'Tell me why you wished to lie with me, Maude.'

There was a silence as she considered her words. He had found that he liked that about her. What Maude said was usually worth waiting for. 'I could not help myself,' she said eventually. 'I know that for you this was just another interlude, and I expect nothing more from you than the pleasure you have already given me.' Her words were hurried, as if she were trying to get them over with.

Instead of denying this, William allowed her to say what she had to. After all, there was more than an element of truth to it.

'I am aware that you will marry Louise de Moresby and there is no place in your life for me. That's as it should be. It's just that...' Maude took a deep breath. 'It's just that I wanted to know what it would be like to spend some time in your arms. That's the truth of the matter.' Her honesty blazed from her eyes and William almost yielded to kissing her violently and denying the truth of her assessment. But he could not do that for he would hurt her badly. He would indeed marry Louise and become a rich landowner, but he would not use Maude.

'And was it worth it?' he asked, pulling her face towards him.

She giggled. It was such a feminine sound that it completely took him by surprise. A gentle hand stroked his face, lingering over the rough patches where the stubble was. 'Do you search for compliments, my lord?' Her fingers moved to his hair and pushed it back from his face. 'The truth is that I think I need more time to assess the situation.'

'More?' he responded weakly, finding his body rousing

to those words. 'You have a most demanding nature, Maude. Has anyone mentioned that?'

His mock admonition made her laugh and she rolled into him. 'By the Face of Lucca, my lord, do you never stop with your complaints?' She sighed dreamily as his mouth nuzzled at her neck and his hands moved to her breasts.

Maude pushed him back a little. 'I wish only to enjoy the moment, William, nothing more.'

The serious tone of her voice made him flinch a little. He had grown to care for this strange girl—perhaps even more than that—but those were feelings he could not afford to indulge in. 'I would not cause you pain, Maude. Lying with you again may have grave consequences for you that would hurt you further.' He sat up.

'Go home with your brother and Edwin, Maude. And know that you have given me pleasure far beyond anything else I have known.' He reached out to smooth back some wayward locks of her hair. It hurt, he realised, to leave her to a future without him. It could be no other way.

He kissed her for the last time, intending to pull away. His body and Maude's had other ideas. The fire in his blood caught alight once again and William found himself pushing her almost violently down into the bed. Had Maude resisted, he would have stopped, but she did not. The woman gave one of those breathy sighs that roused him so much and drew him to her. 'I can't help it, Maude,' he groaned into her ear. 'This once more. Just this once.'

Her answer was to smile gravely into his eyes and slowly open to him. Even as he thrust into her, William acknowledged that he was no better than the villagers, no better than the meanest peasant. He was as much a prisoner of his desires as they were. That was the last coherent thought he had before he yielded to oblivion.

\* \* \*

'My lord!' His squire's dull voice penetrated the door and their consciousness. It was clear that Thomas knew exactly what had happened since he remained doggedly on the outside. 'My lord, I must speak with you.'

William sighed heavily and extricated himself from Maude's arms. 'A moment, Thomas.' He looked down at Maude. 'I think it best if I go. There is much to be done.'

His dark hair was sticking out in all directions and he looked like a young boy. Maude reached out to push it into some semblance of order. 'Aye. I think you are right.' She could not bear to think of leaving but she had to. 'Philippe will need tending. If he is well enough, we shall leave later on.'

He nodded and smiled. 'Do not go without seeing me, Maude. I would take my leave of you privately.'

It was several moments before Maude was able to answer him. The lump in her throat seemed to have grown. 'Aye. I promise.'

With one lingering look at her, William climbed out of the bed and began to pull on his discarded clothes. 'What is it, Thomas?'

'The priest, my lord. He begs to see you over a private matter.'

Dragging his tunic over his shirt, William sighed wearily. He splashed a little cold water over his face, skimmed it with a drying cloth and ran his fingers through his hair. Maude stared at him in astonishment. This was not how he usually prepared himself in the mornings. Without looking back, he strode to the door.

'Very well, Thomas. I have much to say to the priest, too. Private or public, it makes no difference. Where is he?'

He barred Thomas's view of the room and Maude most effectively and shut the door firmly behind him.

Maude stretched out in bed. She felt wonderful. Nothing

could take away from her what she had shared with William de Rohan. She could now die a happy woman.

Philippe was looking remarkably cheerful for a man who had been so close to death. Badly bruised and thin, he grinned at her from his pallet in the hall.

'So, you've finally come to see to my needs.'

Maude frowned at him. 'Sick men are supposed to be quiet and acquiescent, Philippe. I take it you slept well, then?' She moved to sit at his side. Her eyes surveyed him thoroughly, lingering over the bad cuts and swellings that covered his face and hands. No doubt there would be far worse she had not yet seen.

He reached forward to pull her close to him and kissed her. 'I thought I would never see you again, Maude. He would have killed me.'

'Aye,' she whispered. 'I know it. I did my best to help you.'

He pulled back to look at her. 'From what I've heard, you've been lucky to have survived as long as this. What exactly has been going on, Maude? The truth.'

His eyes looked at her directly and she could deny him nothing. There had always been the truth between them.

'This I have to hear.' Edwin of Silverdale sauntered behind her and placed a fatherly kiss on the top of her head. 'As I recall, you were going to explain why you weren't in the de Courcy keep with my daughter.' He came to stand before them, his back to the fire. The light smile was deceptive, Maude knew from experience. Edwin might appear simple and easygoing, but he was not a man you could fool easily.

Maude blushed a little. This was not going to be easy for she had no wish to bring his anger down on Elfie. Leaving out several minor details, she told them what had happened over the past six weeks. When she had finished, the two men stared at her silently.

'So, de Rohan is betrothed to an heiress, then?' Edwin asked.

'Well, nearly,' she replied carefully. 'He plans to announce his marriage plans on Midsummer Eve. There's to be a fair and all the nobles in the county have been invited.' It hurt to talk about it, but Maude knew that if she couldn't do it now, she never would.

Philippe bore a puzzled expression on his face. 'You didn't mention the name of this beautiful heiress. Surely it isn't Douce Woodleigh, after all?'

Maude cleared her throat. He would have to know some time. 'No. It's Louise de Moresby.'

She hadn't thought it possible for Philippe to go any paler, but he did. 'I see.' His voice was distant and wintery. 'And does she agree?'

'He will make her a good husband, I think.' What else could she say? She reached out to squeeze his arm gently. 'I know how you feel about Louise, but—'

'No,' he interrupted, 'you don't. I had a lot of time to think about my life whilst I was with Gant. I promised myself that if I survived this, I would marry her come what may. Kidnap her if necessary.' There was a challenge in the stiff line of his jaw that Maude recognised from old.

'No, you'd do what was best for Louise. And in this case it happens to be William de Rohan.'

Philippe subsided into gloomy silence.

Edwin placed a large hand on her shoulder. 'You look tired yourself, Maude. Time at home will be the best cure for you both. Things often have a way of improving with some love and care.'

Maude nodded. 'Are you well enough, Philippe?'

Philippe sank back. 'Aye.'

At that moment, the doors to the hall were pulled open. Brian FitzCount and a smaller man of slighter proportions accompanied him.

FitzCount nodded at them all curtly, his face and clothes covered in mud. The rain was still falling heavily and showed no signs of abating. 'Glad to hear that de Rohan came to no harm in my absence,' he said to Maude.

Maude stood up and faced him. 'I didn't realise you harboured such doubts about me, my lord.'

FitzCount merely raised his brows. 'Caution is always wise in such times, wouldn't you say?'

His companion nodded, turning flint-like, cold eyes on the group before him. 'Most wise, FitzCount, and certainly if the northern lands are as wild as I hear.'

Judging by the look on his face, Maude surmised that the man viewed them all as being highly suspicious characters. She bristled a little under his close scrutiny. 'The north is no worse than any other part of the country, I've heard.'

Hastily, FitzCount placed an arm about the shoulders of the man. 'Let me introduce you to Theobald Bertolini. He is in charge of the King's safety. There have been certain suspicions about this area for some time.'

The man sketched out a bow, but there was little warmth in his smile. He had an ascetic appearance—thin to the point of wiriness, with fine grey-brown hair and a thin, hard line of a mouth. The cold eyes assessed them before sweeping over the rest of the hall.

'Where is de Rohan? I would discuss the events of last night with him.' His voice was as stiff and austere as the man.

Maude shrugged. 'He wanted to discuss something with the priest. They'll be somewhere close by.'

FitzCount's eyes rested on Maude's tousled hair and

flushed skin, before turning his attention to the other two men. Quickly, she introduced her brother and Edwin, and was pleased at the reaction in the two newcomers.

'Can you confirm that Piers de Vere and Geoffrey Gant were responsible for the attack on Robert Woodleigh?' FitzCount approached the pallet and towered over Philippe.

'Aye. Lady de Vere has much to say on the matter of her husband, too. She went in search of de Rohan earlier.'

Bertolini stilled. 'And they are dead? Both of them?'

Philippe shook his head. 'De Vere for certain. Gant slipped away at the beginning of the battle. I've made enquiries this morning, but no one saw his body.' He sat up and dry washed his face. 'My sister and I have a personal matter to settle with Gant.'

Maude could feel her skin turn icy. If Gant was still at liberty, then there was all manner of things he could do to de Rohan. Where was he?

Just at that moment, Gundreda de Vere entered the hall. The change in Bertolini was immediately apparent. The harsh lines were suddenly softer. 'Gundreda! Lady de Vere! It is a real pleasure to see you again.'

Despite several nasty bruises on her face and rips in her gown, Gundreda was almost as pretty as ever. The rather haunted look she wore merely added to her mystery. 'My lord Bertolini. I had not thought to ever see you again.'

Her voice had an edge of hysteria to it and Maude suspected that Gundreda would soon burst into tears. She did.

Bertolini hurried to her and drew her to a seat before the fire. 'Sit here, Gundreda. Can you tell us what happened?'

Maude glanced up to notice that the only man taken in by Gundreda's act was Bertolini. The others were watching her with distinctly cynical expressions.

Gundreda's sobs had now subsided a little and she was wiping her tearstained face with her sleeve. Red-eyed and

red-nosed, Gundreda sniffed loudly and stared up beseech-
ingly at Bertolini. There was something desperate about her
expression. 'My husband said he would kill me if I did not
do as he said, and I was very afraid of him.' There was
indeed a glimmer of shame behind the confident veneer
which caused Maude a moment's pity. Gundreda stood up
and folded her arms about her whilst she stared into the
fire.

'I know you men will scorn me for my weakness, but I
was not able to fight him.' She half-smiled to herself at
some memory. 'He even had me beaten on our wedding
night, just so that I knew what would happen if I did not
obey him in the smallest matter.'

'And what did happen between your husband and de
Rohan?' FitzCount's voice broke through the silence.

'He and Gant were supposed to take either the girl or de
Rohan and accuse them of the murder of Robert Woodleigh. They were to be killed and their bodies brought back
here as evidence. Once here, Piers was going to insist on
a complete search of the keep. Several silver marks had
been left in different chambers. The villagers have long
since been suspicious of him, thanks to the girl, and the
priest can provide a whole list of his treacheries.'

'But why didn't you say anything?' Maude demanded
starkly. 'You had plenty of chances and William would
have listened to you.'

Gundreda looked at Maude, the hurt shining from her
eyes. 'You have no idea how dreadful it could be to live
with a man who is evil to the core, do you? Aye, I've heard
all about you and your reputation, but at least you had some
freedom. Do you see this?' She pointed to the bruises on
her face. 'He had his squire do this. A boy of no more than
sixteen years. Piers loved to humiliate me. He frightened

me so much. You cannot conceive of the depths he would go to hurt me and I did not want to die.'

She drew in a deep breath. 'Piers knew that William loved me and took great pleasure in forcing me to do things that would hurt him.' She jerked her head back to stare up at Bertolini. 'What will become of me now?' The tears fell again like raindrops down her bruised cheeks.

Bertolini's claw-like hand came to rest on her shoulder. 'I am most grateful for your co-operation and your courage, Gundreda. No doubt the King will wish to see to your needs for the future. Don't concern yourself.'

She smiled up at him gratefully, understanding the situation perfectly. 'You are too kind, my lord,' she sniffed.

'But Gant?' interrupted Maude. 'If he still lives, then he will try to kill de Rohan. I know him. He is mad. We must find him and quickly.'

Bertolini was more absorbed by Gundreda de Vere than anything she had to say. The others stared at her sceptically. 'Long gone by now,' pronounced FitzCount.

'But...'

Edwin smiled at her. 'Go search for him and warn him then, Maude. Perhaps FitzCount can send out a patrol later to see if there are any signs of Gant.'

FitzCount nodded gravely. 'Later. Riddell and the men seem in need of rest.'

'Very well,' muttered Maude anxiously. 'I'll go myself.'

It was a relief in many ways to quit the hall, but the rain was unpleasant and she did not relish trudging about in such weather after William. For once she would have liked him to see her clean and fresh, not mud-spattered and filthy. A wild, almost hysterical barking at the gate of the keep drew her attention.

Hoel was struggling to contain the dog he seemed to

have adopted. Almost clawing his way under the gate, Merlin clearly was desperate to get to something on the other side.

'Gant!' The dog hated Gant and would bark whenever he was nearby. He had to be here. Maude ran to the gate and grabbed the arm of the guard. 'Where's Lord de Rohan?'

He must have sensed the urgency in her voice, for the smile he wore disappeared immediately. He pointed out towards the river. 'Over there. With the priest.'

Maude jumped up. She could see three figures on this side of the river. One was being supported by the other two. She was sure it was de Rohan. 'Hoel, get Riddell and FitzCount to send help. Lord de Rohan is being attacked.' Without waiting for an answer, Maude hauled the gate open. The guard and Hoel stared at her.

The dog pelted down the path towards the river. It had to be Gant. One or two of the villagers had stopped, open-mouthed, to watch what was going on. Maude arrived breathlessly to see a very unconscious de Rohan being punted on the ferry by the priest and Gant. The dog yelped and barked furiously at his enemy.

'Leave him be!' she screamed across the distance between them.

At the sound of her voice, all eyes save William's turned to her.

'I wondered how long it would be before you came to the rescue, my little witch.' Gant's hate-filled voice cut through the rain. He stood, proud and haughty, with his feet planted wide apart on the wooden planks of the raft. The priest guarded the lifeless body of de Rohan with a malicious smile.

'Nothing can help you now. De Vere is dead and his

wife has told them all of your part in the plot. Killing de Rohan is pointless.'

Maude moved closer to the river's edge as the ferry headed towards the middle where the current was strongest. Gant simply laughed. 'He had my lands, but I'll not let him keep them. After all, we both know the trouble I've gone to to hold on to them. They meant nothing to this popinjay. The lands here were everything to me. I had earned the right to keep them.'

Maude watched them float further away, her terror of the water overtaken by her fear for de Rohan. None of the crowd made any move to stop them.

'I'll kill you if you touch him, Gant.' Her eyes fixed on him. Her hate grew by the second.

'Ha! We both know you could never cross this river, Maude. The accident saw to that, didn't it? I'm safe from you.'

'Accident! That was no accident! You deliberately killed your brother just so that you could have the land for yourself.'

Gant smiled softly, almost to himself. 'It was necessary.' The priest must have said something, judging by the frown on his face. 'God spoke to me. He told me to do it. The land was always meant to be mine. My brother didn't love it as I did.'

'He did, but you killed him as you killed both my brothers.' Maude stepped closer, unable to quite put her foot in the cold, fast-moving water. 'I vowed to kill you for that.'

'Your brothers' deaths were unfortunate, Maude, but effective. It all worked out well in the end. I got the land and the glory and you took the blame.'

His words had carried to the villagers standing by the river's edge and Maude could hear the muttering behind her. They were the least of her worries. Her attention was

held now by the movements of the priest. They were right
at the most dangerous point of the river and Father Michael
had stood up. Clearly upset by this unexpected revelation,
he was remonstrating wildly with Gant.

'You lied to me,' he shouted. 'You lied. The Lord will
show no mercy to killers and liars.'

The raft swayed and rocked precariously as the two men
began to fight. Suddenly, the priest launched himself at
Gant. They landed on the edge of the ferry, causing a heavy
swell of water to sweep over the whole raft. Within seconds
the ferry had tipped over and shed its human cargo.

'William!' Maude searched wildly for any sight of him.
Suddenly she caught a glimpse of his bright tunic. Without
thinking, she waded into the water and swam. Her clothes
were heavy and the dark water was muddy and freezing. If
she didn't get to him soon, he would be dead.

It seemed like hours before she reached the spot where
Maude thought he must be. Not far away, she caught a flash
of blue. Straining every muscle in her body, Maude almost
threw herself those last few feet and grabbed for him. He
was snatched further away by the tide. 'William,' she
screamed. 'Swim! William!'

Almost crying with fear, Maude pushed on again and
again until, suddenly, there he was. William was making a
weak effort at swimming to her. Blood was flowing from
a cut on his forehead, but he was still alive. Sending up a
prayer of thanks, Maude grabbed for him and this time she
held on to him. 'I have you, William. Hold on to me.'

The water was cold and deadly and carrying them
quickly to the bend in the river. With the extra burden of
William and her waterlogged clothes, Maude knew she
would never be able to swim to the banks.

'The rope, Maude. Get the rope!'

A familiar green, slime-covered rope rose not far ahead.

She glanced awkwardly to the bank. Hoel had raised the rope. They were safe. She had only to float to the rope and hold on.

Maude dragged William, spluttering and coughing, to the rope. Placing both his hands firmly under hers, she wrapped herself around him and waited for help.

Without warning, a thick hand grabbed at her hair from behind and she screamed in terror.

'We can die together, Maude. All three of us can die together.' Gant's rasping voice echoed in her ears. He tightened his grip.

'No. You won't have him,' she stuttered. As she spoke, Maude could see FitzCount and Riddell running towards them. They would be there to save William in seconds. Freeing one hand, she reached for the knife in her belt. It slipped from its sheath. Gant was going to pull them all under unless she let go. Then it would just be her and Gant. As it should be.

'Hold on, William. FitzCount is coming. God keep you, for I love you.' Her words were spoken softly in his ear before she let go of him. Turning suddenly, she came face to face with Gant. His blue eyes blazed with delirium as he threw himself at her. His hands gripped her neck and Maude could feel them sink deeper and deeper into the black water.

With every bit of strength she possessed, Maude struck at Gant with her knife, but it seemed to do no good at all. He was too strong and his grip on her neck tightened. Finally, Maude knew it was all too late. Blackness engulfed her.

## Chapter Sixteen

William sat at his table, staring morosely at the cheerful, chattering courtiers assembled before him. By rights, he should have been overjoyed that at last his ambitions were being realised. The King had sent a group of his favourites to share his table, so pleased had he been with William's success in confounding de Vere. Further, more useful, rewards would be forthcoming later. Under normal circumstances, William would have sat back to revel in the restoration of the King's favour.

Bertolini had accompanied Gundreda to the King, professing de Rohan's courage and cunning in foiling de Vere. This volte-face was the result of obtaining de Rohan's promise not to ask for Gundreda's hand in marriage. On the contrary, William had done all he could to encourage Gundreda to view Bertolini as a most favourable marriage prospect. It seemed she had.

Gorgeously attired in bright silks, the courtiers had turned his humble hall into a rich banquet full of overripe beauty and gaudy colour. In fact, they all looked rather ridiculous and he actually preferred the simplicity of his hall. How Maude would have laughed to hear that confession.

Maude. His memory was still very hazy about what had happened that day. Was it only two days ago? It seemed longer, mused William. He remembered being hit over the head by the priest and had vague memories of being thrown on to the ferry. Of the fight and landing in the water, he remembered nothing at all. The only words that stuck in his mind were the softly spoken words Maude had uttered as she let go of him. 'God keep you, for I love you.' They had found no trace of her since then.

William could deny it no longer. He loved Maude, too. He had been fascinated by her almost from that first moment when she had glared at him through her black eye with most of the bailey floor smeared over her. The rest seemed to have followed quickly.

A group of highly desirable young ladies were vying with each other to catch his eye and for once William could not respond. He could no longer summon up his courtier's act at will. None of this was important any more. He had learned that much with Maude.

With a weary sigh, he pushed back his seat and rose to stand by the fire. He was not cold, but there was a nagging, empty feeling that would not leave him alone. He leaned against the wall and stared into the flames.

By the Face of Lucca, he missed the wench. Until Maude had disappeared, he had not realised just how much he had grown to love her. He would give a king's ransom if he could tell her what he felt for her.

They had searched for hours for Maude until FitzCount had bodily dragged him back to the keep. The whole of yesterday they had continued the search but there had been no sign of her. It was most unlikely they would ever find her body now. He gritted his teeth as the pain of her death washed over him. She had died, terrified of the water as she was, trying to save him from Gant's madness. The only comfort was knowing that Maude was at rest with her brothers and her parents.

He glanced over his shoulder to watch Philippe de Vaillant. Quiet and watchful, he reminded William greatly of Maude. Despite his thin, gaunt features, he was building his strength and recuperating in body at least. Apart from a lack of food and several minor broken bones, Philippe was emerging from his physical ordeal well enough. Maude's death had taken its toll on his spirit, though, and William was fearful that he would waste away again through a broken heart. Remembering what Maude had said about him and Louise de Moresby and under the guise of requesting her help with his sickness, William had hoped the reunion between them would ease Philippe's grief just a little.

He thought it had been an inspired decision, but now he was not so certain. Initially, Philippe had shown a glimmer of joy at the first sight of Louise. Her response had been far more radiant than William had ever seen. A very different reaction to the pleasant smile she had always treated him to, he acknowledged wryly.

From then on, however, Philippe's reactions to her changed. He dealt with Louise's puppy-like enthusiasm with a gentle patience and affection that betokened more brotherly affection than lover-like passion. He ignored Louise's adoration of him and showed more than a passing interest in one of the comely serving girls. Whenever Louise encouraged him to eat or drink something nourishing, he would brush aside her suggestions as childish and do the opposite. Louise did everything she could to help him, to tend him and to attract his attention, but all Philippe did was upset her.

William could see the girl was becoming increasingly distressed by Philippe's attitude, but was bearing up with stoic resilience. When Louise's attention was directed elsewhere, however, William had noticed that Philippe's demeanour changed. For a few brief seconds, he would stare at the girl with such love in his eyes that it hurt. As soon as Louise turned to him, however, the shutters came down again and he would resume his hurtful ways.

William pondered this for a while. It wasn't hard to work out, though. Perhaps because he was so wrapped up in his own grief, he had failed to understand the simple reasoning behind Philippe's behaviour. Everyone expected William to announce his betrothal to Louise de Moresby at the Midsummer Eve fair. Indeed, he had himself until two days ago. Now it all seemed so senseless. No matter how much Philippe wanted Louise, she was to be the wife of a richer man who enjoyed the favour of the King. Philippe had little to offer Louise and, much as Philippe loved her, he was thinking of the best for the girl herself. William knew he should have felt some twinge of jealousy, but he did not. There was no room in his heart for anything other than pain.

Casually grabbing a cup of wine from a passing servant, William frowned moodily into the fire. The wine was strong and soft—it was the sort Maude had loved best. Drinking deeply, he knew he couldn't marry Louise. He could do nothing for Maude now, but there was something he could do for her much-loved brother. He had to accept Maude's death, but he did not have to ruin any more lives with his ambition.

'Sir William?' Thomas de Moresby had risen to join William at the fire. His face was grave as William looked up to acknowledge his presence. The older man cleared his throat as he handed him a document. 'The agreement is to stand, I hope?' Sir Thomas watched William carefully.

'But, in truth, I do not think your heart is in the match, Sir William.'

Flushing a little, William managed a rueful smile. 'I would cause your daughter no pain, Sir Thomas, for she is as lovely as a man could wish for. However, it is plain to me that she would prefer to take de Vaillant as husband.'

The two men turned to watch the couple. 'He would make her a good husband and I own I like him well enough,' admitted Sir Thomas. 'But I have to think of her interests in the future.' He shook his head. 'De Vaillant is naught but a mercenary, when all is said and done. How can I give her to the lad when I cannot be sure he'll settle to manage my lands? Nor would he bring anything to the marriage and I know the lad has his pride.'

A faint smile crossed William's lips. 'I'll vouch for him and provide an adequate sum that will satisfy you. The King will be certain to favour him for his part in foiling de Vere.'

Sir Thomas stared at him in plain confusion. 'Why would you do this?'

William shrugged. 'I have been slow to realise, Sir Thomas, that contentment stems more from who you are with than what you have. I wish it was a lesson I had learned earlier.'

The sealed document in Sir Thomas's hand wavered before he placed it in his waist pouch. 'Aye, Maude was a rare sort of girl, Sir William. She will be sorely missed by those of us who liked her.' His blue eyes were full of genuine regret as he squeezed de Rohan's shoulder. 'I'll speak to Louise later. No doubt you'd prefer to tell de Vaillant yourself about these plans for his marriage.'

William nodded. 'I'll do it on the morrow, Sir Thomas.'

FitzCount strode through the hall, raindrops shimmering over his hair and cloak. The noise and laughter died down as he made his way to William. William stood up straight, half-fearful, half-hopeful at the news he could be bringing.

As soon as he came close, William could see in Fitz-Count's dull eyes that the news was not good. 'Nothing, William. We've searched every part of that river for miles. However, we've found the priest. He's dead.'

William looked away with a heavy heart. There was no hope now. Even if Maude had survived the water, she would never have survived the cold. 'My thanks, Brian.' He looked up at the cold, pinched face of his friend. 'Warm yourself and take some wine. I'll send some more men out in the morning.'

A commotion at the door caused them to turn. Riddell burst in, scattering tables, courtiers and dogs in his haste. 'My lord, we have news!'

William had never seen the normally taciturn Riddell looking so animated. He raised a weary brow, assuming it was perhaps another message of goodwill from the King. Everyone was silent now. 'Well?' He pushed himself away from the wall, drawn reluctantly by Riddell's inexplicable cheeriness.

Riddell beamed at them, his blunt face ruddy in the candlelight. 'It's Alfred and Hoel, my lord.'

His heart lurched and William placed his hands on the table for support. 'Have they found her?'

For an answer, the captain stood to one side and gestured to the doors. In strode Hoel and that woeful dog of his, closely followed by Alfred. He carried a wretched bundle of rags in his arms.

'Aye, my lord. The dog found her.' Hoel beamed up at de Rohan. 'She and Gant were together. Gant's dead,' he confirmed gravely, 'but Maude still lives. She lives,' he repeated, seeing that his lord had not yet understood his words.

'Put me down,' came a muffled voice. The bundle of rags squirmed.

'No, my lady.' Alfred's voice was firm and he held on to the rags more tightly.

'Maude?' William's voice was little more than a whisper. 'Maude?' He strode forward and pulled the rags from Alfred's arms.

'By the Face of Lucca, William, I am filthy. Put me down.' Dark, swollen eyes peeped out from beneath a mass of matted hair.

His heart racing, William could not believe his ears. His beloved Maude lived. 'By the Face of Lucca, wench, you'll do as I say.' He could almost feel her strength ebbing from her as he held her.

'Don't be ridiculous. I'll ruin your clothes.' A faint smile crept across her lips, before her eyelids fluttered and then closed. She had fainted or fallen into a deep sleep. Maude might be alive, but only just.

'We found her caught in the deep roots of a tree close to the bend in the river. She and Gant were wrapped close together. His neck was broken by the roots and he was all tangled up. I reckon that's how she managed to survive. If she hadn't have held on to him so tight, Maude would have been swept away like the priest.'

Philippe and Edwin pushed their way through the crowd. 'Get the herb-woman,' shouted William, his fear for her life rising. Maude was freezing cold and there was every chance she could die of the fever.

The three of them peered down at Maude's filthy, battered face and knew it would be most unlikely she would survive this.

Maude awoke from her terrible dreams to find the face of her beloved William just an arm's length away. He started at her sudden movement and came to bend closer to her.

'Not dead, then?' he muttered, pushing strands of her hair from her face. Those were the words he had first said to her in his hall, all those weeks ago.

'Not yet,' she whispered. 'But judging by the pain, I still think it most likely.' It was a real effort, but Maude could not stop herself from smiling. She was alive and William was there!

'Sleep now, Maude. Build your strength. I shall watch over you and protect you.' He smiled at her tenderly and Maude closed her eyes. She felt at peace.

Philippe's voice broke through the haziness. 'I'll take her home with me as soon as she's fit to travel. Maude needs rest and time to heal. There'll be time to discuss all this later, when she's well enough. I'll not have you upsetting her.' There was an almost belligerent tone to his voice that Maude had rarely heard before. It only came out when he was upset.

Edwin spoke next. 'Aye. Philippe's right. Give her time to think. She's not up to making decisions in this state.' His voice was soft and reasonable, but Maude still wondered what on earth they were talking about.

'Very well. You are her brother and her friend and I'll not gainsay you.' William sounded most weary. 'I'll give her until the Midsummer Eve fair.'

'You'll give her as long as she needs,' interrupted Philippe. 'Things have changed now and Maude needs to consider many other options besides you.'

Edwin, clearly sensing the rivalry between the two, stepped in. 'First things first. Let's get the girl home.'

'Philippe?' Maude's croaky voice broke into the discussion, silencing them all. She was tired and confused and

her head hurt. All that she remembered was that her beloved William no longer needed her and was to marry Louise. Unable to face him in her weakness and her pain,
Maude reached out for Philippe. She wanted to escape.
'Take me home, Philippe,' she mumbled. 'I want to go
home.'

Maude remembered very little of what happened next.
She woke up in a covered litter, travelling over the stony
paths to her own keep. The old herb-woman was at her
side, wiping her brow with some fresh-smelling liquid that
made her feel more human. The rest of the journey passed
by in a pleasantly drowsy fog. Her arrival at the keep was
met with delirious shouts of welcome from everyone, even
Bronwen.

Bronwen had bundled her quickly inside and had her
carried to her own familiar bed. It felt so good to be home,
surrounded by everything she had known all her life. Nothing could fill the aching void that William had left, but she
could grow content with her lot, in time.

As the days passed, Maude grew stronger. The fever
abated and the ache in her limbs reduced. Chafing to walk
one morning, Maude struggled to sit up.

'What do you think you are doing, Maude de Vaillant?'

Bronwen's bossy voice reached her from across the
room.

'I'm trying to get to the window,' Maude said patiently.
'I want to see outside.'

With a long-suffering sigh, Bronwen moved to Maude's
side. 'Very well. It will do no harm, I suppose.'

It sapped all her strength, but it was well worth the effort.
The sun shone in a beautiful blue sky. The sea beyond was
a lovely turquoise green and the breeze was fresh and

tangy. Breathing deeply, Maude closed her eyes. 'It feels good to be home, Bronwen.'

Bronwen pushed some of her hair back, her dark eyes clouding a little. 'It's good to have you back, Maude. I missed you and worried about you, you know.'

Maude grinned at her. 'Well, it's good to know I'm appreciated at last.' She reached out to touch her hand. 'I thought of you often and hoped you would understand. Where's Philippe?'

He had been a frequent visitor, entertaining her, amusing her, telling her stories of his old escapades. He did not mention Gant, though, and his time in captivity. His omission was beginning to worry Maude.

'Oh. He had to go. There was a summons from the King.' Bronwen was looking strangely sheepish and would not look her in the eyes. She busied herself in tidying Maude's hair instead.

'From the King? What about?'

Bronwen helped her to the chair before the fire. She didn't answer until she was settled comfortably. Finally, Bronwen straightened up and went to tend to the fire. As she bent down, Maude could see the silver strands that threaded through the thick dark hair. Bronwen was getting old, she realised. 'It was about Piers de Vere and Geoffrey Gant, he said.' She stood up and turned to face her. 'He went with Lord de Rohan.'

Maude could feel the blush steal over her cheeks at the mention of William's name. She had not allowed herself to think of him, for the pain of missing him was far worse than she could ever have thought possible. 'Do you...do you know how long they'll be?'

'Well, I think he mentioned something about Midsummer Eve.'

At that moment a loud knock on the door stopped their

conversation. Madselin of Silverdale walked in, her arms full of flowers and medicaments. 'Maude! I'm so pleased to see you getting better again. You must know how we all feared for you, my dear.'

In a cloud of lavender scent, Madselin bent over and kissed Maude on the cheek. Her pretty face was smiling as she surveyed Maude's countenance. Maude managed a weak smile. Madselin was always kind but at times could be overwhelming. She had found it best to stay as quiet as possible in such moments. That was what Edwin did, anyway, and it always seemed to work well on his wife. 'You're still pale, of course, but after such an ordeal, we would expect that.' She looked up at Bronwen. 'Have you fed her any meat yet?'

'Aye.'

Maude could see Bronwen bristling a little at the implication, although she knew from experience that Madselin meant no slight. Reaching up to squeeze Bronwen's hand, Maude just smiled. 'Bronwen is tending me with the greatest of care, Madselin. I could ask for no better.'

The flush of pleasure in Bronwen's dark face was reward enough for such words.

Madselin beamed at the pair of them. 'Well, I must say that your sojourn in de Rohan's keep has certainly had a beneficial effect on your manners, Maude. We can only hope it's long-term.'

Maude was amused to see Madselin had completely missed Bronwen's look of mortification. 'Lord de Rohan was a most charming man. He would often point out my lack of social grace,' said Maude tersely.

'Ah, well. I expect you enjoyed yourself thoroughly,' carried on Madselin blithely. 'To be in the company of such a courtier must be a delight. One can get a little bored with the lack of such men round here.'

'It's quieter here, certainly,' said Maude carefully. 'I doubt Lord de Rohan plans to stay in the area long. Once he marries, he will return to court most likely.'

Madselin sat on the bed opposite Maude and shook her head. 'Oh, I don't think so, Maude. Edwin was telling me that Lord de Rohan refused to accept the gift of a larger estate in the south and has brought in some sheep for his estate up here.'

'Sheep?' repeated Maude faintly. 'Why would he bring in sheep? He knows nothing about them.'

Madselin smiled blankly. 'I have no idea. Perhaps I can tell you more next week. We have received an invitation to his Midsummer Eve fair. Most of the local nobility have been invited.'

Maude could feel her skin go cold at the thought of that Midsummer Eve fair. There were still two days left before it took place, but her heart was already beginning to break. 'Will you go, then?' she asked quietly.

'Of course. Now that he's a rich man, we're hoping that there may be some suitors amongst his entourage for our Hawissa. It's time to think of her betrothal already.'

'But Hawissa is just a child,' said Maude with a frown. 'It's far too early to think of such things.'

'Not at all. But with de Rohan announcing his betrothal at the fair, I suspect there will be a lot of disappointed young women. The King has rewarded him well for breaking de Vere's power.'

'Aye. Louise is a lucky girl,' she murmured, suddenly feeling very cold and tired.

Bronwen was instantly at her side. 'That's enough of that talk, young lady. To bed.'

Maude nodded gratefully. By the look in Bronwen's dark eyes, she had seen more than she let on but was allowing her the respite of her bed.

Madselin hauled herself to stand up. 'Of course. I'm sorry for tiring you, my dear, but I'm pleased to see you making a recovery.' With a brief kiss, she took her leave of Maude and Bronwen.

When the coverlets were placed around her and the candles snuffed, Maude looked up at Bronwen. 'Did I get an invitation to the fair, Bronwen?'

Sitting at her side, the Welsh woman tenderly pushed back the strands of hair from her eyes. 'Not yet, Maude, but I have no doubt you will see him again, and soon.'

Maude blinked as sleep began to claim her. 'Did you see it in your fire, Bronwen?'

'Aye, my love. I saw everything.'


'My lady!' One of the servants rushed into the solar as Maude and Bronwen were sitting quietly. Maude had recovered enough to rise from her bed and dress. Eschewing her normal habit of breeches and tunic, Maude had put on a long gown. It was Midsummer Eve and she felt the need to mark it.

Maude looked up at the pink-cheeked girl as she almost skidded to a halt before her. 'What is it, Freya?'

'There's a sheep at the gate, my lady. And a soldier. He demands to see you.'

'Me?' Maude stared at the girl in disbelief, wondering perhaps whether some of the villagers had begun their own celebrations early.

'Aye, lady. The sheep has a green ribbon round its neck.'

Not believing a word of this, Maude joined Bronwen at the window and looked down at the gate below. Sure enough, there was a sheep with a green ribbon and a soldier who looked remarkably familiar. 'Riddell!'

'You know him, then?' Bronwen frowned down at the soldier.

'He's Lord de Rohan's captain.' Maude was frantically smoothing down her gown and pushing her hair into some sort of order. 'I'd best go down and see what he wants.'

Her heart was racing as she made her way unsteadily down towards the gate. Riddell just stared down at her for a moment in disbelief as he took in the gown.

'Riddell. I had not expected to see you here.' Her eyes stared distractedly at the bleating sheep, who did indeed have a green ribbon around its neck. 'Do you have need of anything?'

Gathering his wits, the captain dismounted and faced Maude. Managing something approaching a smile, he bowed at her. 'I'm come to offer you the sheep as... er...part-payment of my lord's debt to you.'

Scarlet with embarrassment, Maude was not sure whether Riddell had any inkling of the meanings behind those words. 'Did he say what debt he was referring to?' she said faintly.

Riddell shook his head and his expression reverted his more comfortable grimace. 'Nay, my lady. I had the impression it was an old one, though,' he added almost helpfully.

The sheep offered her no more than a dull gaze before going on to bleat pitifully. 'And...what am I meant to do with the sheep, exactly?'

'Lord de Rohan wishes you to collect the rest of the debt today. At his keep.'

'Today?' Maude could hardly keep the excitement from her voice. Whatever his terms, she would meet them. Anything to see him again, anything to be with him, no matter for how short a time.

'Right now, my lady. I reckon he'd be pleased if you went as you are.'

Somewhat nonplussed by Riddell's independent observation of William's preferences as to her attire, Maude merely nodded. 'Very well, but I don't think I could ride the whole way.'

Riddell bowed his head. 'There's a litter just beyond the hill. Lord de Rohan felt it wouldn't be right for you to see it straight off, if you get my meaning.'

'Oh, yes, of course.'

Bronwen and several of the servant girls stood behind her smiling. 'Go now, Maude. This is your destiny.'

For a moment or two, Maude and Bronwen stood looking at each other until eventually Maude nodded. Bronwen was right. William was her destiny.

It was several hours later when Maude, Riddell, her guards and the sheep arrived at the newly built bridge at the foot of the de Rohan keep. Home, thought Maude. It's just like coming home and for the first time in a long while, she smiled.

As they clattered across the wooden bridge, the villagers began to run towards them. Peering out at them from the litter, Maude could hardly believe her eyes. There were none of the usual frowns and malicious glances. All she could see in their eyes was laughter and joy.

Maude glanced up at Riddell with a question in her eyes. 'There's been a few changes here, my lady,' he responded. 'Alfred's the head-villager now and things are much better. We all understand each other. Well, most of the time, anyway.'

'Oh.' Her eyes gazed up at the keep and the village. It all looked much the same, but the atmosphere was indeed much changed. There was contentment here.

'My lady!'

'Alfred!' She was overjoyed to see his large frame approaching the litter. 'It's good to see you again. Things are very different, I hear.'

His broad smile said everything. 'Aye. The villagers wanted me to tell you that they were sorry about all the things that they said when you were here. The priest and Gant had been telling them lies for years and they feared for their lives. They want to know if you will forgive them.'

She grinned at him. 'Aye, Alfred. Tell them I understand and there is an end to it all.'

'Come, my lady. We must hurry now.' Riddell's grave voice interrupted them. 'Lord de Rohan awaits you at the standing stones.'

Alfred and the villagers stood back and waved, making Maude feel as important as a princess. It was a moment or two before she realised just what Riddell had said. She remembered the last time she had been at the standing stones—she and William had enjoyed a happy few hours there.

'My lady.' The litter had stopped and Riddell was offering his hand to help her out. 'Lord de Rohan requests that you walk the last part on your own.' He looked at Maude's pretty gown and her thin leather shoes dubiously. 'I could carry you, if you can't.'

She smiled. 'That won't be necessary, Riddell.' Her blood was glowing in anticipation of seeing him again. Whatever the man's plans, she would enjoy the time she had with him.

Leading the sheep over the rise of the hill, Maude was quite breathless. Before her stretched the lush valley full of…sheep. Maude could hardly believe her eyes. The man had actually filled his land with sheep.

'Well, my lady. A sight for sore eyes, don't you think?'

She stilled at the sound of his voice. 'William?' Turning, Maude was stunned at the sight before her. Instead of the vain peacock she was used to, William de Rohan was dressed in plain brown breeches and a simple shirt. Only his hair remained long in defiance of the King's order. Handsome as ever, he walked towards her slowly, drinking in her gown and her tangle-free hair.

'Is this you, Maude? I hardly recognise you.' He grinned and then reached to pull her braids. Gently he drew her close to him so that she was no more than a finger's length from his chest.

'Nor I you.' Suddenly she felt awkward. This was not at all the same as it was before. There was a feeling between them that was strange and uncomfortable. Her throat grew dry and she closed her eyes. 'I know you will think me bold, William, but I would very much like you to hold me.' Her voice sounded wobbly and odd.

Wordlessly he wrapped his arms about her and held her tight. Nothing mattered other than being there at that moment. Nothing at all.

'Maude, my love. We must talk.' He pulled his face back a little and stared down at her.

Maude could say nothing but managed a nod. Gently he picked her up in his arms and carried her to the standing stones. There, laid out before them, was a picnic.

When he had placed her on the blanket, William set about serving her with delicious food and wine. They talked of the keep and the changes that had been made. Hoel and Thorston had been sent to talk to the King with her brother and he hoped they would be back in time for the fair.

Unable to bring herself to talk about the fair and his impending betrothal, Maude decided she could no longer put off asking about the reason for this unexpected trip to his estate. 'What exactly did Riddell mean when he said it was part-payment of a debt? I had thought all our debts were paid in full.'

For a moment their eyes held and William reached out to touch her face. 'No, Maude. You saved my life. I owe you far more than I can ever repay. But the King, grateful for my reprieve, has gone some way to remedy the situation.'

Sitting by William, Maude was finding it hard to concentrate. 'I don't quite understand.'

'He wishes to make you a present of this estate.'

Maude could only blink. 'This estate? But…it's yours. I'd heard that you were staying here and…' Her voice faltered. 'Oh, I suppose when you marry you'll go to your wife's lands?'

William smiled faintly and looked across the valley before them. 'Well, I think that depends very much on your decision, Maude.'

'Decision?' Completely confused now, Maude looked at him blankly.

He hesitated. 'There is just one stipulation attached to accepting the King's gift.'

'There is?'

Sighing heavily, William moved to push her braids back. 'Tiresome though it might be, I think you should consider it most carefully, Maude.'

Frustrated beyond belief by his words, Maude pushed him away and frowned at him suspiciously. 'What stipulation, William?'

'You must marry.'

Well, that was not at all what she expected to hear. Her blood froze at the very idea. 'How could I do that? I have no wish to marry at all.'

'Quite,' came the careful reply. 'But the King did not feel this was a keep suitable for a woman on her own and he—'

'By the Face of Lucca, will you tell me whom I am

supposed to marry?' Glaring at him now, Maude moved closer to him. 'You are doing this on purpose to tease me, William de Rohan, and I do not appreciate it.'

'Me. You must marry me, Maude. It does make perfect sense.'

The silence between them stretched for several minutes. 'What did you say?'

William took a deep breath. 'He has made you an heiress, Maude, but it is conditional on you marrying me.'

'None of this makes any sense at all. Why would he force you into marrying me? You were to marry Louise de Moresby.'

'Ah, yes. Well, I must tell you that Louise is now married. It happened quite suddenly, I believe.'

Maude stared at the man before her. 'What! Whom did she marry?'

'Ah…your brother, I believe.'

'Philippe! They eloped?'

William shook his head. 'Not at all. They received the King's blessing and plan to come to see us shortly.' He reached forward and pulled her to him. 'Now, I have as yet received no confirmation that you accept the King's stipulation, Maude de Vaillant. I can see that I shall have to revert to recommended methods of persuasion.'

'William, you wanted to marry a lovely, charming and young heiress. Years of your life have been devoted to realising this ambition. I cannot believe that you agree to this for one moment.' She stared at him. Maybe he had been hurt whilst he was in the water?

'Well, you're young and an heiress, Maude. Two out of four isn't bad.' He grinned at her vexed expression. 'I'm sure that with time I can work on the other two.'

'So, you want this marriage between us, then?'

His face suddenly became serious. 'Aye, I do. I love you,

Maude.' He pulled the thongs at her braids until they un-ravelled. 'I persuaded the King that marriage to you was most definitely in my best interests. After all, life being what it is in the north, you can't beat having a bodyguard who is also your wife. Most prudent, I told him.'

'Prudent! You told the King it would be prudent to marry me?'

'Well, yes. And the King saw my point. He agreed. In fact, the document says we must marry on Midsummer Eve if you are to inherit your fortune.'

'So, you marry me for my money, after all?'

William just laughed. 'I'll tell you about it some time, my lovely Maude. But for now, I'm done with talking. I can see I shall have to resort to persuasion, after all.' Deftly his fingers untied the laces at her neck.

'William,' she hissed, 'what are you doing? It's the mid-dle of the afternoon and people will see us.'

'Mmm? Well, you'd best agree to marry me, then, so it won't matter what they see, will it?'

He began to place gentle kisses at the base of her neck and Maude was finding it hard to concentrate. Suddenly, she stiffened in his arms. 'William, was that a proposal…or a proposition?'

He grinned. 'Both,' he said firmly, 'since I intend to take full advantage of your services. Right now.'

She pushed him back once again. 'You do realise our clothes are not compatible.' Her hand swept down to in-dicate her pretty gown and his sensible attire.

'By the Face of Lucca, Maude, I have no intention of allowing you to keep your clothes on for much longer. Now tell me you love me and let me kiss you.'

She smiled at him and placed her arms around his neck. 'I do love you, William. But as yet, I'm really not quite sure why.' Marriage to one of the King's new men was going to be a sore trial, she could tell, but she was prepared to sacrifice all, if necessary. And she hoped very much she would have to.

\*     \*     \*     \*     \*

# SPOT THE DIFFERENCE

Spot all ten differences between the two pictures featured below and you could win a year's supply of Mills & Boon® books—FREE! When you're finished, simply complete the coupon overleaf and send it to us by 31st December 1998. The first five correct entries will each win a year's subscription to the Mills & Boon series of their choice. What could be easier?

**Please turn over for details of how to enter**

F8C

# HOW TO ENTER

Simply study the two pictures overleaf. They may at first glance appear the same but look closely and you should start to see the differences. There are ten to find in total, so circle them as you go on the second picture. Finally, fill in the coupon below and pop this page into an envelope and post it today. Don't forget you could win a year's supply of Mills & Boon® books—you don't even need to pay for a stamp!

**Mills & Boon Spot the Difference Competition**
**FREEPOST CN81, Croydon, Surrey, CR9 3WZ**
EIRE readers: (please affix stamp) PO Box 4546, Dublin 24.

Please tick the series you would like to receive if you are one of the lucky winners

Presents™ ❑ Enchanted™ ❑ Medical Romance™ ❑
Historical Romance™ ❑ Temptation® ❑

Are you a Reader Service™ subscriber?    Yes ❑    No ❑

Ms/Mrs/Miss/Mr ................Initials ...............................
                                    (BLOCK CAPITALS PLEASE)
Surname.................................................................................
Address ................................................................................

...............................................................................................
............................................Postcode..........................

(I am over 18 years of age)                              F8C

Closing date for entries is 31st December 1998.
One application per household. Competition open to residents of the UK and Ireland only. You may be mailed with offers from other reputable companies as a result of this application. If you would prefer not to receive such offers, please tick this box. ❑

Mills & Boon is a registered trademark owned by Harlequin Mills & Boon Limited.

# *Historical Romance*™

## *Coming next month*

### REBECCA'S ROGUE
### by Paula Marshall

*A Regency delight!*

Will was the perfect candidate—desperate
enough to marry Rebecca for her money and
agree to her conditions, but handsome enough
that it was easy to convince society that they had
married for love—almost *too* easy!

### DEAR DECEIVER
### by Mary Nichols

*A Regency delight!*

Who was Emma Woodhill? And why did
Dominic care especially when he was sure that
Emma was lying to him and he was engaged to
marry someone else? But he *did* care—fiancée or
no fiancée.

## On sale from 13th July 1998

*Available from WH Smith, John Menzies and Volume One*

# Penny Jordan

## COLLECTOR'S EDITION

The *Penny Jordan Collector's Edition* is
a selection of her most popular stories,
published in beautifully designed volumes
for you to collect and cherish.

*Available from Tesco, Asda, WH Smith, John Menzies,*
*Martins and all good paperback stockists, at £3.10 each -*
*or the special price of £2.80 if you use the coupon below.*
*On sale from 1st June 1998.*

Valid only in the UK & Eire against purchases made in retail outlets and not in
conjunction with any Reader Service or other offer.

---

# 30ᵖ OFF
## COUPON
### VALID UNTIL: 31.8.1998

## PENNY JORDAN COLLECTOR'S EDITION

9 904170 250306 >

0472 01316